Now the decent old sheriff was dead, along with most of a family. Who knew how many those human blowflies had left dead or injured up the street, before they'd finished their raid.

The dying man moved his hand to Prophet's and squeezed his wrist. It wasn't much of a squeeze, but Prophet could tell the man had something important on his mind. "Get . . . get her back . . . for me. P-please."

Prophet squeezed back. "I will. You can count on that."

Then the man's hand slid away from Prophet's wrist, and slowly, as though he were drifting to sleep, he slumped sideways to the floor and lay still.

Prophet stood and turned toward the front of the store, where several townsmen had gathered in the aisle, looking shocked and wary.

He'd get his guns and be on the trail in a half hour. Then he'd hunt those renegades and turn them toe down hard—with not a scrap of mercy and no concern for monetary reward—if he had to ride all the way to hell and thrash the devil with a stick to do it.

Berkley titles by Peter Brandvold

RIDING WITH THE DEVIL'S MISTRESS
ONCE UPON A DEAD MAN
DEALT THE DEVIL'S HAND
ONCE A RENEGADE
THE DEVIL AND LOU PROPHET
ONCE HELL FREEZES OVER
ONCE A LAWMAN
ONCE MORE WITH A .44
BLOOD MOUNTAIN
ONCE A MARSHAL

Other titles

DAKOTA KILL
THE ROMANTICS

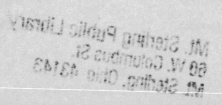

RIDING
WITH THE
DEVIL'S MISTRESS

PETER BRANDVOLD

B

BERKLEY BOOKS, NEW YORK

This is a work of fiction. Names, characters, places, and incidents either are the product of the author's imagination or are used fictitiously, and any resemblance to actual persons, living or dead, business establishments, events, or locales is entirely coincidental.

RIDING WITH THE DEVIL'S MISTRESS

A Berkley Book / published by arrangement with
the author

PRINTING HISTORY
Berkley edition / June 2003

Copyright © 2003 by Peter Brandvold.
Cover design by Jill Boltin.

For information address: The Berkley Publishing Group,
a division of Penguin Group (USA) Inc.,
375 Hudson Street, New York, New York 10014.

ISBN: 0-425-19067-6

BERKLEY®
Berkley Books are published by The Berkley Publishing Group,
a division of Penguin Group (USA) Inc.,
375 Hudson Street, New York, New York 10014.
BERKLEY and the "B" design
are trademarks belonging to Penguin Group (USA) Inc.

PRINTED IN THE UNITED STATES OF AMERICA

10 9 8 7 6 5 4 3 2 1

For Routh and Lawrence Cline,
with love from their Yankee son-in-law

They wandered in the wilderness in a solitary way;
they found no city to dwell in.

—Psalms 107:4

Heaven has no rage like love to hatred turned,
Nor hell a fury like a woman scorned.

—William Congreve

1

LOU PROPHET REINED his horse off the trail and up a hill carpeted in deep, tawny grass. At the hill's crest, he halted the line-back dun beneath a tall, scraggly oak tree with swollen buds. Several crows took flight from the tree, complaining like Satan on Sunday.

"Sorry, crows," Prophet said, reaching for the spyglass bound to his saddle with rawhide. "Some of us don't have all day to sit and quarrel in oak trees. Some of us have jobs to do—ain't that right, Mean and Ugly?"

The horse twitched its ears, one of which had been frayed in a fight with an uppity thoroughbred a few weeks back. Prophet fished the glass from its case, rubbed the lens on his greasy shirt, and brought the piece to his right eye, slowly adjusting the focus.

"There we go," Prophet mumbled as the backside of the roadhouse swam into view. It was a weathered-gray two-story structure fronting a frothy, green lake. The shore of the lake was littered with ice chunks swept off the water by a recent spring thaw. Seagulls dipped over the chunks and over the heads of the three men gathering the ice in a blue box wagon.

Behind the roadhouse sat a privy, several wood stacks, and two dilapidated storage sheds surrounded by barrels and crates of all shapes and sizes, as well as two rusted wagon chassis. There was a chicken coop with several pullets running around, and a pig pen which stunk like the devil's supper.

"Whew! Never could see raisin' pigs."

Prophet lowered the spyglass, returned it to its case, and sat leaning over the saddle horn, critically studying the roadhouse.

When he'd decided that there was no time like the present, he grabbed the shotgun hanging by a leather lanyard down his back and breeched it, making sure both barrels shone with ten-gauge buckshot. The shotgun, a Richards coach gun, was sawed off only an inch above the walnut forearm, and Prophet had found that the barn blaster, backed up by the Colt Peacemaker on his right thigh, was often the best friend a bounty hunter could ask for—at least in close-range situations.

When he was dealing with a little more distance, he called his Winchester '73 into action. He shucked the rifle from the saddle sheath now, making sure it, too, was fully loaded, then returned it to the boot. He might need it later. Gripping the short-barreled barn blaster in his right hand, the big, lean, broad-shouldered bounty man in rough, sun-faded trail garb kneed Mean and Ugly down the hill toward the roadhouse.

As he neared the hulking structure, Prophet began to hear a tinny piano clattering inside. The raucous notes rose above the wind as it ushered the waves against the lake shore, and above the sound of the pullets scratching for seeds around the coop. Behind the hog pen, Prophet tied his horse to an iron-rimmed wagon wheel lying in the weeds, then started for the roadhouse along the path cut to the privy.

The back door to the place opened onto a storeroom on

the left, a makeshift sleeping area, probably for a swamper or stable boy, on the right. Prophet opened another door to the main room, stepping inside and pulling the door closed behind him. Above him rose a staircase. Before him, eight or nine men dressed in wool sweaters and cloth caps sat around the dozen or so tables, smoking hand-rolled cigarettes and cheroots and clenching soapy beer mugs in their gnarled fists.

A young lady in a low-cut red dress and with a matching red ribbon in her cinnamon hair banged away on the piano. To her left was a long mahogany bar behind which stood the apron, who froze when he saw Prophet, a dirty towel shoved inside the glass he was drying. Prophet grinned to put the man at ease, and stepped up to the bar, glad there was a mirror in which he could keep an eye on the room.

The others had, one by one, taken notice of him now. This being a stage stop as well as a watering hole for woodcutters who worked at the sawmill on the east side of the lake, they were used to comers and goers. Most of the men turned back to their cards or their beers or their conversations.

Two did not. Prophet wasn't sure if these two, who sat at a table not far from the piano-playing brunette, were the same two depicted on the wanted dodgers in his saddlebags—wanted-poster renderings were infamously shoddy—but he had a feeling he'd know soon enough.

"What'll you have?" the barman asked him. He was tall and dull-looking, with a waxed mustache, carefully combed black hair, and pale, sunken cheeks.

"Give me a shot of your best whiskey and a bottle of your best beer," Prophet said jovially, tipping his hat back with a grin but keeping one eye on the two faces peering at him in the mirror.

One had a boyish, oval face with a wispy mustache and glassy blue eyes. The other had a long narrow face with a full mustache and chin whiskers. Neither wore the cowl-necked sweaters or high, lace-up boots of the woodcutters. They appeared more like the two Kansas drovers-turned-bank-and-stage-robbers Prophet had been chasing since Dodge City, where his friend, Wyatt Earp, had put him on their scent.

"Boilermaker it is," the barman said as he dumped whiskey into a shotglass and popped the top off a stout beer bottle.

"Good and cold," Prophet said when he'd sipped the frothy beer.

"Keep it in the cellar," the barman said, going back to his glass drying.

"That your boys cuttin' ice yonder?"

The man nodded. "They'll dust it down, toss it in the cellar, and I'll be settin' up frosty brews for these boys"—he gestured at the woodcutters—"on the Fourth of July."

"Nothin' like a cold beer on the Fourth," Prophet said conversationally.

He kept an eye on the mirror as he and the barman rambled on about the weather and the farming in the country, and about the fishing on the lake. Prophet stopped abruptly when he saw the two cowboys gain their feet behind him, shoving back their chairs. He turned around and put his back to the bar, bringing up the shotgun across his belly and fidgeting his thumbs across the hammers.

Over the heads of the raucous woodcutters, the two drovers locked eyes with him. The one with the chin whiskers turned, grabbed the girl's left arm, and said something Prophet couldn't hear. She looked at him, scowling, then stood reluctantly as the whiskered man pushed her toward the stairs. The younger man with the glassy blue eyes followed them, eyeing Prophet with one hand on the walnut grips of the pearl-handled Colt tied low on his thigh.

When the piano had fallen silent, the woodcutters did too, and looked to see what was happening. They followed the cinnamon-haired girl and the two men with their eyes, frowning curiously.

"Hey, she was just startin' to carry a tune," one of them quipped as the threesome mounted the stairs.

That broke the tension, and the others laughed.

"Carryin' a tune is not her only job," another one said in a Norwegian accent heavy enough to sink a clipper ship.

More laughter.

Prophet fingered his shotgun, wondering how to play this so the girl wouldn't get hurt. The younger man stopped halfway up the stairs, crouching as he clawed his six-shooter from its holster, and aimed it over the railing, the barrel forming a black hole directed at Prophet's face.

Prophet crouched as the revolver spat flames and smoke, barking and shattering the mirror behind the bar.

The bounty man straightened, brought the barn blaster to his shoulder while thumbing back the rabbit-eared hammers, and squeezed the right trigger. The shotgun thundered and jumped, ripping a hole the size of a Mexican sombrero through the younger man's chest, throwing him back against the blood-splattered wainscoting and rolling him down the stairs.

The girl halted on the landing, screaming and dropping to her knees. The man with the chin whiskers grabbed at her arm, but seeing Prophet turn the shotgun on him, let her go, cursing her loudly. He turned and ran to the second story.

Prophet followed him, hurdling the dead man at the bottom of the stairs and passing the frightened girl on the landing. When he came to the second story, he slowed, creeping between the two rows of closed doors in the hall, the floorboards squeaking under his boots.

There were three doors on each side. One stood ajar,

the crack bleeding light from a window within the room.

Prophet extended the Richards's short barrel, nudging the door wide. Before him stood the man with the chin whiskers. He held a naked red-haired girl with nubbin breasts and freckles. He stood behind her, clutching her left arm tightly with his left hand and snugging the barrel of his Smith & Wesson to her head with the other.

In the room's small bed lay another man, his head and shoulders pressed to the wall, clutching a wool blanket to his neck. He lay frozen, expressionless, and pale. His wide eyes shuttled between the outlaw and the bounty hunter.

The girl was crying and begging the outlaw to let her go.

"It's all right, Miss," Prophet said, staring into the cold, sneering eyes of the man behind her. "He'll be gone in a minute."

"She's the one's gonna be gone," the man spat through gritted teeth, "if'n you don't drop that gut-chewer."

Sweat rolled down Prophet's cheeks as he stared at the revolver snugged up to the girl's jaw, its hammer locked back, the man's dirty finger crooked over the trigger. Prophet had little doubt that if he didn't set the shotgun down, the man would kill the girl.

Of course, giving up his shotgun would mean giving up his ghost as well—the man would shoot him outright—but what else could he do? He didn't want to be the cause of this innocent whore's demise.

As the bounty hunter prayed for a miracle, his heart pounded, and the sweat glistened on his dusty forehead.

"All right," he said finally, with a distraught sigh. He depressed the right trigger, thinking, "Okay. This is it. It's been a nice run . . ."

As he crouched, lowering the shotgun to the floor, images of his Georgia childhood reeled through his brain. The outlaw grinned widely, showing small, hard, yellow teeth. The man extended his revolver toward Prophet. The bounty hunter stared wearily down the bore, wincing at the imminent, life-ending bullet.

The outlaw laughed. He squeezed the trigger.

At the precise moment the gun barked, the whore screamed.

Prophet couldn't tell for sure what had happened, because he'd closed his eyes. But he figured the whore must have nudged the outlaw's arm, for instead of pinking the bounty hunter's forehead, the bullet had seared a shallow trough along his cheek and notched his earlobe before thunking into the door behind him.

Prophet stumbled back and opened his eyes.

"You goddamn whore!" the outlaw raged, punching the naked girl and sending her sprawling across the bed with another scream.

Prophet reached for the shotgun. The gunman wheeled and fired as the bounty hunter raised the two-bore; the slug slammed into the Windsor chair Prophet was crouched behind. Seeing that the fight was going to involve the shotgun once again, the outlaw turned and dove through the room's single window, landing on the porch roof in a rain of glass. He scrambled to his feet, cursing, and ran to the edge of the roof.

Prophet bolted to the window, thumbing back the shotgun's right hammer. Standing at the roof edge, shuttling his worried gaze between Prophet and the ground below, the outlaw squeezed off a wild round at the bounty hunter. Prophet poked the shotgun through the window and fired as the man threw himself over the edge.

Scrambling through the window, Prophet made it to the edge of the roof as the outlaw, clutching his buckshot-peppered shoulder, gained his feet and started limping across the yard toward the corral, where several saddled horses ran in circles, shaking their manes at the gunfire.

Prophet raked his Peacemaker from his holster. "Stop or prepare to meet your maker, you bucket o' bat shit!"

His yell was followed by the sound of screaming horses. Prophet glanced right, frowning.

Two startled Percherons and the blue ice wagon were barreling across the yard, on an interception course with the outlaw. There was no driver, and the heavy geldings were pulling away from a small gray shed as though the hounds of hell were nipping at their hocks.

Not quite believing what he was seeing, Prophet stared in awe as the gunman, hearing the horses, stopped in the middle of the yard and turned to his right. The marauding team closed on him like a shaggy, blue-tailed comet.

The man opened his mouth but didn't have time to scream before the horses ran him down. Crumpling beneath their hooves, he was pummeled and snatched up by the hitch, dragged a hundred feet east of the roadhouse, and spat turdlike from under the box.

The rolling, mangled heap came to a dusty rest under a cottonwood as the wagon continued over the hill and out of sight.

Dust sifted down in the yard. All was quiet but for the breeze, a few spring songbirds, and the muffled sobs of the whore.

Prophet heard the tentative shuffling of boots on the porch beneath him, where the woodcutters had gathered to watch the festivities. At length, someone whistled. Someone else cleared his throat guiltily.

"Guess I shoulda set the wagon brake."

2

IT WAS FULL dark when Prophet dropped down off a low hill, trailing the horses of the two dead outlaws, the outlaws themselves hanging belly-down over their saddles, hands tied to their feet. He walked Mean and Ugly across a log bridge over a narrow stream and passed the first of several tar-paper shanties of the town of Luther Falls.

The bartender back at the roadhouse had told Prophet that Luther Falls was a mellow little village where he'd find the only sheriff within a two-hour ride. So Prophet had loaded up his cargo and headed northwest.

Luther Falls did, indeed, look mellow enough, with its tight little houses spewing piney chimney smoke, the windows lit with the warmth of familial associations. It was an hour past supper, but the smells of roasted meat and coffee still clung to the cool night air.

Cows bellowed in corrals, occasional dogs barked, and chickens clucked in coops not far from backyard privies. In one window that Prophet passed, well-dressed ladies sang hymns around a piano, open songbooks in their hands. The sight warmed his heart after what he'd been through back at the roadhouse, and he was glad he hadn't ridden into this God-fearing little town, his ghastly cargo in tow, in broad daylight.

Prophet followed the meandering road, no more than two pale wagon tracks under a sky filled with small, hard stars, to the business district. He pulled up before a clapboard hovel with a peaked roof and a shingle over the boardwalk announcing SHERIFF. He was happy to see a dim lantern glow in the window.

"How can I help you, stranger?" a man's voice called behind him.

Dismounting, Prophet turned to see a stout gentleman in a suit, a long deerskin coat, and a fur hat angling across the street toward the jailhouse. He was carrying saddlebags over his shoulder and a full-length shotgun in his hand. A briar pipe jutted from his mouth, puffing a rich, aromatic smoke.

"I'm looking for the sheriff," Prophet said.

The man had stopped to look over the two bodies draped over the horses on Prophet's lead line. "You found him. And I'd say you have a little explaining to do, Mr. . . ."

"The name's, Prophet, Sheriff. I'm a bounty man. These two men are wanted for robbery and murder in Kansas and Missouri. I've been following them since leaving Dodge City three weeks ago. My friend, Wyatt Earp, put me on their trail. He and Bat Masterson were too busy to go after them themselves."

"Earp and Masterson, eh?" the sheriff said, obviously impressed. "They're friends of yours?"

"Wyatt is," Prophet said. "Bat and I . . . well"—Prophet grinned—"Bat ain't too fond of bounty men."

The sheriff puffed his pipe in the darkness. "Never been too fond of bounty hunters myself." He paused. "But I reckon if ole Wyatt Earp put you on their trail . . ."

"Ran 'em to ground in the Johnson Lake Roadhouse south of here," Prophet said. "You can include that information in your cable."

"What cable?"

"The one I'm hopin' you'll send to Wyatt, tellin' him I found his men—Benny Mack and Jack Montoya, last of the Montoya Gang—so he'll send me the reward money."

The sheriff stared at Prophet thoughtfully, scratched his head, glanced at the bodies draped over the saddles, then said, "Come on. We'll hash this out inside."

Prophet turned and followed the sheriff into the jailhouse, a cramped, one-room office with a battered rolltop desk and a heavy, locked door which no doubt lead into the cell block at the building's rear.

"Have a seat," the sheriff said as he shrugged out of his deerskin coat and hung it on an antler rack near the door. "Mighty cold tonight. Looks like ole winter's raisin' its hackles one more time."

Prophet sat in the hide-bottomed chair beside the desk, the old chair creaking under his weight. The bounty hunter sighed, wanting to get this business over with quickly, so he could relieve himself of the bodies, pad out his belly with grub somewhere, down a few drinks, and crawl into a hot tub and a warm bed.

"I forgot how cold April could be this far north."

"Yeah, we get cold blasting down from Canada pret' near till May," the sheriff said, rubbing his hands before the stove, which someone must have recently stoked. "If I had my druthers, I'd be down in New Mexico or Arizona, where I was raised. Problem is, I married me a woman from Minnesota—one of them ornery Swedes." The sheriff winked at Prophet and curled his white mustache with a playful grin. "She's due set on stayin' on here with her family, and there's not a thing I can do about it but complain."

Prophet smiled, relaxing a little. The sheriff seemed to

be warming to him, and that wasn't always how things panned out for bounty hunters. The grisly nature of the bounty hunter's trade often made him an outcast, disdained by many. It always seemed a little odd to Prophet that the ones who resented him most were lawmen—men whose jobs he presumably made easier by bringing in the riffraff they themselves didn't have the time or resources to hunt.

He guessed it was probably due to jealousy, for bounty hunters, unlike lawmen, came and went as they pleased, hunted whom they pleased when they pleased, unconstrained by time or jurisdictional boundaries. In many ways, it was a dream life. The only problem was, you had to be a singular, solitary breed to live it. A man who didn't mind giving up the comforts of hearth, home, and family for a life lived on the owlhoot trail, where you could die any second of any minute of any hour, and no one would be the sadder. . . .

"Coffee?" the old sheriff asked as he poured himself a cup at the stove.

"Why not?" Prophet said, glad the man was being friendly but really wanting to get on with his business.

That didn't happen, however, until the sheriff had given Prophet a full cup of steaming coffee, hot and strong enough to seal a roof with, plunked down in his swivel chair, and talked about the evening he'd spent riding out to Mrs. Larson's ranch five miles west of town.

"She thinks Indians are stealing her pullets," the sheriff said, blowing ripples on his coffee. "She's been thinking that for the past five years. I've told her over and over again that if Indians were stealing pullets, why would they just steal hers? I mean, her neighbors Mrs. Hanson and Mrs. Peterson and Mrs. Munson all have pullets, too. Why aren't the Indians getting theirs?"

The sheriff gave a snort and plucked at the curled ends of his mustache, his face flushing with amusement. "So I finally ride out there this afternoon, have a look around the place. I see the dog Mrs. Larson got when he was just a pup, snoozing on the porch, stretched out like Caesar at his favorite bath. And I get to thinking, this Indian problem started occurring about the same time this dog came along. He's old and fat now—fatter than most country dogs get on table scraps and mice.

"So I ask her where the dog sleeps, and she tells me, and I climb into this old falling-down hog pen she's got down by the stream that runs behind her place, and what do you suppose I find, Mr. Prophet?" The sheriff's blue eyes flashed with amusement.

"Feathers?"

The sheriff leaned back in his chair and roared, nearly spilling the coffee in the cup he squeezed in his small, fat hands. "About five years' worth!"

He roared again, snorting. Regaining his senses, he said, "When I got back to the house, that dog was gone, and I have a feelin' he won't be back. Not if he knows what's good for him!"

Wheezing with laughter, the sheriff got up, refilled his coffee cup, topped off Prophet's and plopped back down in his chair. "Sorry about that, Mr. Prophet. It gets kinda quiet around here—especially at night—and I just felt like cuttin' loose with a big windy. Where in the hell were we, anyway, before all this chicken business grabbed hold of my tongue?"

Prophet reminded him that they had been discussing the cable he hoped the sheriff would send to Wyatt Earp in Dodge City.

"Well, goddamn!" the sheriff exclaimed, rubbing his hand across his mouth. "You want me to send a cable to ole Wyatt Earp, eh?"

"Yes, sir. Explaining how I captured the prisoners, brought them to you, the nearest official peace officer, and turned them in for the bounty."

"Well, I'll be goddamned," the sheriff repeated, obviously overcome with the idea that he would have anything—even a telegram—to do with the venerable lawman of Dodge. "Wyatt Earp, eh?"

"That's right, Sheriff."

"Why don't you send the cable your ownself?"

"I need a lawman to corroborate my story." Prophet smiled. "Otherwise I reckon I could tell him I got his men when I really didn't."

"How much these boys have on 'em, anyway?"

"Five hundred apiece."

The sheriff whistled and stared at his scarred desktop, thinking. "Why don't you just bring 'em both back to Dodge, show Earp himself their ugly faces?"

Prophet tipped his hat forward to scratch the back of his head. "Well, it's a little warmer down there than it is up here, Sheriff. . . ."

"Oh, I see. I suppose they'd get a little ripe on you, eh?" He chuckled.

Prophet nodded. "I have a feeling that by the time I got there, they wouldn't be very recognizable."

"Yeah, I hear the faces and eyeballs are the first to puff up," the sheriff said speculatively. "I wouldn't know." He leaned toward Prophet as if to share a secret. "You know, I've never had to hunt down and kill a badman as long as I've been sheriff of this little town? And that's five years this July."

"Pretty quiet around here, eh?"

"Nice and quiet," the sheriff said, packing his pipe. "Too quiet, you might even say. Sometimes I don't know why I'm even needed. Just to make people feel safe, I guess."

"And to hunt down pullet-thievin' Injuns," Prophet added with a smile.

"There you have it." The sheriff lit his pipe. "Well, if a cable's what you need, Mr. Prophet, I should be able to manage that much. As long as those men are who you say they are, that is."

"Just describe them a little," Prophet said, rising from his chair and donning his hat. "Wyatt knows what they look like. Besides, there's plenty of booty in their saddlebags that'll pin handles on 'em, too."

"All right, Mr. Prophet," the sheriff said, puffing his pipe and nodding. "Will do."

Prophet shook the man's hand and asked where he could stable his horses. The sheriff told him where Dawson's Livery was located, and added, "You might as well leave your expired hooligans over there, too. We have an undertaker, but he turns in early, and I don't see any reason to wake him. I'll call on him in the morning and have a look at those boys myself. Then I'll get Henry over at the telegraph office to send your cable."

"Much obliged, Sheriff. I think I'll wait around here for the money. Nothing else to do. Uh, if you don't mind, that is."

The sheriff scrutinized Prophet as he puffed his pipe. "You don't look too bad. A little rough around the edges, maybe. Maybe what you need is a week or two around decent, God-fearin' Norwegians. Bore your hide off, but smooth the kinks out of your soul." A whimsical smile shone far back in his eyes.

"That might be just what the doctor ordered for me, Sheriff," Prophet chuckled. "Say, I don't believe you gave me your handle."

"Beckett. Arnie Beckett."

"Pleased to make your acquaintance, Sheriff Beckett. Now, I just have one more favor to ask. Where can a man get him some supper and a stiff drink and then a good night's rest?"

"Well, the snakewater you can get over at Herman Waterman's a block west and across the street, but you better hurry. He's the only saloon in town, and he closes at nine.

City ordinance. We're strict Lutherans around here, you understand."

Beckett gained another wry expression and pulled at his mustache. "As for the rest, you'll find Mrs. Cordelia Ryan's boarding house a half mile north of here. It's the biggest house out that way—a big, green, clapboard affair with a white picket fence. Nice house. Even nicer lady, but strict as all get out. The widow doubles as the school teacher, and she'll paddle your butt if you're bad, so mind your p's and q's."

"Oh," Prophet said, feeling a little disheartened. He liked the idea of resting up in a nice, quiet town, but he wasn't so sure about the tight reins. He was known to carouse a little on his time off . . . to lift his tail and stomp.

Oh, well. Like Beckett had said, a week or two among good, God-fearin' folks might be just what he needed to iron the kinks out of his soul.

After he'd brought the outlaws' saddlebags into the jail and set them along the wall by the sheriff's desk, he headed for the livery barn, where he rented a stall for his own line-back dun, laid the outlaws out, and sold their mounts for twenty dollars apiece.

Since it was getting late, he decided to forgo the saloon, heading instead for the boarding house. If the old biddy who ran the place didn't confiscate his liquor, he could have a nip or two in his room, from the bottle of Kentucky rye he always packed in his war bag, for emergencies. . . .

3

CORDELIA RYAN'S BOARDING house—all three stories of it—was lit up like a Dodge City brothel on Saturday night. Piano music filtered into the yard as Prophet pushed through the gate in the picket fence, mounted the wide porch, and knocked on the door.

He had to knock again before the door finally opened. A gorgeous young woman in a lacy purple dress stood before him, looking curious. She appeared to be in her early twenties, and long black hair parted in the middle framed her exquisite oval face.

"Yes?"

Prophet's tongue was stuck to the roof of his mouth as his eyes wandered over the scrumptious figure. He hadn't been with a woman since Dodge City, three weeks before, and he certainly hadn't expected to find one like this in Luther Falls—with a shape like that, and eyes like black diamonds.

"Uh . . . pardon me for bothering you so late in the evening, Miss, but I was wondering if I could speak to a Mrs. Cordelia Ryan?"

"What can I do for you?"

Prophet shuddered like a dry drunk on July fourth. "You're . . . you're Mrs. Cordelia Ryan? The widow?"

She smiled and gave her head a little ironic inclination. "I'm the Widow Ryan, as they call me around here, yes. What can I do for you, sir?"

His eyes raked the long, well-built body one more time, his jaw hanging to the bib front of his filthy cotton tunic. "Pardon me for saying so, ma'am, but you sure don't look like no widow I've ever seen."

She gazed at him tolerantly, giving her eyebrows a queenly arch.

"Uh . . . sorry," he said, abashed, feeling self-conscious in his filthy trail clothes, with the shotgun hanging from the lanyard down his back, his saddlebags draped over his shoulder, and the Winchester held at his side. "I've been on the trail for quite a few days." He shifted his rifle to his left hand and offered her his right. "I'm Lou Prophet, Miss . . . uh, Mrs. Ryan. I'll be staying in Luther Falls for a few days, and I was wondering if I might be able to rent a room here in your fine establishment."

Her brown eyes dropped to his hand, as if inspecting it for ringworm, then lifted her own—small, delicate yet strong, and long-fingered—and gave Prophet's big paw a curt shake. She measured him for several seconds, sucking her delectable bottom lip. Finally, her eyes returned to his.

She said quietly, "What is your occupation, Mr. Prophet?"

"Occupation, ma'am?" He'd been afraid she'd ask that.

She arched her brow once again. It was the only thing about her that bespoke the fact that she was also a school-teacher.

"Well, ma'am, I'm . . . I'm a bounty hunter."

"A bounty hunter." It was a statement, not a question. Prophet smiled wanly.

"Do you hunt wolves, Mr. Prophet?"

"Uh . . . no, ma'am. I don't hunt wolves."

She didn't say anything for a time. Her eyes glistened. "And what brings a bounty hunter to Luther Falls, Mr. Prophet?"

Prophet sighed. He had a feeling he'd be bunking with Mean and Ugly tonight. "I, uh . . . brought in a couple of . . . uh, men . . . to Sheriff Beckett."

"I see. Were these dangerous men, Mr. Prophet?"

"I'll say they were, ma'am."

"And you brought them to justice."

Prophet sighed again, but this time there was more hope in it. "Yes, ma'am, I certainly did," he said proudly.

She appraised him again, her eyes looking him up and down, running along the Winchester in his hand and across the Peacemaker and wide-bladed bowie on his belt, making him feel like an ape in a French boutique.

She sighed at length and lifted her chin. "I have a room on the third floor I guess you could take for a few days. As long as you follow my rules, Mr. Prophet."

Prophet removed his hat and held it over his chest. "I'm a rule-follower from way back, ma'am. Yessiree."

"The charge is two dollars per night, payable in advance, and there is no drinking on the premises." She paused, wryly observing his reaction. To his credit, though his heart was breaking, he maintained a neutral expression.

Gravely, she continued. "There are no women other than wives allowed in my rooms with the menfolk, just as there are no men other than husbands allowed in the rooms with my ladies. Breakfast is at seven o'clock sharp, supper at six. If you'd like dinner, you must inform me by nine o'clock of the previous evening. There is no smoking or eating in the rooms, and no singing or playing guitar or other musical instruments after ten P.M."

She paused, watching him.

"Sounds fair as cream to me, ma'am," he said, despite

his reluctance. If she hadn't been so damn attractive, and he in such need of a real bed, he would have turned around and headed back to the livery barn. He sure did want that drink. . . .

"Are you sure you can abide my rules, Mr. Prophet?" She seemed to be reading his mind.

"Like I said, ma'am," Prophet said, his eyes dropping against his will to her bosom, "I'm a rule-follower from way back. Why, my momma used to tell me—"

Drawing the door wide and stepping aside, she said, "I'm sure she did, Mr. Prophet. Why don't you come in and sign the register. Then I'll have Annabelle heat some water for a bath."

"Much obliged, ma'am. I reckon I do smell about as bad as my horse, an' he was born smellin' like . . . well . . ."

Prophet let it go. Beautiful women always made him nervous, gave him a real case of hoof-in-mouth disease, in fact.

Adjusting the heavy saddlebags on his shoulder, he followed her into a small office with an ornately carved rolltop desk. While she got out her register and prepared a pen, Prophet looked through the open French doors to a parlor, where several well-dressed gentlemen and ladies were dancing to piano music. Around a table sat several other men in business suits, smoking pipes or cigars and reading newspapers and magazines. Two gents looking as old as the Minnesota hills sat off by themselves, playing checkers and scowling.

"Real nice setup you have here, Mrs. Ryan."

"Thank you, Mr. Prophet," she said, handing him a freshly dipped pen. "After you've had your bath, you're welcome to join us."

Prophet snickered and, holding the saddlebags awkwardly over his right shoulder and taking his rifle in his left hand, stooped over the desk to sign the register. "Oh,

I don't reckon I'd fit in with this bunch, ma'am." He regarded her eyes, in which the light from the desk's Rochester lamp danced like starlight on a summer lake, and his throat swelled. Good Lord, what a creature!

"Uh, if you don't mind me askin'," he said, his curiosity piqued, "how did one as young and lovely as yourself come to run a boarding house in Luther Falls?"

"I'm charmed by the compliment, Mr. Prophet," she said, though she didn't look charmed. "My husband, Archibald Ryan, owned the first sawmill here in Luther Falls. He was somewhat older than I, and died two years ago—only a year after we married, I'm afraid."

"Oh, I'm sorry, ma'am."

She nodded solemnly. "This was our house," she said, glancing around. "Can you imagine?"

Prophet wagged his head and whistled.

"I certainly couldn't have lived here alone, so I turned it into a boarding house. I have several year-long residents."

"They look right comfortable, Mrs. Ryan."

"I do try my best." She turned to him and caught him staring at her. "The charge is two dollars, Mr. Prophet."

"F-for wha-what?"

"The room, Mr. Prophet."

"Oh!"

He cleared his throat, chagrined, and gave her enough coins to cover several nights. Holding up a key on a gold ring, she said, "Your room is number twelve."

He accepted the key and started edging away, feeling like a dog slung around by its own tail but reluctant to stop feasting his eyes on this woman.

"Good night, Mr. Prophet. I'll summon Annabelle for your bath straightaway."

"Much obliged, Mrs. Ryan."

"Uh, Mr. Prophet?"

Prophet stopped at the newel post at the bottom of the

wide staircase and turned around. "Yes, ma'am?"

She gazed at his saddlebags with a schoolmarm's suspicion. "Did I mention there could be no consumption of spiritous liquids on the property?"

Prophet swallowed, his right knee quaking. "Yes, ma'am. You sure did."

She smiled a smile that had no doubt taken its toll on the men of Luther Falls. "See you in the morning for breakfast at seven o'clock, Mr. Prophet."

"Seven o'clock it is, ma'am."

"Sharp."

"Sharp."

At once madly in love with her and scared to death of her, he turned and started up the stairs. He would have turned cartwheels through the parlor if she'd asked him to. No wonder her husband was dead. Married to such a browbeating vixen, he'd probably gone mad and cut off his own head with a rusty saw.

On the third floor, Prophet found his room, went in, and fumbled around until he got the bracketed wall lamp lit. Neat and comfortable, the room sported a double-sized, four-poster bed with a canopy, an oak wardrobe, and a washstand with a built-in cupboard and a deep porcelain bowl. The two sashed windows were covered with heavy mauve curtains, and there was even a writing desk upon which sat a leather-bound book, its title in gilt lettering: WUTHERING HEIGHTS.

Prophet stood for a full minute taking it all in. He hadn't stayed in a room this grand since wintering in Denver three years before.

Shaking his head, he hung his rifle and shotgun on the wall pegs between the two windows and dropped his saddlebags on the bed. He tossed his hat off and sat next to the bags, eyeing them cunningly, staring at the bulge his bottle of rye made in the left pouch.

Should he or shouldn't he?

Guiltily, he glanced around the room, as if there were a peephole somewhere and she were watching him.

"Oh, for Chrissakes!" he groused aloud, opening the flap and producing the bottle. "She's just a woman like any other—born to be hornswoggled."

He popped the cork and took a long swig, the air bubbles rising toward the lip. He took another drink and, feeling relaxed, kicked his boots off and scooted up against the headboard, resting there, his eyes on the canopy as he very slowly but surely anaesthetized himself against the wear and tear of the trail.

He wasn't sure how much time had passed before he became aware of footsteps in the hall. A loud, single knock on the door.

"Yoo-hoo," a shrill voice sounded. "Bath time!"

Jesus, he'd forgotten! His heart leaping into his throat, Prophet slapped the cork back on the bottle and looked around for a place to hide it. Finally slipping it under his pillow, he got up and opened the door.

A woman very closely resembling an Oklahoma mule skinner—her shoulders were that broad, her face that haggard—said, "Bath time, Mr. Prophet," in a high singsong.

She pushed her way into the room, a tin tub in one hand, a bucket of cold water in the other. While Prophet gazed on, befuddled, she set the tub on the floor, hefted the bucket in her big, well-muscled arms, and poured the water into the tub.

"There we go—nice and cold to start out. Gets the circulation going. Now I'll go down for some hot!"

With that, she waddled out of the room, shuffling from side to side, wide shoulders working like a yoke on a pair of contrary oxen, and disappeared, not closing the door behind her.

Prophet stood there, staring at the door. What was he supposed to do? Climb into that damn ice melt? He'd had enough river baths. No thanks. He'd wait for some hot water to temper the cold.

Which was what he did, inciting a Norwegian-laced tongue-lashing from the beast known as Annabelle. He smoothed her feathers, however, by offering a silver dollar gratuity in return for as much skin-peeling hot water as he could take and the tub could hold.

Then he locked the door behind the retreating Annabelle, climbed into the tub, his skin reddening instantly, and sat there in the steaming suds for close to an hour, sipping from his bottle on the floor. All he wanted now was a cigar, but he guessed he could do without, under the circumstances. He certainly didn't want another surprise visit from Annabelle, who could no doubt inflict some serious damage with those maul-like fists of hers.

And then there was Mrs. Ryan . . . Cordelia. If she found him smoking in here, let alone drinking, she'd sure as grit in a sandstorm throw him out with his horse. But it was nice to think about her . . . the way her eyes sparkled and the way her full bosom heaved under all that velvet and lace.

He was sound asleep and dreaming about her beneath two quilts and the softest, cleanest sheet he'd ever experienced, when he awoke to a creaking sound in the hall. Then there was a tinny clicking, as though someone were trying to unlock his door.

Shit!

He reached for his gun on the bedpost, but it wasn't there. He'd gotten careless and left his gunbelt on one of the pegs across the room.

Shit!

"Who the hell is it?" he asked as he heard the door squeak open in the darkness, instinctively expecting a bullet.

"Sh."

"What?"

"Be quiet. It's Cordelia."

"What is it?"

He heard the door squeak shut and softly latch. As his eyes adjusted to the dark, he saw a figure move toward him, heard the sibilant sound of rustling silk. Smelled laurel in full bloom. . . .

The figure moved toward him and stopped beside the bed. "You've been drinking. I can smell the whiskey."

His heart pounded and his head swam. "Uh . . ."

"Your punishment is you must make love to me."

He heard the cloth moving again, and then he saw her figure before him, the dim light from the window revealing proud, delicate shoulders thrust back behind heavy breasts, the dark nipples staring him down like a pair of .44s.

His pulse throbbed in his throat. There was a low humming in his head. His throat had gone dry as the Sahara during a sandstorm.

She reached down, found his hand, and brought it to her breast. "You want to. I know you do. I saw the way you looked at me earlier."

"Sorry . . . I . . ."

"I haven't had a man in two years, Mr. Prophet."

He didn't know what to say to that. He rubbed his thumb around on her nipple, which quickly grew erect beneath his touch. She looked down at it, saying, "I've never met a man here I wanted to be with . . . as much as I wanted to be with you as soon as I saw you."

He could hear her breath quicken as he worked at her nipple. She brought both her hands to his, cupping it and her breast both, "You mustn't tell a soul. Promise?"

"I promise."

"Slide over."

He slid over.

"Tell me one thing," he said, running his hand down her impossibly smooth thigh. "Am I dreaming?"

She laughed huskily and bit his lip, pushing him back on the bed.

4

THE NEXT MORNING, Prophet woke to the sounds of someone shuffling about the room. He turned his head on the pillow and opened his eyes.

Pale dawn light seeped around the edges of the curtains. In the smoky dusk of the room, Cordelia held her silk wrapper out before her, tossing it around to find the front. Her breasts jiggled as she did so, and Prophet groaned with desire.

"Where . . . where you going?" he asked her.

"Well, good morning," she said cheerfully.

She drew the wrapper on and sat on the edge of the bed, leaning down and kissing Prophet's lips, running a rough hand through his hair. Her wrapper yawned open, exposing her breasts, and Prophet took them in his calloused palms, fondling them gently and kissing each nipple in turn.

"It's early," he said, his voice muffled by her bosom.

"I have to go down and help Annabelle with breakfast," she said, making soft sounds of delight as he buried his nose in her cleavage.

"Come back to bed," he urged.

"I can't," she laughed, drawing her wrapper closed and pulling away. "But I'll be back again tonight—you can bet your boots on that!"

Prophet grinned and smacked his lips at the prospect, watching her lithe form fairly float to the door, her long black hair rippling down her slender back.

"Oh, Lou?" she said, turning around.

"Yes, my pet?"

"What are your plans for the day?"

"Don't have any," Prophet said, stretching luxuriously.

"Then would you mind—? Oh, I hate to ask this."

He lifted his head from the pillow. "Ask what?"

She thought for a moment, then shook her head. "No, I can't." She started twisting the doorknob.

Prophet pushed up on an elbow. "What is it, Cordelia?"

She stopped again and turned to face him. "Well . . . I was just wondering . . . You see, the man I had taking caring of chores around here is laid up with a kidney ailment, and . . ."

"And you need something done. What?"

"Oh, Lou, what will you think of me, asking a favor after we've . . . ?" She let the sentence trail off and drew her shoulders together, bunching her breasts.

"Ask away," he said absently, swallowing as he stared at the flesh exposed by the open wrapper.

"The door to the privy won't shut all the way. I think the boards are warped." She had a pained look on her face. "Would you mind taking a look at it? I mean, since you don't have any other plans for the day and all?"

Prophet ran his eyes up and down her scrumptious figure once more. "I would be more than happy to fix anything you got ailing, Mrs. Cordelia Ryan."

"Oh, Lou!" she said, running back to the bed and kissing his cheek. "You're a dear!" She went back to the door, began opening it, then closed it again gently, half-whispering, "Until this evening, my stallion . . ."

She blew him a kiss and left.

Thoroughly bewitched, Prophet rolled back on the pillow with a big grin on his face.

As soon as he'd polished off a big plate of ham and eggs and fried potatoes, and washed it down with hot, black coffee, he got started on the privy door, which was so badly warped by moisture that he had to remove it, take it apart in the maintenance shed in the backyard, and replace two boards and a handful of screws before putting it back together and remounting the knob, which he also took apart and oiled.

Before he put the door back on its hinges, he gave it a fresh coat of paint. That done, something didn't look right. The problem was the fresh white paint on the door no longer matched the dull, gray paint of the rest of the privy. It bothered him to the point that he went ahead and painted the whole privy.

"Now, if that ain't the best lookin' two-holer in town, I'm not the middle son of Homer and Minnie," Prophet said, stepping back to admire his handiwork.

"Oh, Lou?"

He turned. It was Cordelia standing on the house's back porch. "Annabelle was cleaning a room upstairs and found a cracked window." She thrust her lower lip out, pouting.

Prophet sighed and offered a wry smile. "Be right there."

By the time Prophet had replaced the window, repaired several pickets in the fence surrounding the boarding house, plastered several cracks in the parlor's ceiling, cleaned the kitchen chimney, and hauled a load of food staples back from the mercantile, stacking it all in the basement storage room, he was ready to saddle Mean and Ugly and head back out on the owlhoot trail for a little rest and relaxation.

But he was rewarded that evening by the finest meal—

young chickens roasted in white wine and butter and a dessert of peach cobbler and ice cream—he'd ever eaten in his life. And the coffee Annabelle brought him on the porch afterward, where he sat smoking with the two older, chess-playing gents from the evening before, was liberally laced with a sweet liquor—a clandestine gift, he knew, from Cordelia.

The gift she gave him later was just as clandestine but not nearly as subtle. Slipping into his room after everyone else in the house was long asleep, the old gents' snores resounding in the walls, she snickered into her hand, ripped off her wrapper, threw herself atop him, and hissed, "Come, my stallion—throw the blocks to your sweet Cordelia!"

He did, and paid for it again the next day, so that by the time he'd finished repairing the house buggy's left front wheel and greasing both axles, his back was squawking like an old goose. Rather than head back into the boarding house, where surely Cordelia or Annabelle would have another chore for him, he washed at the outside pump, donned his hat, unrolled his shirtsleeves, and walked south toward the business district. He thought he'd have a beer and the free lunch in the town's only saloon, maybe even indulge in a game of five-card stud—if such impious dalliance was allowed in Luther Falls.

On the way to the Sawmill Saloon, he saw Sheriff Beckett sitting in the sun outside the jailhouse.

"Mr. Prophet," the sheriff greeted him. "Haven't seen much of you lately. Thought maybe the widow had done run you out of town." Beckett laughed.

"No . . . not yet," Prophet said with a baleful sigh, shoving his hands in his pockets. "She's workin' on it, though."

Bathing his face in the warm midday sun, the sheriff glanced up at the bounty hunter. "Yeah, she can be mighty tough. It's either her way or no way. Think that might be why she hasn't remarried. Tends to scare men off with all her rules and regulations. Why, you so much as clear your throat wrong over at the big house, and she'll read you from the book till you're blue in the face."

"That she will, Sheriff. That she will."

"Been toeing the line over there?"

"I guess you could say that."

"Must be doin' all right," Beckett mused, looking Prophet over humorously. "Otherwise, she and ole Annabelle would have sent you out on a long, greased pole." He laughed again and shook his head.

"Yeah, I guess I'm doin' somethin' right, Sheriff," Prophet grumbled with an unreadable irony. "Say, how long do you think it'll take for my money to travel from Dodge?"

"Well, it's a fair piece, and this time of the year the roads can be a little muddy. I'd say a week at the earliest."

"A week, eh?" Prophet mused with an air of disheartenment. He'd figured it would take that long but was hoping he was wrong. He wanted to exit these parts before Cordelia decided she needed a new roof. He didn't think that even at his relatively youthful age he could roof her house and grease her wheels at the same time. "I reckon if it rains, or if there's some official holdup, which there usually is, it could be two or even three weeks before I can start looking for my reward money."

"I'd say that's about right."

Prophet sighed. "Thanks, Sheriff." Favoring his back, he started toward the saloon.

"What's your hurry?" Beckett called after him. "The widow's treating you all right over there, isn't she?"

Prophet gave the man a dismissive wave and continued across the street to the Sawmill, where he enjoyed the free sandwiches, pickled eggs, nickel beers, and several three-for-a-nickel cheroots. There were no gamers, however. Just two regulars—retired sawyers by their ratty clothes and missing fingers—playing backgammon beside the woodstove. The bartender told Prophet the gamblers were still out chopping trees and wouldn't be in until after six or so.

"That's all right," Prophet said, shoving his chair out, extending his legs, crossing his ankles, and lacing his fingers over his belly. He smiled at his third beer sitting before him, beside his empty plate. "I'll wait for 'em right here."

He was halfway into his fourth beer when he heard a commotion down the street. A man yelled, a woman screamed, and then two pistol shots sounded.

Prophet looked at the bartender, who was sitting beside the chess players, reading the paper. The man had looked up and was staring out the window with a curious frown.

"What was that?" Prophet said. In ranch country, it could've been cowboys hoorahing the town, but since this was mainly a honyonker and woodcutting area, and since the weekend was still three days away . . .

"I don't know."

Two more pistol shots split the midweek somnolence, and Prophet got to his feet and walked to the door, followed by the bartender in his sleeve garters and the two old backgammon players. Across the street, the dentist stepped out of his establishment to gaze around curiously, as did the blacksmith and the barber and the little gray-haired lady who ran the fabric shop.

They, like Prophet and the others from the Sawmill, turned their gazes eastward down the town's main drag, where at least twenty men on horseback were milling around on agitated horses before the mercantile. Two more men were on the broad loading dock fronting the place. The two appeared to be fighting with a long-haired girl, who screamed.

One of the men yelled something and smacked the girl across the face. When the girl went limp in his arms, he carried her down the steps to the street, where the other men were heeling their mounts back and forth before the place, six-shooters drawn and raised above their heads.

Several squeezed off shots skyward, just making noise.

"Now what in the hell is that all about?" the bartender said as he scratched his noggin.

"Looks like a damn holdup, if you're askin' me," Prophet said, all his senses suddenly coming alive but not quite believing what he was seeing.

"In Luther Falls?"

"I admit things look a whole lot more like Dodge City suddenly, but . . ." He was already walking down the street, instinctively heading toward the fracas, his gaze on the men milling before the mercantile.

"What are you doing with the girl, Day?" one of the horsebackers yelled.

"What do you think I'm doing with her?" another man returned as he climbed into his saddle, hefting the girl in his arms like a feed sack and throwing her over the horn.

"No!" the girl cried. "No!"

An older woman ran out of the mercantile, screaming, "You can't take my baby! Please, no! *No!*"

The man with the girl calmly drew his revolver from his hip, raised it to his shoulder, aimed, and fired. The gun clapped, smoke puffing. The woman who had run halfway down the steps of the loading dock stopped suddenly as though she'd forgotten something. She sat down and rolled to the side.

The girl screamed.

That's when Prophet realized beyond a shadow of a doubt that these men were highwaymen and that they were not only robbing the mercantile, they were kidnapping the girl. Here—in Luther Falls!

He'd run half a block, his heart pounding, when he saw the sheriff turn the corner on his left. Not wearing his suit coat or hat, Beckett was carrying his shotgun. He'd probably been eating lunch at home when he'd heard the gun-fire.

"Good shootin', Day!" one of the horsebackers shouted.

Day laughed and holstered his gun. "Come on, Dave, we got the money," he yelled at the store. "Leave the candy alone!" He laughed and shook his head.

"Yeah, come on, Dave. Let's skedaddle!" another man yelled at the store while several others shot their six-guns in the air.

Walking down the side of the main drag opposite Beckett and a half block behind him, Prophet reached for his revolver but grabbed only denim. His heart skipped a beat when he realized the Peacemaker wasn't there. He'd hung it in his room at the boarding house, having decided it would only get in his way while he toiled for Cordelia.

Besides, who needed a gun in this idyllic little berg?

The blunder mocked him now as he made his way quickly toward the dozen gun-toting firebrands itching for war.

He'd pulled up at an awning post a block from the mercantile when another man walked out of the store, grinning and holding two big paper sacks in his arms.

"Hit the mother lode, boys!" he whooped, holding the bags aloft.

"Come on, Dave. We ain't got all day."

"What's the hurry?" Dave said as he took his reins from one of the men riding horseback. "I say we see if there's a gun shop in town. I could use a new Smith & Wesson."

Standing by the awning post as other shopkeepers gathered on the boardwalks, mumbling, frightened, and confused, Prophet gritted his teeth. These firebrands seemed to think they could ride into town and do as they pleased. What was here was theirs for the taking. They showed no fear whatsoever, and very little urgency. If they knew there was a sheriff in town, they certainly paid no heed to the fact. Their guns were drawn, but mostly for show and to make some noise.

The disregard these men showed for law and order in Luther Falls could not have been lost on Sheriff Beckett, whom Prophet watched creep to the side of a buckboard wagon parked before the butcher shop, about a half block away from the mercantile. Old Beckett laid the barrel of his barn blaster over the side of the wagon box, taking aim.

"Don't do it, Beckett," Prophet thought, warning bells tolling in his head. "There's a dozen of them, and you've only got the two loads in that farm gun."

Prophet looked around for a gun, but no one was wearing one.

More whooping and gunfire erupted from the men before the mercantile, drawing Prophet's frantic gaze. They were all mounted now, and starting down the street, heading his way. They fired at windows and shingles as they rode, whooping and hollering like mad spirits released from hell, the hooves of their horses pounding the hard-packed street.

Prophet shot a glance at Beckett, taking aim across the side of the wagon. "Don't do it, Sheriff!" Prophet shouted.

It was too late.

He heard, "Stop! Sheriff!" and then the roar of the shotgun. It brought the firebrands to a skidding halt. Turning their horses toward the wagon, they opened fire, smoke puffing in huge clouds above their heads, the sound of their mocking laughter mixing with the racketing of their six-shooters and the confused whinnies of their horses.

"Well, that does it," Prophet thought, the skin on his neck pricking in earnest, lead filling his boots. "The crazy old coot's finished."

As the laughing men resumed their course down the street, Prophet turned to the four shopkeepers cowering a few feet away, behind water troughs and shipping barrels. "Doesn't anyone have a goddamn gun?"

A little man with a big, waxed mustache regarded him fearfully behind a stack of crates. "I got one inside."

"Get it, goddamnit! Move!" Prophet shouted.

The man ran into his millinery and was gone for what seemed like a long time as the firebrands trotted their horses paradelike down the street, shooting every window they spotted and even killing several horses tied to hitch racks.

"Hurry up!" Prophet shouted as the group passed.

He turned around just as the hatmaker reappeared, stooped and cowering, his face white, handing an oily, lumpy rag to Prophet. Crouching behind a water trough, Prophet opened the rag to find a Navy Conversion .36 with cracked grips and a rusty barrel. He hefted the gun in his right hand, not sure if the old cannon would blow his hand off but at the moment not caring. He bounced up from behind the trough and ran into the street as the procession made its way westward.

"Take one from me, you goddamn scurvy swine!" he shouted, thumbing back the hammer, squeezing the trigger and feeling the old hog nearly buck his hand off, springing his wrist.

In spite of the pain, he loosed two more shots before all the riders were out of range. So much black powder hung before him that he couldn't see if he'd hit anything. One of the riders at the end of the bunch turned in his saddle to return fire at Prophet, but apparently thinking he wasn't worth the effort, he turned back around and followed the others out of town.

Silence fell as the thunder of the horses receded in the distance. It was just as quickly shattered again as a woman commenced screaming.

"Arnie! Oh, Arnie!"

Prophet turned to his right and saw a woman standing

beside the wagon the sheriff had used for a shield. She wore a gray gingham housedress, an apron, and a lace-edged bonnet she must have thrown on in a hurry, for it was untied.

"No! Oh, Arnie!"

Prophet headed that way, hoping there was something he could do for the sheriff. It didn't take long to see there wasn't.

Beckett sat behind the left rear wheel of the wagon, his back to an awning post. He could have been napping, his chin on his chest, but for the four holes in his face, another in his throat, and at last three more in his chest. He was a bloody mess, and the wagon had been honeycombed with lead, the two horses killed and lying in the traces, in pools of their own viscera.

Prophet grabbed the woman's arm and led her up on the boardwalk—Mrs. Arnie Beckett, widowed in an eye blink.

"Take her home and call the undertaker," Prophet told one of the men who'd gathered at the wagon, looking as jittery as raw recruits in the aftermath of their first battle.

Unsteadily, the man led the crying woman off.

Prophet walked around the dead horses toward the mercantile. When he got there, he stopped before the woman lying slumped on the steps and checked her pulse. It was an instinctive move running contrary to logic, for the small, neat hole dripping blood between her eyes told him she was dead.

He mounted the steps and went inside to see who else had been the victims of the gang's violence. Inside the door, he stopped and looked around at the aisles of clothes and other dry goods, at the upended barrels of flour and nails and scattered displays of soaps and smoking pipes and chewing tobaccos. Nearly all the candy barrels and bins had been upended as well, the rock candy and licorice and jawbreakers scattered about the floor.

A guttural groan lifted from the back of the store, toward the counter, and Prophet moved toward it. Down the aisle he saw a man in a bloody apron sitting with his back to the counter. A tall, lanky man with short, black hair pomaded to his scalp and parted in the middle, he held his hands across his belly. Prophet winced when he saw that the man was literally holding his guts in his hands.

"Jesus Christ!" Prophet sputtered, kneeling before the man. Hearing someone mounting the steps, he turned and yelled through the door, "Someone get a sawbones— quick!"

He turned back to the wounded mercantile proprietor, who was shaking his head. His eyes were vacant and glassy. Blood bubbled from his mouth.

"No . . . use," he rasped. "I'm a . . . gon-er."

"Hold on, buddy," Prophet said, squeezing the man's shoulder. But he knew the man was right. Back during the Little Misunderstanding, he'd seen similar wounds. They were as deadly as they were painful, and this man didn't have a chance.

"My wife?" the man said. His chin was dipped to his chest.

Prophet hesitated. "Fit as a fiddle."

The man gave a halfhearted chuff, reading the lie. "That's . . . that's . . . what I . . . f-figured."

The man paused as if to conserve his strength. He took a rattling breath and said, "D-daughter?"

The daughter was apparently the blond girl the lead rider had ridden away with, thrown callously over his saddle and screaming for her life.

"I'm gonna get her back for you," Prophet said. His jaw was set hard as he stared down at the dying man, his heart breaking for all the hell that had happened here . . . for what? There couldn't have been more than fifty or sixty dollars in the cash drawer.

Now the decent old sheriff was dead, along with most

of a family. Who knew how many those human blowflies had left dead or injured up the street, before they'd finished their raid.

The dying man moved his hand to Prophet's and squeezed his wrist. It wasn't much of a squeeze, but Prophet could tell the man had something important on his mind. "Get . . . get her back . . . for me. P-please."

Prophet squeezed back. "I will. You can count on that."

Then the man's hand slid away from Prophet's wrist, and slowly, as though he were drifting to sleep, he slumped sideways to the floor and lay still.

Prophet stood and turned toward the front of the store, where several townsmen had gathered in the aisle, looking shocked and wary.

"Ole Hank," one of them said slowly. "He dead?"

"He's dead," Prophet said, brushing past the townsmen and heading for the door. When he got there, he pushed through the screen, descended the steps past the dead woman, and headed for the boarding house, moving quickly.

He'd get his guns and his possibles and be on the trail in a half hour. Then he'd hunt those renegades and turn them toe down hard—with not a scrap of mercy and no concern for monetary reward—if he had to ride all the way to hell and thrash the devil with a stick to do it.

5

"SHIT!"

Prophet reined Mean and Ugly to a halt in a cotton-wood copse along the grassy, southern bank of the Otter-tail River. The sun was going down, but making the sky even darker was a plum-colored storm curtain beating in from the west.

The curtain was streaked with pearl rain. From the size of the cloud topping the storm, it was a mean one, too, and would no doubt obliterate the tracks of the men Prophet was following, had been following for the past hour and a half, since leaving Luther Falls in a wind-splitting gallop.

"Lou, you be careful," Cordelia had admonished him from her front porch as he'd sprinted off down the street toward the livery, saddlebags over his shoulder. "That's the Red River Gang!"

He hadn't had time to go back and have her fill him in on just who in hell the Red River Gang was, but the tall Scandinavian who ran the livery barn had given him the quick lowdown while saddling his horse. Turned out the

Red River Gang was a group of renegades led by Handsome Dave Duvall and Dayton Flowers—both murdering
outlaws whom Prophet had heard of down in the Indian
Nations. Wanted by federal marshals out of Fort Smith,
they'd fled the southern plains to the north, where they'd
been running hog-wild for the past six months, raiding
settlements up and down the Red River between Wahpeton and Grand Forks in eastern Dakota Territory.

"They always raided more into Dakota than Minnesota," the liveryman had groused as he cinched Prophet's
saddle. "No one ever expected 'em to show their ugly
souls in Luther Falls. I mean, there ain't nothin' here
worth thievin'!"

Well they had a girl and some candy and the satisfaction of having turned a quiet little town upside down, and
that's probably a good day's work for that bunch, Prophet
thought now, as he sat watching the storm growing on the
horizon.

"Shit!" he repeated, knowing he was going to have to
seek shelter soon, probably throw a lean-to together to
keep from getting soaked.

He looked westward, the direction the gang's tracks led.
It was a vast, flat, brown prairie out there, relatively fea-
tureless but for the Ottertail River twisting through,
sheathed in high brush and cottonwoods. The gang was
following the river toward the Dakota border, and Prophet
figured they'd hole up, too, probably in a bend much like
the one Prophet sat along now, cursing the weather and
the lateness of the hour.

If he stopped now, he wouldn't be able to get started
again till the morning. No point tracking those men in the
dark and risk losing their trail—a trail that would prove
hard enough to follow after that squall hit.

He turned his horse back into the trees, dismounted,
and stripped the gear off Mean and Ugly, and hobbled
him. There was plenty of tall grass around, and the river

offered water, so he knew the horse wouldn't wander far. It was starting to rain, and the wind was kicking up by the time he'd rigged a lean-to with the tarpaulin in which he'd wrapped his bedroll. He'd chosen a campsite in a slight hollow with a big, uprooted cottonwood along one side, and the shelter kept him from getting soaked, although wind prevented him from building a fire.

Fortunately, the heaviest wind lasted only ten minutes or so. When it had tapered off, Prophet went out in the spitting rain to gather dry wood, returning with several small branches that had been sheltered by heavier limbs. He piled the wood outside the lean-to, then carved out a small hole in the center of the shelter, surrounded it with rocks he gathered from the river bank, and built a fire.

He didn't dally in starting a pot of coffee heating, with which he'd try to chase the damp chill from his bones. While the pot gurgled and sighed in the coals, he produced the bacon Cordelia and Annabelle had packed for him, and started it frying in his skillet. When the bacon was done, he fished the strips out of the grease, packed them and several extra dollops of grease from the pan in three fresh biscuits, and his supper was made.

He ate hungrily and washed his makeshift but delicious meal down with tar-black coffee, watching the rain, hearing the drops clatter on the tarpaulin. What was foremost in his mind, though, was the image of Sheriff Arnie Beckett riddled with bullets, and the dying mercantile proprietor feebly trying to hold his innards in place and begging Prophet to save his daughter.

That he'd do, by Ned. If it was the last thing he did in this world.

Most of Prophet's manhunting jobs had been pure business transactions which he'd carried out with cool objectivity. He'd rarely been a witness to the deprivations his quarries had committed and which had led to their being wanted by the law.

This was different. He'd seen what the Red River Gang had done, the brutality they'd carried out with the abandon of boys teasing a schoolyard snake. He'd seen the men and horses they'd killed, the property they'd destroyed, and the girl they'd carted off like the candy Handsome Dave Duvall had hauled out of the store.

And because he'd seen it in person, without being able to do a damn thing about it at the time, his hunt for them was personal. He figured all or most of the men already had high bounties on their heads, but he didn't care about that. What he wanted first and foremost was to free the girl. Then he wanted to see the renegades either behind . bars or dead.

How he'd execute such a task, he wasn't sure. There were at least twelve of them and only one of him. Eventually, lawmen would be alerted to their trail, but the group had no doubt cut the telegraph lines out of Luther Falls, so for the next few days, at least, Prophet would be on his own.

For probably a hell of a lot longer than that. He doubted this godforsaken part of the country had any badge-toters with enough rawhide to face down the Red River Gang. Federal marshals would probably be called in, but that would take days, and it would take the marshals at least a week to get here, even longer to pick up the gang's trail.

No, Prophet was alone for now, on the trail of twenty ruthless killers. And he had no inkling of a plan. . . .

"But then again, I'm not much of a planner, anyway," he said to himself, setting his cup on a rock and fishing in the breast pocket of his buckskin tunic for his Bull Durham and rolling papers.

He smoked and watched the rain, and after dark he checked on Mean and Ugly, banked the fire, and rolled up in his soogan. The next day dawned clear and cool and fresh-smelling after the rain. Prophet woke to geese honking on the river and ducks jawing at the geese.

He got up and ate a hurried breakfast, downing several cups of coffee and smoking several cigarettes before rigging out Mean and Ugly. He'd taken down his lean-to and was all packed and mounted by the time the sun poked its bright orange top above the western hills.

Fortunately, the rain hadn't lasted long enough to obliterate the renegades' trail. It had made it fainter, however, and Prophet had to be extra vigilant, keeping his eyes glued to the grassy sod. He couldn't just rely on the flattened grass trails normally left by horses, for the wind and rain themselves had flattened plenty of grass. Several times he had to stop and dismount to spy hoofprints or horse apples in the sod.

About nine o'clock in the morning he approached a creek meeting the river from the south, and stopped suddenly when he smelled smoke from a cookfire. He reined the line-back dun to a halt, sniffing the air and looking around. Shortly, he reined the horse to his right, into the trees along the river. He dismounted and tied the horse to a branch.

Shucking his Winchester, he started walking westward through the trees, stopping every now and then and listening for voices. He couldn't believe the Red River Gang would be holed up this late in the day, but if they were as cocky as they'd appeared, maybe they were careless enough to make stupid mistakes. . . .

Prophet moved forward, holding his Winchester across his chest, avoiding branches and deadfalls which would make noise if stepped on. He kept his ears pricked, listening, and sniffed the air as he followed the smell of the fire.

When he'd walked a hundred yards, he stopped and crouched down, his eyes widening. About twenty yards ahead, blue smoke curled through the branches of the box elders and cottonwoods. There were no voices, which might mean the gang had left their camp without extinguishing their fire, but Prophet wasn't taking any chances.

He ducked behind a tree, laid out a course that would bring him to the camp while zigzagging between trees, and started off, quietly levering a shell into his rifle breech. When he came to the last tree in his course, he crouched low, removed his hat, and slid a look around the cottonwood's wide bole.

His heart tapped rhythmically when he saw a man sitting on the other side of a smoky fire, his back to a natural levee. He was half-bald and unshaven, and his head was thrust back, his face bunched, as if in pain. A wool blanket was draped across his shoulders.

Prophet looked around, but it didn't appear to be a trap. Nearby was a single horse, but there were no other riders in the area.

Thumbing the hammer of his Winchester back, Prophet stepped out from behind the tree. "Keep your hands where I can see them, old son."

The man gave a start, his head snapping level. The blanket fell from his shoulders as he grabbed at the pistol on his right hip with his left hand. It was an especially awkward maneuver, because he wasn't wearing a cross-draw rig.

"Stop!" Prophet shouted, squeezing off a shot and ripping a widget of sod and leaves from the levee about six inches to the man's left.

That froze him, and he looked at Prophet belligerently. "What the hell do you want?"

For a minute, Prophet wondered if the man was just a farmer or some drover riding the grub line. But then he saw the blood on the man's right arm, which was red from his shoulder to his wrist.

"I want you, if you're part of the Red River Gang," Prophet said, taking another cautious glance around, making sure he and the wounded man were alone.

"The Red River Gang?" the man said with a caustic laugh. "Who in the hell are they?"

Prophet studied the man and knew he was one of the dozen he was looking for. He glanced at the arm. "What happened there? You take a bullet?"

The man looked at his own arm and laughed again. "Yeah, I was out huntin' and wouldn't you know it—I dropped my damn gun, and it went off on me. Hit me in the shoulder, bored a route down the bone, and came out my wrist."

"You dropped it and it hit you in the shoulder, did ye? That's some fancy gun you have there." Prophet couldn't remember hearing or seeing any of the townsmen return fire. He had a feeling he'd hit this man himself, with that old Colt Navy the hatmaker had given him.

"It's the darndest thing," the man said, shaking his head.

Prophet walked slowly up to him, pointed the barrel at his face, reached down, and lifted the revolver from the man's holster. It was a Colt Army with gutta-percha grips. Prophet wedged the gun in his belt and said, "Get up."

The man lifted his eyes to Prophet and snarled, "Go to hell, you bastard. Can't you see I'm bleedin' to death here?"

"I'm taking you to the sheriff over in Wahpeton. Maybe, if the man's nice and doesn't mind wasting town funds on the likes of a shit dog like yourself, he'll hire a sawbones to tend that arm. Have you good as new for the hangman." Prophet was seething, and he had to try with all his might not to drill a slug through the man's skull and leave him here for the hawks. "Get up."

"Sheriff? What sheriff? I didn't do nothin'."

"Get up!"

"Can't you see I'm—?"

"If you're not standing in three seconds, I'm sending you to the smokin' gates."

"All right, all right," the man said with a sigh. "But I'm tellin' you, Mister—you're makin' a mistake." Painfully, without Prophet's help, the man donned his hat and gained his feet. "I don't know what you think I did, but I'm innocent as the baby Jesus."

Prophet went around behind the man and patted him down, finding a knife in a sheath down his back and a hideout gun in the well of his left boot. He also found three new gold watches in his jeans pockets, a new pocket knife, and several shiny trinkets.

"Innocent as baby Jesus, eh?" Prophet chuffed. "Move!" he ordered, pushing the man toward his horse.

The dapple-gray was unsaddled, so Prophet tacked it up while the man watched with an angry sneer on his pain-ravaged face. He was slick with sweat, and Prophet didn't doubt an infection had set in. He had a mind to put him out of his misery and leave him here, but a cold-blooded killer the bounty hunter was not.

When Prophet had the man on his horse, he tied his wrists to his saddle horn and bound his feet to his stirrups. He led the dapple-gray back to Mean and Ugly, who nickered at the strangers and lifted his tail aggressively at the dapple-gray.

"Friendly horse you have there," the outlaw remarked.

"Ain't he?" Prophet said, yanking the line-back's head away from the dapple-gray's ass, and mounting up.

Trailing the outlaw, who grunted and groaned in pain, his head either sagging to his chest or tipped back on his shoulders, Prophet tracked the main group along the river. He had a feeling they were headed the same place he was headed—the little town of Wahpeton, which sat at the point where the Ottertail and Bois de Sioux rivers converged to form the Red on the Dakota line, about ten or fifteen miles away.

If that's where they were headed—and there wasn't much else to head for out here—they and Prophet would be meeting real soon.

6

THE HONEY-HAIRED BLONDE rode a sleek black Morgan horse, as fine in head as a Swiss mantle clock, as deep in barrel and haunch as a mountain grizzly. She walked the well-trained mount across the wood bridge, traversing the diminutive Rabbit River, and kicked him into a canter, then a gallop. When the town came into sight around a bend in the muddy wagon trail, she slowed the frisky Morgan back down to a trot.

As she passed the post with a crudely painted sign with the word CAMPBELL painted in green letters, she turned her head from side to side, noting the handful of modest frame buildings lining the recently graded railroad bed.

There were no tracks in the grade yet, but the girl had heard that the St. Paul & Pacific would be laying rails through these parts before the summer was out, connecting the Red River Valley with Minneapolis and Chicago and other points east.

Why anyone would care that this backwater hole in hell was connected to anything, the girl had no idea. But then, she didn't care, either. She didn't care about much of anything at the moment but the four horses tethered to the hitch rack before a two-story building sitting between the brick depot and the post office, with enough space on each side for one or two more stores.

The sign over the building's veranda announced THE PHILADELPHIA hotel, and she thought the name mighty uppity for such a humble pile of boards. Stopping her Morgan about fifty yards before the white-painted building, she gave it a close study, ignoring the subtly fearful tap of her pulse in her wrists and neck, the cool-warmth of apprehension creeping up the backs of her thighs.

If anyone had been out on the street of this ambitious little railroad stop, they might have wondered what had brought this girl here—a pretty blonde in her late teens riding a tall, broad-chested black Morgan. They might have thought she was a farmer's daughter come to buy some flour or eggs at the general store, for she wore a round, felt farm hat with a chin thong, a weathered brown poncho, and the kind of long, gray skirt favored by farm women.

The fine horse would have thrown them off, however. The Winchester carbine poking out of her saddle boot would have stumped them, too, for few girls rode around this country armed with rifles, let alone Winchester carbines.

Running her tongue along her upper lip and inhaling deeply, steeling herself, the girl kneed the Morgan over to the hitch rack. She dismounted, while keeping an eye on the hotel's single door and its single frosted window. Her hands trembling slightly, she looped the reins over the rack.

Turning, she faced the building for several seconds before walking resolutely to the door, twisting the knob, and pushing it open. She closed it quickly with only a cursory glance around the room, and made for a table near the wall on her left.

She took a seat with her back to the wall, planted her elbows on the table, and rested her chin in her hands, taking the time now to glance around.

There was a bar along the right side of the room, and lined up at the bar, their backs to her, were the four men who belonged to the four horses outside. They hadn't seen her yet. Only the barman had seen her—a stocky man with sandy hair and an ostentatious mustache wearing sleeve garters and a white apron. He gazed at her with a question wrinkling the bridge of his nose.

The four men standing at the bar noticed the barman's gaze and turned to follow it to the girl, who smiled, removed her hat, and tossed it on the chair beside her. She shook her head, tossing her long, blond hair out from the collar of her worn poncho, then replaced her chin in her hands.

The barman cleared his throat, lifted his chin, and called, "If you're waitin' for the stage, Miss, it don't get here till tomorrow noon."

"I'm not," she said.

Puzzled, the barman glanced at the others. The others glanced at each other. Then the man farthest on the girl's left said, "Maybe she's waitin' for the train."

The others laughed.

"Nope. I ain't waitin' for the train, neither," she said. "I'm just waitin'." Her voice was at once girlish and mature; it was a trait that made her appealing to men. Especially men, she had found to her horror, like the ones before her now: denim-clad hookworms.

The others shared glances again, chuckling. The four along the bar elbowed each other, snickering. Finally, one picked up his beer mug and made his way to the table, weaving a little, sucking in his gut and adjusting the holster tied low on his thigh. He had curly hair under a battered hat with a funneled brim, and his brown eyes were bleary.

"Well, you must be waitin' for somethin'," he said when he'd stopped before her, grinning down at her stupidly.

"No, not really," she said. "I was just passin' through and thought I'd take a breather, maybe have a sarsaparilla"—she glanced at the barman—"if you have any, sir."

The man before her laughed. Turning to the barman he mocked, "If you have any, sir."

The three men at the bar laughed. The barman turned to them, and he laughed, too.

The man before her turned to her and planted his left fist on the table, regarding her lewdly, running his eyes over the two pert swellings in her poncho. "Why don't you have a beer with me?" he said. "I'll buy."

"I don't much care for spiritous liquids, sir," the girl said. "My grandmother raised me to believe they were brewed by the devil and imbibed by the damned."

More laughter. The man standing over the girl smiled down at her, showing his brown teeth. "Well, now, how in the hell would she know? I bet she never drank anything stronger than goat's milk. And I bet you haven't neither, have you, sweetie?"

The girl didn't respond to this. She returned the man's gaze levelly, her hazel eyes wide and innocent.

"Where you from and where you headed, angel face?" the man asked.

"I'm from Minneapolis. My dear grandmother passed away last week, and I'm off to Montana to find Aunty Gert."

The man turned to the others. "She's off to Montana to find her Aunty Gert," he said, his voice teeming with irony.

"Ask her if she wants some company," one of the others at the bar called.

"You heard him, sweetie," the man said. "You want

some company out to ole Montany, looking for Aunty Gert?"

"No, thank you, sir. But thanks for asking."

"Well, how about a beer, then?" the man standing before her said.

"No, thank you. Like I said . . ."

"Yeah, I know what you said." The man turned to the bartender. "Dave, bring the little miss here a sarsaparilla, an' put it on my tab."

He tossed the girl's hat off the chair beside her and sat down, turning to face her. She nearly choked on the beer stench of his breath, but kept her gaze even and innocent.

"Thank you," she said.

When the bartender came with the sarsaparilla, setting the glass before the girl, the man sitting beside her said conversationally, "So you're heading to ole Montany, eh, my sweet?"

The girl sipped her drink noisily. "That's right," she said, wiping her pretty, wide mouth with the back of her hand.

"Better be careful in ole Montany," the man said, half turning to his compatriots at the bar. "Montany's full of one-eyed snakes."

One of the men at the bar sprayed beer from his mouth. The others chuckled and jostled each other.

"One-eyed snakes?" the girl asked.

The men at the bar guffawed.

Smiling, the man seated beside the girl said, "That's right. There's a whole bunch of 'em out ole Montany way. You'll want to be careful." He turned a cockeyed look at her. "You mean to tell me you've never seen a one-eyed snake before?"

The girl thought about it, rolling up her eyes. "Nope. I don't think so." Frowning, she looked at the man seriously. "Are they a type of sidewinder?"

The men at the bar were laughing so hard they had to

grab the zinc counter to keep from falling down.

The man sitting next to the girl dropped his head, then brought it back up, tears rolling down his cheeks. "Yes, ma'am. I guess you could say they're a type of side-winder." He paused and squinted his eyes, as though a thought had just occurred to him. "Say, maybe you should see one, so you know what they look like. That way, if you see one along the trail, you'll know to avoid them."

The girl sipped her sarsaparilla and shrugged noncom-mittally.

"Yeah," the man said, turning to his friends for counsel. "Boys, don't you think this girl should see a one-eyed snake, so she'll know what to avoid out in ole Montany?"

"I think that'd only be prudent," one of the men said through a belly laugh.

"Why don't you come upstairs with me, honey?" the man beside the girl said. "And I'll show you a one-eyed snake."

The girl set her glass down, frowning. "They have one-eyed snakes in Minnesota, too?"

"Well," the man smiled. "There ain't as many of 'em hereabouts, but I've got one upstairs . . . in a special cage." He put his hand on the back of her chair. "Come on. I'll show you."

He turned to the bartender. "Say, Dave, can I have a room for, say, half an hour?"

"Five minutes, more like," one of the man's friends interjected.

"Yeah, but it'll cost you," the bartender said.

"Put it on my tab." Turning to the girl, the man said, "Come on, little honey. Let's go upstairs, and I'll show you my one-eyed snake."

The girl rolled her eyes to the side as she sipped her drink, thinking about it. "Nah. I better not. My grand-mother told me never to go off with strange men."

The man grabbed her arm, standing. "Come on, little

honey. I'm gonna show you my one-eyed snake."

"No," the girl objected as he dragged her to her feet. "I told you, my—"

"Yeah, I know what you're grandmother said," the man said, pulling the girl away from the table. "But granny's worm food now, and it's time you had you a good look at one of them ole one-eyed snakes you're gonna be seein' plenty of out in ole Montany."

The men at the bar whooped and yelled.

"No!" the girl cried, yanking her hands from the man's iron grip.

"Hey!" the man shouted, his face creased with sudden rage. He turned sharply and smacked her hard with his right fist, sending her sprawling across two chairs. He grabbed her, yanked her to her feet, bent down, and threw her over his shoulder. As she kicked and yelled, pounding his back with her fists, he made his way to the stairs at the back of the room.

"I'm second," one of the men at the bar called.

"I'm third," yelled another, raising his fist after the man disappearing with the girl up the stairs.

"Guess you know what that makes you," the bartender said to the fourth man.

Above them, the girl cried for help.

7

"WELL, I'LL BE damned," Prophet said.

Mean and Ugly's reins in his hand, he was hunkered on his haunches, studying the horse sign in the sod. He looked around, then lifted his gaze westward, turned it south, and sighed. With a gloved finger, he poked his hat back from his forehead and scowled.

"They split up."

He heard a snicker. Turning his head, he saw the man sitting the speckle-gray behind Mean and Ugly. The man was smiling through the pain of his shattered arm.

"What the hell are they doin' splittin' up out here?" Prophet asked him.

"None o' your goddamn business," the outlaw groused, wincing as more pain lanced his arm.

Prophet stood and walked over to the man. "I bet I could make that arm hurt worse," he speculated.

The man looked at him with bright fear in his eyes.

"I bet all I'd need to do," Prophet said, lifting his right hand to the wounded man's right wrist, "is give your arm a little yank."

He tugged on the man's sleeve. The man yelled, "No! No, goddamn you!"

Prophet looked into the man's face, smiling wistfully. "Well, sure enough, I could. Now, tell me, why would those four that split off from the main group be headin' south?"

"I don't know," the man yelled, his face bleached with misery.

"Oh, come on," Prophet said. "I think you do."

He reached up and gave the man's right wrist a pull. The outlaw whipped his head up, howling. Panting, he said, "Ow! Goddamn you, it hurts! Oh, Jesus, don't do that!"

"Tell me where those four went. What's south of here?"

"I don't know . . . well . . . goddamnit . . . I reckon they either cut out for Campbell or Tintah. I reckon Campbell, seein' as how there's a saloon there an' all . . ."

"You think they just split off for a drink?"

The scowling firebrand considered this and shrugged. "I reckon they're thirsty. Ole Newt and Barry—they can't be without a drink for long, an' they ran out of whiskey around the fire last night. Campbell's only about three miles south. Wahpeton's still another ten miles or so west."

Prophet ran his thumb along the line of his unshaven jaw, considering this. He should probably follow the main group, but he didn't want any of these gunnies getting away. The four would more than likely rejoin the group later—probably in Wahpeton—but that wasn't certain.

On the other hand, if they were drinking heavily in Campbell, they shouldn't be all that hard to take down. It might only take him an hour or so. As far as the kidnapped girl was concerned, she could be with the four as easily as the larger group.

Deciding to go after the four, Prophet unsheathed his

bowie and cut the ropes tying the man's feet to his stirrups
and his wrists to the horn. "Get down."

"Huh?"

"Get down."

"Wha . . . what the hell . . . ?"

Prophet grabbed the man's arm.

"Oh, no! Not my arm! Jesus, I heard you!"

Holding his arm stiffly at his side, the outlaw climbed
down from the saddle. Prophet led him over to a tree,
pushed him down, and tied his arms behind the trunk, the
man screaming and cursing him all the while. Apparently,
the position wasn't very comfortable for his wounded
arm, but Prophet didn't care. The man had been with the
group who'd murdered innocent people and taken a help-
less girl hostage. Screw his arm.

When he'd tied the man's feet together so he couldn't
move around too much and work his hands free, Prophet
led his horse to another tree, tied him there, then mounted
Mean and Ugly, who'd been waiting, ground-hitched
nearby, the dun's white-ringed eyes on the speckle-gray.

"Let's go, hoss," Prophet told the horse, reining him
away.

"You just gonna leave me here?" the outlaw called.

"That's right."

"I'm gonna bleed to death, you damn fool."

"Shoulda thought of that before you raided Luther
Falls," Prophet yelled over his shoulder, kicking Mean
and Ugly into a gallop.

Following the tracks of the four horses, he traversed a
grassy swale and splashed through a slough, scaring up
ducks and geese. A few minutes later, he came to a railroad bed on which no tracks had yet been laid, and followed it west until, mounting a rise, he saw several
buildings, including a brick depot lined out below.

Heeling the dun toward the fledgling town the railroad
surveyors had probably platted last summer, Prophet

pulled his shotgun over his chest and worried a thumb over the hammers. He entered the town at a slow walk, eyeing the buildings still smelling of pine resin. Seeing the five horses, including a black Morgan, tied before the two-story, high-fronted structure touting itself as the Philadelphia Hotel, Prophet reined Ugly that way, dismounted, and tied him to the rack's far end.

"Now don't bite anybody," Prophet scolded the horse, turning to the building's door.

Removing the thong over the hammer of his .45 and holding the shotgun across his belly, he opened the door and stepped inside, raking his eyes quickly around the long, narrow room. In the shadows before him, about twenty yards away, three hard-looking gunmen stood along the bar, facing the wall to Prophet's right. Facing the toughs was the bartender. They'd all turned their heads to look at Prophet, and the expressions on the blunt faces of the hard cases were both curious and guarded—especially when they saw the barn blaster hanging from the lanyard around the bounty hunter's neck.

Prophet took them all in, watching their hands. Above him, he heard something thumping the ceiling and the muffled sounds of a girl or young woman protesting what could only have been the advances of a man. There was the sound of a slap and a shrill cry.

Prophet smiled. "Sounds like someone's havin' a good time, anyway."

"That's just the whore," one of the men at the bar explained. "When she's drunk, she likes it a little rough's all."

"I see," Prophet said. "Would you bring me a shot and a beer?" he asked the barman. He turned and sat down at the nearest table, removing his hat and tossing it on the table before him.

Without saying anything, the barman set a shot glass on the counter and uncorked a whiskey bottle. The three

toughs were scrutinizing Prophet through slitted eyes. One
man eyed the shotgun with a half smile on his face. He
was a fiery-eyed little terrier with sandy blond hair falling
out of his slouch hat. His right hand was on his gun butt,
and Prophet saw that he'd removed the safety thong from
the hammer.

It was fairly obvious why he was here, he supposed,
armed for bear as he was. These three shouldn't be much
trouble, however, grouped up along the bar. He'd wait for
his drink and for one of them to make the first move. . . .

The fiery-eyed little terrier said tightly, "What's the
matter—you don't want to stand at the bar and drink with
us?"

Prophet smiled at him. "No, I don't."

The others didn't say anything. The barman brought the
beer and the shot, setting them on the table before Prophet
and collecting the coins the bounty hunter had tossed
down by his hat. The man moved quickly, nervous about
getting caught in a crossfire. In a moment, he was behind
the bar, backed up to the mirror, his uneasy gaze sliding
between Prophet and the three men before the mahogany.

Overhead, the sounds of the fight had died.

"That ain't very nice," one of the men at the bar said.

"Sorry," Prophet said, lifting the shotglass to his lips
and tossing back half the whiskey. "Didn't mean to hurt
your feelings. It's just that, well"—he set the glass down
and looked at the three from under his brows—"I never
cottoned to drinkin' with wormy dog shit."

Upstairs, someone screamed. Prophet couldn't tell at
first if it was the girl or the man. That's how shrill the
scream was. When it became obvious the long, echoing
cry belonged to the man, the three at the bar slid their
eyes to each other, befuddled. The cry was so enduring,
expressing such pain and horror, that it put even Prophet
on edge.

"Sounds like your friend's getting more than what he paid for up there," Prophet said at last.

"Benny, go see," the little man ordered.

"What about him?" Benny said, eyeing Prophet.

"Forget him for now," the little man returned. "Go see what in the hell's wrong with Barry."

Upstairs, the cry seemed to grow even louder. "Ahhhhhh! No! Ahhhhhhhhhh! Nooooooooo-hoh-hoh-hoh!"

Wincing with apprehension, Benny sidled away from the group and walked to the stairs at the back of the room. "Barry, what the hell's happenin' up there?" he yelled. Receiving only more yelling in reply, he placed a hand on the railing and started up the stairs.

Meanwhile, the two other men stared at Prophet, hands on their guns. "Probably just stubbed his toe," the little man said.

"That can sure grieve ye," Prophet replied.

It was not the little man who drew first, but the man standing to his right. He crouched of a sudden, bringing his six-shooter up and out of its holster. He took too much time, however. All Prophet had to do was thumb back the shotgun's hammers, which he did, turn the barrel a little, and trip the right trigger.

The gun's enormous bark was followed by a loud yelp. The gunman jerked so far backward that he smacked the back of his head on the bar top, breaking his skull with an audible crack. At the same time, the terrier crouched and drew. He, too, was too slow, and a half second later he lay on the floor across his friend, their blood mingling and running in several thick streams across the warped wood floor.

A shot sounded upstairs. A man yelled, and then two more shots followed in quick succession. Something hit the upstairs floor so hard that the hanging lamps danced, swaying shadows.

Prophet looked at the ceiling, then at the barman. "You want any of this?" he said, nodding at the two dead men on the floor.

The barman shook his head. "I just serve 'em liquor—that's all."

"Smart man," Prophet said.

He breeched the shotgun and replaced the spent shells. Then he scraped his chair back, stood, stepped over the dead men, and walked to the stairs. Grabbing the newel post, he gazed up uneasily, the shotgun in his right hand.

He sighed and started up the stairs, taking one step at a time. He tried to figure out what in the hell had been going on up there, but nothing washed.

When he made the landing, he paused, brought the shotgun up tighter to his side, extending the barrel before him. Slowly, he poked his head around the corner, gazing up the last flight of stairs to the second story.

No one was there. He could hear a man's muffled groaning. The air was fetid with gunpowder.

Prophet started climbing again, one step at a time, hearing the groans and the creaking of the steps under his boots. He was halfway to the top when a hatted figure suddenly appeared with a gun.

"Die, devil! Die!" rose a girl's shriek, followed by three swift gunshots.

Prophet ducked and threw himself to the side as one bullet ripped his hat off and another singed his cheek. Losing his footing, he fell back down the stairs, hearing the whine of a bullet slicing the air over his head and chunking into the landing wall, at the foot of which he piled up like dirty clothes.

"Lady, hold on, goddamnit!" Prophet yelled, scrambling to his feet. "I ain't one o' them!"

He looked up the stairs. A fair-faced girl stood there in a black, round-brimmed, bullet-crowned hat and a tattered wool poncho. Blond hair fell over her shoulders, but what interested Prophet most was the fact that she was busy reloading her silver-plated revolver.

"Hold your skirts, kid—I ain't one o' them!" he yelled again as he started up the stairs, tripping in his haste and pushing himself off his hands.

The girl thumbed the last cartridge into the cylinder and was bringing the gun up, thumbing back the hammer, as Prophet reached her. Knocking the gun aside with his left hand, he bulled into her, throwing her backward off her feet. He went down on top of her and tried wrestling the gun out of her ironlike grip. She cursed and punched him with her left fist, hard.

"Goddamn you! Goddamn you!"

Flinching and cowering, Prophet crawled up her body and gained his knees. Finally, he managed to restrain her left arm with his right knee. It took both his hands and the strength of Goliath to peel her fingers open and to finally remove the revolver. When he did, flinging it away, she erupted with a whole new string of curses, and her knees went to work, pummeling his back. Her right hand came up, thrashing him and opening a cut on his lip.

"Goddamn it!" he complained, lowering his head against the renewed onslaught and pinning her right fist to the floor with his left knee.

Now he was high enough on her body that her knees could no longer reach him. She still writhed beneath him, but to no avail. Her face was red with hate and anger, tears of heart-searing rage watering her hazel eyes. He held on and waited for her to wear herself out.

Which she eventually did, but it took awhile. Finally, her muscles relaxed and her eyes focused on him through an acrimonious haze.

He said, "Will you listen to reason now?"

She lifted her head and scrunched her eyes up angrily. "Do I have a choice?"

He climbed to his feet, her gun in his right hand. "Ow," she said, sitting up and massaging her wrists. She looked at him accusingly. "If you ain't one o' them, who are you?"

"Lou Prophet. Bounty hunter. I was in Luther Falls when they robbed the mercantile. Been tracking the group till these four broke off and headed here."

He looked down the hall behind him and saw the body of the man who'd come up looking for Barry. Prophet looked at the girl and jerked his thumb at the dead man. "Your work?"

The girl didn't reply to this. "You take care of the other two downstairs?"

"Yup. What happened to . . . ?" Prophet moved down the hall, at the end of which was an open door. He stood in the doorway and looked into the room, where a nude man lay thrashing around on his belly, his hands cupping his groin. He was crying into a pillow. The bed was soaked in bright red blood.

Prophet turned to the girl at the other end of the hall, who was busy straightening her skirt and adjusting her poncho. "What the hell did you do to him?"

"Gelded him," she said matter-of-factly.

Prophet looked into the room again, then returned his dubious eyes to the girl. "Jesus."

"Yep. I doubt he'll be showin' off his one-eyed snake anymore."

Prophet sighed, shook his head, and started back down the hall. The girl stopped in front of him, extending her open hand. "I'll take my gun back now."

Absently, still thinking about the man in the bedroom, who had been punished thoroughly enough by Prophet's standards, he slapped the gun in the girl's hand. He gave her a long, amazed stare, then started back down the stairs.

8

THE BARMAN WAS waiting at the bottom of the stairs. "What the hell happened up there?" he asked Prophet.

"You don't want to know." Pushing past the man on his way to his table, Prophet said, "Got a sawbones around here?"

"No. Mrs. Jergens handles most of the medical problems."

"Well, you better get her," Prophet said, retaking his chair at the table upon which his beer and half a shot of whiskey still sat.

"I'll send someone for her, and get some help hauling these bodies out."

"There's one more upstairs," Prophet said as the barman headed for the door.

When the barman had gone, Prophet threw back the last of his whiskey and chased it with a healthy swig of the flat beer. He heard steps on the stairs, and the girl appeared at the newel post, gazing at the two dead men on the floor before the bar. Her expression was one of interest and mild admiration, not of the horror that would have been etched on the faces of most girls her age— most women, for that matter.

"Nice shootin'," the girl told him at last.

Prophet grunted. "Can I buy you a drink?"

The girl walked toward him, blond curls bouncing on her shoulders, chin thong swinging against her poncho. She stepped over the bodies, sidled over to a table to Prophet's left, grabbed a glass from it, and brought it over. She set the glass on Prophet's table and sat down in the chair across from him.

"Already have a drink, thanks."

"Sarsaparilla?"

"Yep," the girl said when she'd taken a sip.

Prophet gave a sardonic chuff. Looking at her sitting there sipping her red bubbly water, all peaches and cream skin and blond hair and milk teeth, she could have been on her way home from Sunday school. You never could've guessed she'd sunk three .44 pills into one bad-man and left the other minus his oysters.

"Figured a girl like you'd drink rye straight up with a blood chaser."

The girl's face was expressionless. "Nope—just sarsa-parilla for me, please. That stuff you're drinkin' tastes like badger pee and fuzzies the brain."

Prophet looked at her without saying anything for several seconds. "What's your name?"

"Louisa."

"Louisa what?"

"Why?"

Prophet shrugged. "Why not?"

"I don't like men knowin' anymore about me than they have to for civilized conversation."

"Okay," Prophet said with a sigh. "Then I suppose tell-ing me what you're doin' here and why you killed those two men upstairs is out of the question?"

"Yep." She drained her glass and set it back on the table. Standing, she said, "It was nice meeting you, Mr. Prophet."

"Where you goin'?"

"After the others."

"How do you know where they are?"

"Because I've been following them for most of a year." Prophet frowned, incredulous. "You have?"

"Yep."

"Then I suppose you know they raided Luther Falls yesterday afternoon."

"That's right."

"Where in the hell were you?"

"Outside of town, in an old barn. I trailed 'em to the outskirts of town. I would've warned the sheriff—if there is a sheriff—but I didn't know where they were headed until they were almost there."

Prophet stared at her again, as if at a puzzle he couldn't begin to fathom. "Why is a nice-looking little gal like yourself tracking a herd of gunnies like them?"

"I have my reasons." She turned and started for the door. "Now I best get after the others."

When she'd left, Prophet sat there, his head swirling. Finally, he finished his beer, got up, and walked outside. The girl was heading out of town on the black Morgan that had been hitched to the rack. When she made the outskirts, she heeled the gelding into a gallop, and was soon swallowed up by the brown grass and rolling prairie, heading north.

Prophet turned to his right and saw the barman heading toward the saloon with two men in bib-front coveralls. "Sorry for the trouble," Prophet said to the barman as he untied Mean and Ugly's reins from the rack.

"Wait a minute, Mister," the barman called. "You best wait for the county sheriff. You got some explainin' to do."

"You saw it," Prophet said, mounting up. "You explain it."

He reined the dun around and kicked him into a trot. At the edge of town he reined Mean and Ugly northward and kicked him into a ground-eating gallop. He'd ridden nearly half a mile before the girl came into sight. She'd slowed her horse into a canter, which made it easier for Prophet to catch up to her.

When he was about fifty yards behind her, she heard him and turned around, reaching through a slit in her skirt—for the gun, no doubt. She halted the action when she recognized Prophet, and turned back in her saddle to scowl over the Morgan's ears.

"What do you want?" she groused as he drew abreast of her.

"Same thing you do," Prophet said. "The Red River Gang."

"Why?"

" 'Cause I was in Luther Falls when they rode in and shot up the town. They kidnapped a girl, the daughter of the couple who ran the mercantile. They not only shot the girl's parents in cold blood, but they shot the sheriff, too. A nice old fart named Arnie Beckett."

"You live there?"

"No, I was just passin' through. But I seen it happen. And since there ain't no more law to go after those men, I'm doing it myself. I'm sort of in the profession, you might say."

The girl sighed. "Well, I'm sure there's plenty of bounty on their heads. They've cut a wide swath, that bunch."

"I'm not after the bounties," Prophet said.

The girl looked at him pointedly. "Neither am I."

"You know, I had a feeling you weren't," Prophet said with an ironic wince. "Well, I told you my story. What's yours?"

The girl rode along in silence for a minute, obviously pondering her response. Finally, she said, "They killed my family." That's all she said, and she didn't turn to look at him, but kept her gaze straight ahead at the rutted wagon trail they were following.

"Where? When?"

She sighed heavily. "Last year. Nebraska."

Prophet looked at her, waiting for more. No more came. Finally, he said, "Well, what in the hell made you think you could run them down? You're just a girl, for chrissakes. I bet you aren't seventeen."

"I am seventeen. And being 'just a girl' has come in mighty handy a time or two."

"A time or two?"

"Actually, three times so far."

Prophet tipped his hat back from his forehead impatiently and scowled at her. "What are you saying?"

Louisa shrugged. "I've already done away with three of 'em. Just waited for the group to split up and went after 'em one at a time. One I stabbed in a privy outside Julesburg, Colorado. Another one I caught with a whore in Deadwood Gulch. And the third one, Jimmy McPhee was his name, was trying to get into my bloomers when he stopped to help me with my horse I told him had come up lame. That was in southern Dakota, outside Sioux Falls. Ever been there?"

"Once or twice," Prophet grumbled, staring at the girl, mystified.

"Nasty place, ain't it? I think some Saturday night the sheriff should lock all the owlhoots in the saloons and burn the whole kit 'n' caboodle to the ground. The whole damn town."

"You're a real charmer, Miss Louisa."

She favored him with a cockeyed smile. "Thank you, Mr. Prophet."

"What's your last name?"

"I guess it ain't no big secret. Bonaventure."

"Louisa Bonaventure?"

"That's right."

"From Nebraska?"

"My folks farmed out there, near the Platte River, before the Red River Gang rode through. Of course, they weren't called the Red River Gang back then. That's just been since they moved north to get away from the federal marshals down Kansas and Missouri way."

"They killed your pa and ma?"

"And my two sisters and my brother, James." She squeezed her eyes tightly closed and grimaced, sucking air through her teeth, as though the images in her head were far too much for her to bear. "Let's talk about something else now!"

"Okay, Louisa," Prophet said quickly, seeing the pain she was suddenly in. "I'm sorry." They rode in silence for a while, Prophet reflecting what a tragedy it was that this pretty young girl, who should be churning butter on a porch somewhere and daydreaming about the neighbor boy who sparked her on Saturday nights was instead riding the vengeance trail, her eyes flat and cunning, her innocence lost without a trace.

He waited awhile before asking her if she'd been alone since she'd started hunting the Red River Gang.

"Except for nights with farm folk here and there," she said, the color returning to her cheeks. "I try to stay away from people. Men, especially."

Prophet glanced at her sheepishly. "Well, not all men are bad, Louisa," he said, casting her a reassuring smile. "How 'bout ridin' with me awhile?"

She jerked a suspicious look at him. "Wouldn't you just like that?" She looked him up and down, mostly down. "Why, you got rascal written all over you!"

Prophet flushed, offended. "I do not!"

"Yes, you do."

"Listen, Missy, I've never once in my life laid a hand on a woman who didn't want me to. Never needed to!"

She looked him over again, but this time she didn't say anything and her eyes were hard to figure.

His anger waning—the girl was right to be suspicious of strangers—Prophet shrugged. "I just meant, why not throw in together for a while? We're both alone, and we share the same objective. And hell, considerin' how we cleaned up those four back in Campbell, I'd say we make a pretty good team." He really just didn't like the thought of such a pretty young girl being all alone out here. It gave him a lonely, haunted feeling.

She didn't reply for nearly a minute. "I'd have to think on it. I can't go gettin' mixed up with some stranger."

"You think about it, then," Prophet said. "In the meantime, we might as well ride to Wahpeton together. That's where the gang's headed."

Louisa shrugged noncommittally. "I reckon it couldn't hurt to ride together that far."

"I have a stop by the river, though. I caught one of 'em this mornin', and I left him tied to a tree."

"You did!"

Prophet grinned proudly. "Yes, ma'am."

"Which one?"

"Didn't tell me his name."

"Well, what are we waitin' for?" she said impatiently, spurring the Morgan into a gallop.

They rode hard for fifteen minutes, and then the river came into view over a hill. At first, Prophet couldn't remember where he'd left his prisoner, but then he recognized a landmark and headed toward a clump of trees in a southward curve in the Ottertail.

Riding up to the copse, he dismounted, and Louisa Bonaventure did the same. They tied their horses to low branches, then Prophet followed the trail of bent grass into the trees, Louisa following closely behind.

The prisoner was asleep but woke with a start when Prophet kicked the man's foot. "You still alive?" Prophet asked the man.

The man's voice was raspy and he was breathing hard. "Kiss my ass," he growled. His arm was bleeding badly, the entire sleeve soggy scarlet. His eyes found Louisa, who'd stopped beside Prophet to gaze grimly down at the man.

"Wayne MacDonald," she said.

The man frowned at Prophet. His voice was thin. "Who in the hell is she, and how in the hell does she know my name?"

"I studied the wanted dodgers on all you boys," the girl replied in a tone of withering malevolence. "I could pick each one of you out of a crowded train station. Prepare to meet your maker, you murdering savage."

The girl yanked her silver-plated revolver from a fold in her skirt and aimed it in both hands.

"Hey, wait a minute," Prophet objected, reaching out and shoving the gun down. "What in the hell do you think you're doin', girl?"

"She's crazy!" MacDonald cried. "She's plumb crazy!"

"Get your hand off my gun," she warned Prophet. "This animal raped my mother and sisters."

MacDonald gazed at her with wide-eyed fear and incredulity. "Huh? What are you talkin' about?"

"You know what I'm talkin' about, you dog. Back in Nebraska. Last year. I saw it all—or enough of it, anyway," she added darkly. "And you're gonna die for your part in it, just like all the others are gonna die."

MacDonald looked beseechingly at Prophet, who still had a grip on the girl's gun. "I don't know what she's talkin' about."

Prophet gazed at the man, remembering the raid in Luther Falls, his own anger returning like kerosene dribbled on a guttering fire. "You don't, eh?" he grumbled skeptically.

"Release my gun," the girl ordered Prophet.

Prophet turned to her. Sympathetically, he said, "I'm sorry about what happened to your family, but I can't let you shoot this man in cold blood. I know he deserves to die, but you can't do it."

Louisa's eyes flared angrily. "Just see if I can't! He murdered my family!"

"You can't judge him, Louisa. As tempting as it is, it ain't your place."

"What about the two men you killed with that scattergun back in Campbell?"

"That was different. They drew on me. I was ready and willing to take them alive and haul 'em before a judge, but it came down to either them or me." Prophet shook his head. "You can't kill a defenseless man, Louisa. It ain't right. I won't let you do it."

With a sudden tug, he jerked the gun from her hand. She gave an angry grunt and cursed him, watching as he tucked the revolver behind his own cartridge belts. "I'll return this to you when you've calmed down."

She stared at him, fuming, then stomped off through the trees toward her horse. Prophet waited until he was fairly certain she hadn't gone to get the rifle he'd noticed in her saddle boot, then said to MacDonald, "You worthless pile of dog shit!"

The last thing in the world he'd wanted to do was to be in the position of defending a man such as this. As much as he knew MacDonald deserved to die, his letting Louisa drop the hammer on him would have been the same thing as Prophet doing so himself. And one thing he'd never let himself do, for as long as he'd been collecting bounties on wanted men, was allow himself to play the tempting roles of judge, jury, and executioner. Because once he got a taste for it, he knew, there would be no stopping himself, and before he knew it he'd become no better than the men he hunted.

MacDonald looked up at him and grinned, reading his mind. It was too much for Prophet, and, without thinking, he drew his hand back and smacked the outlaw hard across his jaw, whipping the man's head sideways against the tree.

"Ow!" the man cried. "That hurt!"

"Yeah, well, there's more where that one came from," Prophet groused, cutting the man's tethers and jerking him to his feet. "Move! I wanna hit Wahpeton before sundown."

MacDonald laughed as Prophet pushed him toward his horse. "Then you wanna be dead before sundown."

"How's that?"

"'Cause the whole gang's gonna be there," MacDonald said through a grin. "The whole damn bunch!"

9

WHEN PROPHET CAME to the edge of the woods leading MacDonald's horse, Louisa was waiting there astride her Morgan. "Shit," Prophet said. "I was hopin' you'd ridden on. I don't have time for craziness, girl."

"I don't go anywhere without my revolver, Mr. Prophet." She extended her hand for the gun.

"So you can shoot my prisoner here?" Prophet said, grabbing his saddle horn and pulling himself atop his hammerheaded dun. "No, ma'am."

With her customary bald impudence, the girl said, "If I still wanted to kill him, I could plug him with my Winchester. Could've already done it, as a matter of fact—just as you were coming out of the trees."

Prophet looked at her tiredly. "Where did you learn all this stuff, anyway—shootin' and ambushin' and cuttin' men's balls off? You're only seventeen."

"It's a tough world out here, Mr. Prophet."

Slouched in his saddle, favoring his wounded arm that was giving him tremendous pain, MacDonald looked wary. "Whose balls did she cut off?"

"Man name of Barry," Prophet told him.

"Barry?"

"I think that was his name."

MacDonald blinked with horror. "That little girl cut Barry Little's balls off?"

"He was appropriately named," the girl quipped, flashing another of her icy smiles, then gigging her horse beside Prophet, who had begun heading west.

They rode for an hour in relative silence, the only sounds the chirping of birds in the trees along the river and the painful sighs and groans issuing from MacDonald, who rode behind Prophet and the girl on a lead rope tied to the tail of Prophet's horse.

The day was warm and bright, and they stopped to water their horses in the river. When they were heading out again, Prophet turned to Louisa Bonaventure with a question that had been on his mind since he'd found out who she was and what she was after.

"So Louisa, you've been on the vengeance trail for a year now, and you've killed five of the men you're after. What makes you think you can get them all?"

" 'Cause I've given myself over to it," she said matter-of-factly. "And because I don't have anywhere else to go or anything else to do. And because I know the souls of my folks won't rest until I've accomplished this task."

"Why don't you just turn it over to the authorities?"

She laughed caustically, swinging her head and tossing her hair out from her slender neck. "The authorities, eh? The authorities haven't been able to stop these men in the five years they've been raiding. Not even the marshals out of Fort Smith—Judge Parker's boys—were able to do it. The ones that chase them either end up dead or out of their jurisdictions, and, lost and afraid, they head home with their tails between their legs.

"Besides, that," she continued before Prophet could ask his next question, "I'm better equipped than the 'authorities' are. That gang can smell the 'authorities' from a hundred miles away. None of 'em has any inkling I've been on their trail—sometimes only a half mile behind! Even if they did, they wouldn't know who I was or what I was up to. I'm just a girl, see? That's why it's easy for me to sneak up on them and put a bullet in 'em or stick a knife in their necks." She sighed. "It takes time, though," she added. "I swear, I have to have the patience of Job sometimes."

"To wait for 'em to split up, you mean?"

"Then to catch up with the rest again," she said with a nod, dramatically blowing air through her lips. "They can be a trial, that bunch."

Prophet was regarding her uncomprehendingly as they rode, stirrup to stirrup, along the trail to Wahpeton. At last, he whistled and shook his head. "Miss Louisa, you're the crowned queen of vengeance, if I ever knew one."

"Yessir, I am," she said, extending her open hand to him. "Now, how 'bout returning my Colt?"

"So you can play God with ole MacDonald back there?" Prophet shook his head. "Not on my watch, queenie."

"I don't have to play God with ole MacDonald anymore," the girl pertly replied. "The devil came and got him about fifteen minutes ago."

Startled, Prophet whipped around in his saddle, placing his left hand on the cantle and darting his gaze at the outlaw. MacDonald was slumped forward on the speckle-gray, his face buried in the horse's mane. He didn't appear to be breathing, and the speckle-gray was tossing its head, its white-ringed eyes filled with an instinctive aversion to death.

Prophet clucked and sucked his teeth. Then he threw Louisa her gun and dismounted to dispose of the dead outlaw.

•   •   •

An hour after Prophet had finished burying MacDonald, a job Miss Bonaventure proclaimed the biggest waste of time since the invention of alcohol, they paid a wizened little man in a black stocking cap fifty cents to ferry them and their horses across the Red River, still swollen with snow melt. As they crossed, Prophet found out from the man that he'd ferried eight men and a girl across the river about three hours before.

"They were all looking for a good time in Wahpeton tonight, sure enough!" the man cackled, shaking his head.

"There much in the way of fun to be had in Wahpeton?" Prophet asked with a skeptical air.

Glancing sheepishly at Louisa, the little man sidled up to Prophet and whispered in his ear that there was one tavern and two whores—both German girls—but that the lack of amenities had never stopped the farmers from having a good time when their wives would let them out of their potato fields. He wheezed, cackling, his one tobacco-colored tooth glinting like a raisin in the sun.

"The town have a sheriff?" Prophet asked.

"Sure it does," the man said, offended. "It's the county seat!"

"Much obliged," Prophet said as the ferry scraped the river's west shore, nearly knocking them all, including the horses, off their feet.

When the ferryman had dropped the ramp, Prophet and Louisa led their horses across it and onto the grassy bank near several flooded ash and cottonwood trees and a few old, gray cabins where woodcutters for the riverboats probably lived when the Red lay within its banks.

They splashed through a slough and into the little town of Wahpeton, not much more than a wide, muddy main street lined with hangdog-looking stores before which supply wagons sat. Men in farmers' garb crossed the street between stores, and several glum-looking blanket Indians stood out front of a blacksmith shop, apparently getting the wheel of their dilapidated wagon repaired.

The Indian group was composed of three men, two women, and four children. The children were running around in the mud alongside the shop, chasing chickens. The men were smoking and staring at Prophet and Louisa as the strangers passed before them. The women stared, too, their faces as expressionless as the men's.

Prophet pulled up beside the blacksmith working on the wheel.

"Where can I find the sheriff?" he asked the stout, balding man, who did not turn to look but momentarily ceased hammering the wheel onto the axle.

"One block west, turn right. It's the log cabin beside the bathhouse."

He jerked his head up sharply when a chicken squawked, then turned to the Indian men lounging in the shop's open doors. "I told you to keep your damn kids away from my livestock!" the blacksmith complained.

One of the women turned to the mud-splashed kids and said something in Sioux, only slightly raising her voice, and all four kids stopped suddenly and looked at her.

"Much obliged," Prophet said to the blacksmith, who did not reply but only started hammering again on the wheel.

As Prophet and Louisa walked their horses along the street, glancing from side to side for signs of the men they were after, Louisa said, "What do you want the sheriff for?"

"It's his town," Prophet said. "He should know if there's badmen about, shouldn't he?"

"What's he gonna do about it?"

"I reckon that's up to him," Prophet said, adding, "If there's one thing I learned in my years as a bounty hunter, it's to never step on a lawman's toes. Most of 'em hate bounty hunters the way it is. But you get between one and his quarry without consultin' with him first . . ."

Prophet let it go at that, giving his head a resolute wag.

"I don't think you have to worry about that around here," Louisa said. "The Red River Gang has a way of sendin' local lawman into the hills lookin' for their mommas."

Prophet brought his horse to a halt when they came to a cross street. Looking left, he saw what appeared to be a saloon about a block away. The hitch racks before the place were crowded with horses—more than a dozen of them, all craning their heads around to watch the loud freight wagon passing behind them into the vast, flat prairie beyond town.

"Speaking of which," he said to Louisa, "you think that cavvy belongs to our boys?"

Louisa studied them coolly, then turned to Prophet, arching one of her eyebrows. "Who else?"

Prophet nodded and looked right, and pointed. "That must be the jail over there." He gigged his horse toward the sheriff's office, but stopped when he saw that the girl wasn't following him.

When he hipped around in his saddle, she said, "You go ahead. I'm gonna go in that general store over there and scrounge up some foodstuffs." She reined her horse left, heading south down the street toward the general store, which sat kitty-corner to the saloon.

"You be careful," Prophet yelled.

She didn't so much as turn, just kept riding. Prophet chuffed ruefully at the girl's independence, then continued toward the sheriff's office—a long, low cabin with the words RICHLAND COUNTY SHERIFF in gold-leaf lettering on the hovel's only window. There was a heavyset young man sitting on the gallery, to the right of the window. Shaggy blond hair tumbled out of his shabby bowler hat, and a shiny silver star hung from his ratty wool vest over an even rattier white dress shirt. He leaned forward on his bench, elbows on his knees, rolling the barrel of a Spencer carbine between his hands like a pool stick.

"Who are you?" he asked, casting his weary, blunt-faced glance at Prophet reining up at the hitch rail.

"Name's Prophet, and you and me got trouble, if you're the sheriff."

"I ain't the sheriff, I'm just the deputy," the young man was quick to respond, casting another cautious glance to his right, toward the saloon at the other end of the street. "You aren't part o' that bunch down the street, are ye?"

Prophet said he wasn't. "Where's the sheriff?"

The young man—about nineteen or twenty, Prophet guessed—measured him from the doughy gopher holes of his eye sockets, then jerked his head to his right. "Out back. He's plantin' his garden."

"Kind of early for gardenin' in these parts, ain't it?" Prophet said, crawling out of his saddle.

"That's what I told him," the young man grunted.

As he tossed his reins over the hitch rack, Prophet considered the lad nervously rolling the carbine between his hands, then, with a knowing smile, headed around the building to the back. He found a tall, middle-aged man in suspenders and a washworn undershirt raking a patch of freshly turned earth. The man's gray hair was thin on top, and he wore a beard, Prophet saw as the man turned to him.

"What the hell do you want?" the sheriff asked, narrowing his eyes with the same wary expression his deputy had offered. Obviously, both men knew what kind of snakes had ridden into town, and were more than a little jumpy.

"Don't worry, Sheriff," Prophet said, raising his hands in a gesture of acquiescence. "I ain't part of that crew down the street. I'm after them, as a matter of fact. Yesterday, they raided Luther Falls. Shot a couple and kidnapped a girl of about fourteen or fifteen years old."

The sheriff's eyes dropped, scouring Prophet's chest for a badge. "You a federal?"

"No, I'm a bounty hunter."

The sheriff stared at him, holding his rake across his chest. His eyes were gray and old, and his chin jutted like a sharp rock. "You alone?" he asked finally.

"Well . . . not exactly, but close enough."

"What the hell does that mean?"

Prophet studied the man from across the black, wet garden that smelled of worms and fresh earth and which a pair of robins eyed from the eaves of the jailhouse. Prophet could see the man wanted no part of the Red River Gang, and the bounty hunter didn't blame him. He'd probably farmed most of his life, and when the sheriff's job had opened, he'd probably figured why not take it? Beats following mules around a potato patch. It was a pretty typical state of affairs, Prophet had found, and one that contradicted the newspapers and dime novels that had the easterners believing every town was Dodge City and every lawman was Wyatt Earp or Bat Masterson.

Prophet waved and, turning, said, "Never mind, Sheriff." He should have listened to Miss Louisa, but he always figured that giving the local lawmen a courtesy call would save him trouble in the long run.

"They send me federals, I'd go in there after those bastards," the sheriff said.

"It's all right, Sheriff," Prophet said over his shoulder.

"Hell, I have a wife and a daughter, and my deputy just had a baby!"

"I hear ye, Sheriff."

"If I wired Bismarck today, they wouldn't have federals here till next Wednesday!"

Prophet threw up a hand, waving, and walked back to the front of the jail, startling the deputy as he approached the veranda.

"Jeepers, you scared me!" the lad said.

Prophet untied his reins from the hitch rack. "Sorry, kid."

"What'd the sheriff say?"

"He told me you just had a baby."

The lad grinned. "Sure did."

Prophet crawled into the leather. "Boy or girl?"

"Girl. Named her Sonya after my mother, God rest her soul."

"Greet her and her mother for me, lad," Prophet said. "And stay away from that saloon tonight."

10

FROM THE SHERIFF'S office, Prophet gigged his horse southward, toward the mercantile, keeping a wary eye on the saloon.

He stopped his horse suddenly when he heard the general store's door open and saw two women walk out. One was Louisa carrying a small burlap bag. The other was a silver-haired lady in a brown dress and a crisp white apron. Louisa and the woman were chatting amiably, though Prophet couldn't quite hear what they were saying until they both stopped at the edge of the boardwalk, before Louisa's Morgan.

"Now, you go back down the street one block, and hang a left and then another left," the lady said, one hand on Louisa's shoulder and the other pointing east. "My house is the big white one with the red barn behind it. You can't miss it because it's the only place out there!" The woman laughed as though at the funniest joke she'd heard in years.

"Oh, thank you, Mrs. McBride!" Louisa exclaimed, gazing into the woman's eyes with all the ingratiation the girl could muster. "I can't tell you how pleased Poppa and Momma will be when they hear how well I was taken care of on my journey back homeward."

"An innocent child like yourself should not be allowed to journey so far from home!"

"Oh, believe me, Mrs. McBride, it was a truly hard decision for Poppa and Momma to make. But with all their infirmities, they simply were unable to make the trek themselves. And I really wanted to go."

"Well, I'm sorry your grandmother has passed, child."

"Yes, but, you know what, Mrs. McBride? I think her passing was made more comfortable by having her only granddaughter at her side."

"Oh, I'm sure it was, I'm sure it was," the old woman cooed, drawing Louisa to her great bosom, hugging her and patting her back. Brushing a stray tear from her cheek, she said, "Well, I think you'll find mine and Mr. Mc-Bride's home quite comfortable, child. Run along now. It's the second-story room to the left of the stairs. The hired boy will probably have a fire going in the hearth, so you can heat water for a bath. Have the boy stable your horse in the barn with plenty of hay and oats."

"Thank you, Mrs. McBride. As meager as my means, I don't know how I'll ever be able to repay you."

"Your gratitude is thanks enough, child." The old woman gave Louisa a gentle shove toward her horse, adding, "Hurry along now, dear. You look positively exhausted."

"Yes," Louisa said, lacing her voice with a weary trill as she untied the Morgan's reins from the hitching post, "I do feel a bit worse for the wear."

The girl mounted up and, waving to the old woman, turned the Morgan into the street. When she saw Prophet sitting atop Mean and Ugly and staring at her with a look of amazed disbelief on his unshaven face, she stuck her tongue out at him and gigged the Morgan into a trot.

Prophet turned his head to watch Miss Bonaventure disappear around the corner, a grim smile on his face. A survivor, that girl. Turning back to the old woman, who remained on the boardwalk before the general store, staring at him with her gnarled fists on her hips and a scowl on her face, Prophet gigged his horse toward her and reined up.

"Ma'am," he said with a tug on his hat brim, "you have any idea where a poor, weary traveler might find a soft bed for the night?"

Brusquely she said, "Down by the river there's plenty of soft grass, young man." She wheeled around on her stout, black shoes and disappeared into the store.

"Much obliged, ma'am," Prophet grumbled at the door slamming closed.

He turned to the saloon sitting on the corner of the next block. The horses remained at the hitch rack, and, knowing what he knew about the gang inside, the poor animals would probably remain there all night, saddled and bridled. From the sound of the whoops and muffled laughter from inside the place, he suspected the gang was having one hell of a time. The girl they'd kidnapped was probably in one of the upstairs rooms, no doubt going through a hell administered by each of the drunken gang members in turn.

The thought set Prophet's blood to boiling, but there was nothing he could do to help her at the moment. If he walked in there now, he'd be dead in two minutes.

Prophet rubbed his bristly jaw. Shit.

He thought it over and decided the first thing he had to do was free the girl, and the best time to attempt that was after dark, at least three hours away. The gang would be fairly drunk by then, and his chances of stealing into the place unseen would be fair to good. His chances of getting her *out* without being seen were probably only poor to fair, but he had to try it, and he didn't have much time.

The girl was living on borrowed hours. The gang would no doubt head out of here in the morning, and Prophet doubted they'd take her along. They'd get all they could from her tonight, then probably slit her throat and leave her in one of those upstairs cribs to bleed to death.

First thing he had to do was get Mean and Ugly stabled, fed, and rested, so he'd be able to ride later. To that end, he reined the horse back along the way he had come. Seeing a barn and paddock down a side street, he headed that way and paid a lad to bed the horse down with fresh hay and oats. He gave the boy an extra dollar to tie the horse before the general store in three hours. Taking only his shotgun and leaving his rifle and the rest of his tack with the boy, he headed back down the street toward the saloon.

Halfway there, he caught a whiff of something cooking, and followed the smell to a small, tar-paper shack sitting on a weedy lot behind the general store, flanked by stacked wood and a smokehouse. On a crude sign tacked beside the door the word FOOD had been painted in white letters. The place was propped by logs about a foot off the ground, and out from under it came a dog to bark at Prophet and sniff his clothes.

Tripping over the dog, he made his way to the door, pushed inside, and looked around at the three hand-hewn tables and benches surrounding a smoky woodstove. In one corner, an old man and an old woman worked on a plate of roast beef and mashed potatoes with gravy, not saying a word and glancing up only briefly at the stranger. Noting the shotgun, they quickly returned their eyes to their tin plates, muttering in a foreign language.

The meal Prophet was served turned out to be as humble as the setting it was served in, and he left the place fighting down the frothy acid bubbles rising in his chest. Unsteadily, he made his way back to the main street and stopped on the corner just east of the general store.

The sun was nearly down, and there was very little activity on the street. The only horses were those of the Red River Gang, still tied to the hitch rack before the saloon. The animals' heads hung sleepily.

Glancing to his right, Prophet saw that there was no light on in the sheriff's office, and he was grateful for that. He hoped the sheriff and his deputy had gone home for the evening. He didn't want them getting in his way or fouling up his plan to remove the girl from the rooms above the saloon. From the fear he'd seen in their faces earlier, he didn't think he had anything to worry about.

Now, little Miss Bonaventure was another problem altogether. Not having seen her since she'd headed for the room she'd wrangled from the woman who ran the general store, he had no idea what she was up to. But sure as rabbits hopped, you could bet she was up to something. He just hoped she realized what a pit of perdition that saloon was tonight, and stayed away from it. If she did not, she could tie Prophet's plan in one hell of a knot and probably get herself killed to boot.

The bounty hunter scanned the area around him for several minutes, trying to spot a good location from which to keep an eye on the saloon and to wait for a couple more hours to pass. Finally, he headed for the alley paralleling the main street, hung a right, and came up behind the general store.

Seeing that the roof over the store's rear was fairly low, he used a couple of shipping barrels to help hoist himself on it. Adjusting the shotgun hanging down his back, he made his way toward the front, hoisting himself onto the store's second story, and hunkered down behind the false front, which jutted up a good six feet and offered perfect cover from the saloon as well as the quickening spring breeze.

Standing, Prophet could peer over the top of the facade at the saloon, from which tinny piano music prattled above the Red River Gang's raucous revelry. Bright lantern light spilled onto the boardwalk and the heads of the horses stationed there. Shadows flickered in the windows and occasionally the sounds of breaking glass rose.

One of the second-story rooms, whose windows he could see from this angle, was lit, and he fairly shuddered as he imagined what could be happening to the Luther Falls girl in there.

As the minutes passed, the laughter in the saloon grew louder, the yells and shouts more and more boisterous. Someone tried playing a banjo for a while, and gave up amidst a barrage of wild complaints and several gunshots. At one point, a girl screamed, and Prophet, who was sitting with his back to the facade and smoking a quirley, jumped. But then the girl laughed harshly, and he realized it was one of the whores.

The minutes passed slowly. To stretch his legs and stomp the chill from his bones, Prophet rose occasionally and walked around the general store's roof. Then he sat down again and rolled another quirley.

About two hours after he'd begun his vigil, he heard the slow thud of hooves and the tinny clatter of a bridle bit. Standing, he saw the boy from the livery barn leading Mean and Ugly this way down the main drag. The boy tied the horse to the hitch rack directly below Prophet, then, tossing a wary glance at the saloon, slipped slowly off in the darkness.

The sounds in the saloon had grown into a constant, muffled roar, the piano not so much being played anymore as pounded, its discordant notes punctuating the din of the yelling, drunken men. It was time. The noise would cover any made by Prophet, and the senses of the men would be sufficiently dulled that even if they did happen to see or hear him, they'd be less effective at doing anything about it.

He made his way carefully off the roof, trying not to

make any noise and wake any dogs on this side of the main street. The night was black as pitch, for clouds had moved in to cover the stars. He had to be extra methodical in finding the barrels he'd used to hoist himself onto the roof. He got only one foot on one of them, and went down hard on his side, the barrel falling on his right leg.

Fortunately, the barrel was empty and didn't do any damage, but Prophet still cursed his clumsiness as he adjusted the shotgun, made sure his revolver was still on his right hip, the bowie on his left, and headed down the alley. When he came to the main drag, he paused beside the general store, making sure none of the gang was outside, then headed for the saloon.

He was no more than halfway across the street when the saloon door opened and several men started onto the boardwalk under the awning, their voices loud in the quiet night, the piano music and din pushing out behind them.

Prophet froze, his veins filling with adrenaline. He crouched, looked around, and headed for the boardwalk across the side street from the saloon, hoping the shadows of the shop there would conceal him.

Making the boardwalk at a shuffling, crouching run, holding the shotgun across his chest, he pressed his back against the wall of the store and gritted his teeth, watching the three silhouettes of the men across the street, and listening. From their conversation, if you could call their drunken blather conversation, Prophet could tell they hadn't seen him. He knew from experience that men who'd been drinking as long as they had were experiencing the world from a thick, gauzy curtain, their senses deadened.

They were grumbling and cursing about something as they milled before the horses. Prophet waited there in the shadows, frozen, watching and listening, trying to figure out what they were up to. Surely they weren't leaving town at this hour, after all they'd had to drink.

At last, it became obvious they were gathering up the reins of all the horses at the hitch rack, and were leading the horses off somewhere.

"Shit . . . I don't see why this is my job," one of them complained.

"Shut up, Price."

"I'm gonna miss my turn with that girl upstairs."

"You rather have a dead horse to ride tomorrow?"

Price said something in reply, but Prophet couldn't hear it because the three men and the eight horses had drifted off down the street, apparently heading for the livery stable. He'd heard enough, however.

So the girl really was upstairs. . . .

Prophet watched the saloon to see if anyone else came out, then took a breath and ran northward down the side street. After about fifty yards, he stopped, took another gander at the saloon, then headed across the street to the saloon's rear.

There was a slender staircase running up the back of the building to the second story. Peering around in the dark to make sure no one was around or using the privy, which was a pale splotch in the darkness twenty yards north, Prophet put his hands on the railings, trying to cushion his steps, and began climbing.

He took it slow, for the stair planks were badly rotted in places and squeaked like rusty hinges. When he made the second-story landing, he peered into the frost-edged window in the door's top half. Before him was a narrow hall with a shabby rug, faded, peeling wallpaper, an askew picture frame, and a single lantern in a wall bracket. In each wall there were two closed doors. Opening the outside door carefully, Prophet stepped inside.

When all appeared clear, he closed the door behind him and moved forward, hearing the thunderous noise below, laced with the piano's cacophony and a drunk man singing an Irish drinking song Prophet had heard once or twice during the war. It was a lusty song Prophet had liked, but he suddenly didn't like it anymore. Through the soles of his boots, he felt the vibration all the racket made in the floor.

He moved forward, peering at the cracks under the doors. No light escaped the cracks of the first two doors he passed. When he came to the second set, the set closest to the door leading to the stairs to the floor below, he discovered lights bleeding from the cracks under both doors.

He stopped between the doors, breathing shallowly, his heart beating slowly but powerfully, his pulse throbbing in his neck. Now, how in the hell was he supposed to figure out which room the Luther Falls girl was in?

The answer came a few seconds later, in the form of a giggle behind the door to his right.

Okay, she wasn't behind that door, he thought with a sigh, turning to the door on his left. He took another deep breath, lifted his hat, and ran a hand through his sweat-damp hair. He replaced the hat, produced his bowie from the scabbard on his left hip, knowing that, in spite of the revelry below, there was no way he could use the revolver and not bring the whole gang down on top of him.

He began twisting the doorknob but stopped suddenly when he heard boots scuffing inside the room and a deep male voice say, "Shit, she's about as fun as a dead fish."

The man's voice had grown as he neared the door, as did the sound of his footfalls. Obviously, he was about to exit the room.

Prophet looked around, finding nowhere to hide, his heart leaping into his throat.

11

PROPHET STEPPED TO the left of the door, pressing his back to the wall and praying for all he was worth that the man wouldn't see him.

Shit, shit, shit, shi—

The door opened. A tall, broad figure appeared, placing his hat on his head as he stepped through the doorway. Fortunately, he'd put his hat on with his right hand, and that arm had blocked his view of Prophet.

As soon as his hat was on, he turned to his left, pulling the door closed behind him, then continued leftward down the hall. Prophet watched the man's back as he sauntered drunkenly to the door at the end of the hall, opened it to the rabble below, walked through, and flung it angrily closed behind him.

Prophet sighed, tears of relief moistening his eyes. "You know, I don't deserve to be that lucky," he whispered to himself.

Stepping before the door once again, he dried his right hand on his pants, then placed it on the knob and turned it. The door opened, and Prophet quickly entered, drawing his bowie.

As he had suspected when the other man had spoken, another man was there, but fortunately he was sitting on the other side of the bed, facing the outside wall.

The man was pulling on his boots. Without turning to Prophet, he said, "Wait your goddamn turn, damnit!"

Prophet stood there, his back to the door, glancing from the nude girl on the bed, her wrists and ankles tied to each of the four bedposts with strips of cloth, to the man pulling his boots on. When Prophet didn't say anything, the man turned a scowling look at him over his left shoulder.

The scowl grew when the man saw Prophet. His face flushing, the man bolted to his feet, reaching for the pistol on his hip. The gun hadn't cleared leather before Prophet's bowie, spinning end over end, thunked blade first into the man's broad chest.

The man grunted, dropping his pistol and stumbling back against the wall. He raised his hands to the knife as if to remove it, but he didn't have the strength. Lifting his exasperated gaze to Prophet, the man slid down the wall, making a low hissing sound, and died about the same time his butt hit the floor.

Prophet quickly closed the door and went to the bed. The girl, who appeared about thirteen or fourteen, stared up at him with shock-dulled brown eyes. She had a round, cherubic face, and sweat-soaked, sandy blond hair. Her face was bruised, one eye nearly swollen shut. Her cracked lips moved but no words escaped her mouth.

"It's all right," Prophet said. "I'm a friend, and I'm going to take you home." He hadn't finished the last sentence before he'd begun slicing the cloth tethering her arms and feet to the bedposts.

When he was through, he drew a quilt and sheet up from the bottom of the bed, covering her. Then he lifted her off the bed and swung around to the door.

"No," the girl sobbed quietly, shaking her head, shuddering.

"Sh. It's all right. I'm taking you home."

Cracking the door, he peered into the hall. All was clear. Behind the door opposite, bedsprings squawked, and a man and a woman moaned.

Hurriedly, Prophet slipped out of the room and started down the hall, the girl inert in his arms. He was about ten feet from the door when a figure appeared in the window of the door's upper half. Prophet froze.

The door opened, and Louisa stood there, gazing at him expectantly.

"Well, what are you waiting for?" she hissed. "Come on!"

Prophet was incredulous. "What the hell are you doing here?"

"I was waitin' under the stairs when I saw you. I'll cover you while you get her on your horse and get out of here."

"What were you doin' under the stairs?"

"Waitin' for opportunities—what the hell do you think I was doing?" The girl's face widened with anxious impatience. "Will you *go?*"

Prophet exhaled sharply and headed through the door. When he'd stepped onto the landing he heard a man groan somewhere beneath him.

"Help!" a voice croaked.

Again, Prophet froze. Swinging sharply to Louisa, he said, "What the hell was that?"

"Oh, no!" the girl sputtered, her face bleaching as she gazed over the railing. "I thought I killed that son of a bitch."

"Toomer," a man drawled in a trembling voice. "Toomer . . . Da . . . Dan . . ."

Fortunately, the din in the saloon was too loud for the man's voice to carry. But if one of the others was outside. . . .

"Well, finish him, goddamnit!" Prophet snarled.

But Louisa had already started down the stairs, taking no caution on the squawky steps. Prophet went down behind her, watching his feet so he didn't tumble face first with the kidnapped girl in his arms. He'd reached the body just as the man called out again, louder this time, "No! Toom—" Something cut him off.

Prophet watched Louisa move back toward him in the darkness. "Got him," she said, holding up a knife that gleamed wetly in the stray light filtering from the saloon's front.

"Hey, what's goin' on back there?" a man called from the other side of the saloon. "Jack, the gremlins get you, or what?"

"Let's move!" Prophet hissed at Louisa.

He wheeled with the kidnapped girl in his arms, and cut across the side street. Louisa ran beside him.

"Hey, Jack!" one of the gang members called.

Prophet could tell the man was behind the saloon now. He'd find the body soon.

Prophet and Louisa pressed their backs against the building on the corner opposite the saloon. Prophet looked around to see how many men were after them, but he couldn't see anything yet.

Turning to Louisa, he carped, "That was a hell of a crazy stunt, kid. You're gonna get us all killed yet!"

"I thought I killed him dead!"

"Well, you didn't. And . . ." Prophet let his voice trail off, too frustrated for expression. "Listen," he said, "you hightail it back to the room you finagled. Take the back alleys and don't stop for nothing."

"Where you going?"

"I'm taking this girl back to Luther Falls. We can't stay here. Now! Go!"

He gave Louisa a shove and started the opposite way, toward the main street and his horse. He stopped angrily when Louisa called, "Lou?"

He turned to her, a slim figure in the shadows against the building.

"Meet me in Fargo tomorrow night."

Before Prophet could respond, she'd slipped around the building's rear corner and was gone.

Prophet didn't have time to consider the message. Turning back around, he trotted down the boardwalk toward Main Street, shaking his head and hissing, "Crazy goddamn younker!"

He paused at the edge of the main street and took another gander at the saloon. It was lit up like a lone ship at a T-wharf, shadows moving in the windows. Several men were kicking around behind the place, talking loudly enough to be heard above the roar from within.

Prophet ran across the street, frightening Mean and Ugly, who'd been dozing with his head down. With the girl in his arms, he clumsily removed the bridle reins from the hitch rack.

"Easy, boy, easy," he whispered to the fiddle-footed horse.

He turned a stirrup out and peered down at the girl, whose eyes fluttered as she drifted in and out of consciousness, the corners of her eyes crinkled with pain.

"Listen, I'm gonna set you up on my horse, and then I'm gonna climb up behind you. It might hurt a little, but don't yell out, okay?"

Prophet didn't think she heard him, but then her eyes fluttered again, remained open for a second, and she nodded slightly.

"There you go, honey," he said gently, lifting her onto the saddle. "You'll be home in no time."

As he climbed up behind her, she turned her head. "Who . . . ?" she said. "Who . . . are . . . ?"

"I'm Lou Prophet. Easy, now. Just lay your head back against my chest and hold tight to the horn."

He adjusted the quilt and sheet around her legs and began turning Ugly away from the tie rail.

"Hey, you!" someone shouted.

A gun barked, the bullet sizzling the air about six inches off his right ear. Mean and Ugly reared, sidestepping, nearly throwing both Prophet and the girl into the street.

The girl cried weakly, fighting to hold on, and Prophet grabbed the horn and sawed the reins. "Hoah, Mean . . . *easy!*"

Another pistol barked, the slug shattering a window in the general store. Prophet ducked, reining Mean and Ugly leftward into the street. Without Prophet having to slap the iron to him—the dun had been with Prophet long enough to know when they were at death's doorstep—the horse lunged off its back legs and fairly vaulted down the street, heading east at a hungry gallop.

More pistol fire opened up behind them—at least four shooters, Prophet guessed. The hail of bullets sailed around and over Prophet's head as he leaned forward to protect the girl. The slugs kicked dust at Mean's feet, tore into stores and water troughs, and shattered windows, before Prophet kneed the horse southward around the first corner he came to, feeling one of the slugs burn a nasty swath across his thigh.

Well, they'd discovered the body. And then they'd seen him. Putting two and two together, they'd figured the score.

On the plus side, they were drunk, and he was sober as a parson. It would take them a good fifteen or twenty minutes before they found and saddled their horses, maybe longer. What's more, they'd have a hell of a time tracking him in the dark.

He just hoped they hadn't seen Louisa. . . .

He rode a circuitous route through the edge of town, then headed south along the river. The night was so dark

it was hard to see where he was going. He left the partic-
ulars of the route to Mean and Ugly, as surefooted a
mount as Prophet had ever ridden and one of the few
reasons he put up with the cussed beast.

While he rode, his shoulders steadying the girl before
him, who gave occasional weak sighs of complaint and
lolled against his chest, he searched for a place he could
cross the swollen river, knowing the ferryman would be
dead asleep at this hour and that waking him would take
too much time.

Several times he pulled the horse eastward into the big
cottonwoods sheathing the Red, only to find the water far
too wide and deep to cross without swimming. When it
didn't look like he was going to find a shallow enough
ford, however, he said to hell with it, turned the horse into
the river, and gave him the spurs.

The horse balked, snorting and lifting its snout.

"Come on, Mean, you candy-ass . . ."

Grudgingly, as though entering a pool of vipers, the
horse mince-stepped into the water. It wasn't long before
he was up to his neck and Prophet and the girl were up
to their waists.

The girl cried, recoiling at the feel of the water. "Sorry,
honey," Prophet said, putting his hand on her shoulder to
steady her. "We're crossin' the river. You're okay. Don't
frighten Mean. He's scared enough the way it is."

Prophet had a hell of a time staying on the horse and
keeping the girl mounted as well. The water was black
and bone-splitting cold, and the girl sobbed and moaned
in protest, breaking Prophet's heart with her cries of, "No
. . . please . . . no . . ." After all that had happened to the
poor youngun, now she was being swept across a river in
the middle of the damn night. And what was he taking
her home to? Two dead parents and a shot-up store.

The current took them downstream a good quarter mile
before the dun finally planted his hooves and climbed out

of the water, Prophet and the girl dripping mud, their teeth chattering. The bounty hunter brought the shivering horse to a halt on the bank.

"You all right, Miss?" he asked the girl, tipping her gently against his shoulder so he could look into her face.

Her teeth were chattering, her eyes were squeezed shut now, and she said nothing.

"I'm sorry about this, Miss. I'd build a fire and dry you out if we had time, but we don't. You'll be home shortly, though."

He reined Mean eastward out of the trees along the river, the horse splashing through the six inches of water and mud covering the prairie for at least a hundred yards beyond the riverbed. Then he spurred him into a lope.

They rode hard along the pale wagon path, the air cool against his wet clothes, his soaked denims clinging to his skin. The girl moaned often, bobbing against his chest and shoulder. The horse plunged eastward, blowing, his powerful muscles rippling beneath the saddle. The sky was black, and the air smelled of wet earth and budding leaves.

Prophet knew they were close to farms when he detected wood smoke. He would have stopped at one and asked for a warm bed for the girl, but he didn't want to put others in danger. He had to get to Luther Falls and get the girl to Cordelia's, where she would be safe. He doubted the gang would track him that far—twenty-five miles. They were too drunk, and he was only one man, she, one girl.

He stopped to rest the horse after an hour's hard ride. He dismounted and lay the girl against a tree. She was moaning in earnest now, for the ride was torturous.

"I'm sorry, Miss," Prophet said, truly grieved.

"No," she said, wagging her head, lips trembling. "I can't. Please . . . no. Leave me."

"I'm not gonna leave you, Miss . . ."

"Please," she begged, reaching out and grabbing his

hand. She opened her eyes, which gleamed darkly, filled with pleading. "Don't take me back there. I'm sick and . . . and . . . I can't go back there after . . . what they done to me."

"Oh, Miss," Prophet said. "No one's gonna—"

"Please shoot me, Mister!" the girl cried in a gut-wrenching little girl's voice. "I can't ride no more. My insides ache and . . . after what they done to me!" She broke down in tears, sobbing, and Prophet let her lie there, half-cradled in his arms, pleading and sobbing.

Finally, when he'd taken as much time as he dared, he got up, took the horse's reins, and mounted up once again, easing the girl before him on the saddle. She sobbed and shook her head, calling out for her mother—a mother she would never see again. Grimly, Prophet reined the dun back onto the trail and kneed him into another wind-splitting gallop toward Luther Falls.

The girl cried out, grieving, for her mother. Prophet pressed her head against his chest, his jaw set grimly, his eyes hard, and tried to block out her cries as he rode.

He thought of the girl in his arms and of Louisa Bonaventure. How many other children had the Red River Gang torn the souls from?

How sweet it was going to be to make them pay. . . .

12

HANDSOME DAVE DUVALL reined his horse to a skidding halt along the trees on the west bank of the Red River. He squinted into the dark ahead of him, but couldn't see a thing. He didn't think it was only because he'd had more than his share of Wahpeton's coffin varnish, either.

It was just too damn dark. Too dark for riding and too dark for tracking.

Not only that, but it was a damn good night for getting bushwhacked.

He raised his left hand as the others approached at a gallop, nearly running him down. "Hold up, you stupid sons o' bitches," Duvall complained testily. Nothing made him nastier than a good time interrupted, and a good time was just what he and the boys had been having back at the Oasis.

The riders reined up, cursing, yelling to the others behind them to do likewise. When they were all stopped and gathered around him in the dark, Duvall said, "Anyone get a good look at that son of a bitch?"

"I just saw him from behind," called Frank Henry.

"Me, too," said Jack Toomer. "Big bastard. He had the girl."

Handsome Dave Duvall's partner, Dayton Flowers, turned to Duvall with a question in his long, dark face— the at once timid and fierce face of a Welsh parson's boy raised on pious, soul-building strappings. "Lawman?"

"Could be," Duvall said, turning his head to gaze southward.

"U.S. marshal, maybe," said someone from deep in the ring of bleary-eyed riders and snorting horses. Unlike the men, the horses were all fresh; the group had left their own exhausted mounts in the livery barn and stolen the ones they were riding now.

"Maybe we're dealin' with a marshal," Duvall said. "But I have a feelin' we ain't gonna find out tonight. We can't follow him. It's too hard to track him on a night this black, and if we keep pushin' it, we're liable to get bushwhacked."

Dayton Flowers twisted around in his saddle, perplexed. "So what do you want to do, Dave? Your call."

"Who's the soberest among us?" Duvall called to the group.

No one said anything. They glanced around at each other, humorously sheepish. Their fetid breath puffed around their heads and drifted toward the clouds hovering just beyond the haggard tops of the cottonwoods.

Duvall snorted. "Silver? Taber?"

When both men had replied in the affirmative, Duvall said, "I want you boys to ride to Luther Falls. That's where that girl came from, so that's probably where the big bastard is taking her. Get after him and find out who the hell he is. If you can, kill him. If you can't, send me a telegraph in Fargo the day after tomorrow, and let me know what you found out about him."

There was a brief silence. Thomas Taber cleared his

throat and said in his slow, husky bass, "How come you want me to track him, Dave? I had me as much o' the busthead as—"

" 'Cause I just told you to, that's why," Duvall said in a low, menacing voice. "But if you don't want to go, Tom, I'll send someone else."

Duvall spurred his horse ahead and stared pointedly at the bulky, mustachioed rider in the knit cap and buffalo coat. "Is that what you want, Tom? Be sure now. Think it over real good before you answer."

Taber watched Duvall dully, the liquor in his veins making him consider the proposition. He knew Duvall had singled him out because Duvall knew he thought he could lead the group himself if only Handsome Dave had an accident—like, say, a bullet between his shoulder blades. But then again, this was no time for an uprising. Not after all the liquor Taber had consumed and the energy he'd spent on the two German whores and the little blond filly from Luther Falls.

At last, he smoothed his mustache with his thumb and index finger, and conjured a defiant smile. "No, I'll track the son of a bitch. Not only that, but I'll kill him—marshal or no marshal—in my grand old style." He placed his left hand on the enormous Green River knife jutting up from his beaded belt sheath.

Duvall returned Taber's grin. "I had a feelin' you'd put your best foot forward, Tom. And that's just why I picked you, too." He turned to the short, stout half-breed Sioux in the smelly buckskins and black, broad-brimmed hat. "Billy? You got any questions?"

The wiry half-breed said nothing. Customarily focused and kill-hungry, he reined his horse toward the river and gigged it through the trees. Soon Duvall heard Silver's horse splashing in the flood water.

"Well, wait for me, for chrissakes, Billy," Taber

groused as he gigged his horse in the same direction.
"Crazy Injun . . ."

When both men were gone, Flowers turned to Duvall.
"What's the rest of us gonna do, Dave?"

"We head north of Wahpeton, just in case the bastard's
a marshal and there's more where he came from. Hell,
this country could be swarmin' with badge-toters, for all
we know. We'll camp at the first good spot we find, then
head for Fargo in the morning."

When they were riding north ahead of the group, Dayton Flowers gigged his horse up alongside Duvall's. "I
have a feelin' that man was workin' alone, Dave," he said
with a drunken leer. "And what's more, I think ole Billy
and Tom Taber are gonna make chicken feed out of him."

Duvall grinned in return, in spite of his knowing he
was soon going to have to settle things with Taber.

"If anyone can," he said, "it's those two."

Prophet entered Luther Falls around midnight. The town
was dark and silent, and so was Cordelia's boarding
house, looming darkly against the starless sky.

Prophet rode up to the front gate and dismounted, then
reached up for the girl. When he had her in his arms, he
turned through the gate in the picket fence, climbed the
porch steps, and pounded on the door.

He had to pound for nearly a minute before a light
appeared in one of the rooms, then another. He heard
footsteps and saw another light shimmer to life in the
foyer. A large figure appeared behind the frosted glass.

"Go away!" rose a rancorous female voice.

"Annabelle, it's Lou Prophet. Open up!"

The door opened. Annabelle stood there in a powder-
blue duster draped like a curtain over her matronly frame,
a nightcap on her head, and a lantern in her hand. "Oof-
ta! What's dis, Lou?"

"The girl from the mercantile," Prophet said as he pushed his way into the foyer.

"Achter-lever! Poor Lettie!"

"You have an empty room?"

Before Annabelle could respond, another voice said, "Lou!"

Prophet turned and saw Cordelia coming down the stairs in a pink wrapper, her hair falling about her shoulders.

"I have the girl from the mercantile here," Prophet told her. "She's in a bad way."

Cordelia opened her mouth to speak, but stopped, turned, and headed back up the stairs. "Bring her this way."

Prophet followed her to the second floor and down the dark hall dimly illuminated by the candle in Cordelia's hand.

"Lou, where did you ever find her?" Cordelia asked as she opened a door to one of the rooms.

"You don't want to know."

Cordelia quickly drew back the sheet and quilts, and Prophet lay the girl, whose groans were now disconcertingly tremulous and weak, on the bed.

"Oh, Lettie, I'd thought for sure we'd seen the last of you," Cordelia cooed, leaning down and smoothing the hair from the girl's eyes.

She turned to Prophet, her large brown eyes reflecting the light from the candle she'd placed on the bed table. "Has she been . . . ?"

"Yes."

Cordelia turned to the girl, biting her lip. "Oh, my."

"Is there a doctor in town?" Prophet asked.

"There was until the Red River Gang struck," Cordelia said tightly. "They shot him in the knee on their rampage down Main Street; he'll be out of commission for awhile."

Prophet heard footsteps and turned as Annabelle swung

into the room, breathing hard. "I have water heating on the stove," she told Cordelia, bustling toward the bed.

"We'll take care of her," Cordelia told Prophet. "Your old room's open. Why don't you get some rest?"

Knowing it was time for the women to take over, Prophet nodded and left the room, closing the door behind him. Out in the hall, he saw that one of the other doors was cracked. The withered features of an old man peered out, silhouetted by the lamp behind him.

"You find that girl, Lou?" the man asked him in a weathered voice.

"Sure did, Bert."

"Good for you." The door closed.

Prophet headed downstairs, feeling his way in the darkness. As he did so, he felt his exhaustion nearly overcome him, and the swath the bullet had burned on his thigh began barking in earnest as he descended the stairs. His pants were still damp and caked with river mud. He needed to get out of them, but first he had to tend to his horse.

Outside, he stabled Mean and Ugly in the buggy shed behind the boarding house, foregoing the livery stable uptown in case the Red River Gang trailed him here. It was best to stay put for the night.

When he'd stripped the tack off the dun, grained and watered him, and given him a cursory rubdown, Prophet closed the stable doors and headed back to the house. He climbed the stairs to his old room, and, finding the door unlocked, indulged in a smile. He had a feeling Cordelia had left it unlocked just for him.

He went inside, lit a lamp, tossed his saddlebags on the floor, hung his rifle and shotgun on the wall pegs, and peeled out of his clothes, piling them all by the door where Annabelle would find them and haul them off for washing.

He was giving himself a sponge bath with water from

the pitcher on the dresser when someone tapped on the door.

"Hold it—I ain't decent," he said, looking around for something with which to cover himself.

The door opened, and there was Cordelia. "I'll say you aren't," she said, giving her upper lip an ironic curl.

She came in, looking him up and down with those smoky eyes, one eyebrow arched, and closed the door behind her.

"How's the girl?" Prophet asked her, going back to his scrubbing. He was too tired to be aroused by the presence of this gorgeous woman, gazing as she was at his nakedness, as though at prime beef she was considering for a picnic.

"She'll be okay . . . physically," Cordelia said. "Annabelle's going to spend the night in her room." She frowned when she saw the gash on Prophet's muscular left thigh. "Oh, Lou!" she exclaimed, keeping her voice down.

"It's nothin'—just a burn," Prophet said.

"Oh, here, let me," she said, moving to him and taking the sponge from his hand. She dipped the sponge in the basin, then knelt before him, placing one hand on the back of his thigh and dabbing at the cut with the other.

It was a strange sensation, having this fully-clothed woman kneeling before him in all his nakedness, dabbing at the wound, which nipped with every dab of the sponge. Before he realized it, he was becoming aroused, his member stiffening only about a foot to the right of Cordelia's angelic face.

He felt sheepish about it, and tried to ignore it. But then Cordelia noticed it and looked up at him with a wistful smile.

"Must be feeling better," she said.

"I . . . reckon."

She stared up at his face, then slid her eyes to the fully

erect organ, narrowing her gaze and nibbling her upper lip. "Does that need tending, too, do you think?"

"I reckon it thinks so," Prophet grunted.

"I would have thought you were too tired, after all you've been through."

"Me, too."

She got up, soaked the sponge, knelt down, and went to work on him with the sponge, giving assistance with her wonderfully full lips and tongue. By the time she was done, Prophet had discovered religion again, after all these years, if only for a little while.

Clean and satisfied, he crawled into bed. He watched her undress before him, then curl up beside him, her naked flesh against his. They slept entwined in each other's arms until the first light painted the window. Then they made love, very quietly but thoroughly, before she washed, dressed, and bent down to kiss him on the cheek.

"I've waited a long time for a man like you, Lou Prophet," she whispered.

He looked at her, blinking the sleep from his eyes. "You . . . you know I can't stay, don't you, Cordelia?"

"Yes, I know," she said. "That's what makes you even more special." She straightened and walked to the door, where she stopped and turned to him with a mysterious smile in her eyes. "But you can come back whenever you want, and it'll be like you never left."

Then she went out, and Prophet listened to her soft footsteps fade down the hall as he drifted back to sleep.

13

PROPHET SLEPT DEEPLY for another hour and was awakened at around six-fifteen by two old codgers walking past his door arguing. Lifting himself onto his elbows with a groan, his thigh burning, he shoved his pillows up against the headboard, and lay back, arms folded across his belly.

Cordelia was on his mind in all her bewitching tenderness. He smiled, remembering how she'd straddled him, sighing softly as she'd worked against him, her long hair in his face, her swollen breasts in his hands. He wondered whose room was directly beneath his and if they'd heard the bedsprings getting one hell of a workout so late last eve. . . .

Prophet chuckled at the thought, but not for long. There was work to be done.

He sighed deeply and cleared his throat, scowling away the memory of Cordelia's opulent breasts in his hands, and scooting higher against the headboard. It was time to give some thought to his next course of action against the Red River Gang.

Pondering the situation, he remembered Louisa telling him to meet her in Fargo tomorrow. He remembered from his study of a map on a stage station wall some time ago that Fargo lay about fifty miles north of Wahpeton, also on the Red River of the north. Larger than Wahpeton, it had become a major river port for Dakota Territory as well as northwestern Minnesota. The Northern Pacific Railway had laid track through there as well, and the town had become a major stopping-off place for immigrants heading west.

Had Louisa learned the gang was headed that way? She must have. How she had, Prophet didn't bother to guess. The honey-haired Miss Bonaventure was pure-dee hell with the fires out, and if she told him to head to Fargo, you can damn well bet it wasn't for a barn dance.

Thinking of her, he smiled ruefully and shook his head. No seasoned lawmen had yet been able to sink their teeth into that gang, but here she was, knocking them off one by one. How she'd gotten by with it so far was a mystery. Prophet guessed that being such a sweet-talking, innocent-looking girl had helped. And so had her patience, not to mention her methodical, relentless tracking abilities.

Also on her side was the keen yet subtle madness Prophet had seen in her eyes. The girl may have been only sixteen years old in body, but what she'd seen happen to her family had made her soul as old as the moon and stars. He'd seen people age like that during the War Between the States—hell, it had happened to him—and he knew that once that innocence was lost, there was no getting it back.

So Fargo it was, he thought, tossing his covers back and dropping his feet to the floor. In Fargo, he'd meet Louisa and they'd take it from there . . .

He dressed in a clean pair of denims and buckskin shirt, and stomped into his undershot boots as soft as mocassins, then wrapped his gunbelt around his waist and donned his hat. He descended the stairs and nearly ran into Cordelia coming out of the kitchen with a bowl of scrambled eggs.

They smiled at each other lustily. Cordelia saw one of the regular boarders starting down the stairs and cleared her throat. She arranged an impartial expression and said, "Good morning, Mr. Prophet. Sleep well?"

"I sure did, Mrs. Ryan," Prophet said, following her into the dining room and removing his hat. "Very well, indeed." He wanted to inquire about the condition of the girl, but knew it would have to wait until after breakfast. One did not inquire in public about such a delicate matter as rape.

Prophet stepped up to the table and frowned when he saw three strange men seated amidst the regulars before the long, oval table covered with a white cloth, glistening china, and steaming coffee cups. The men examined him critically as Prophet reached for a chair, and the bounty hunter measured them in turn.

They were all so young and well-dressed and carefully groomed, with such confident eyes and smiles, that they reminded Prophet of the young, green, well-bred cavalry officers he'd known back during the Little Misunderstanding. The resemblance was so keen, in fact, he nearly shuddered. The negligent leadership of such men—or boys, rather—had been responsible for the needless slaughter of so many of Prophet's friends and family.

"Mr. Prophet," Cordelia said, when she'd put down the egg bowl, "as you can see, we have three newcomers. They appeared last night, and Annabelle let them in. Gentlemen, would you introduce yourselves to Mr. Prophet and the other boarders while I fetch the rest of the meal?"

"We certainly will, Mrs. Ryan," said the darkest of the three young men. His glittering eyes followed Cordelia's backside from the room before sliding back to Prophet, the trace of a an appreciative leer lingering on his lips.

Immediately, Prophet didn't like him. He was tall, pale,

and thin, with a full head of black hair and a carefully combed mustache the blue-black of anthracite.

"I'm Abel Montgomery," he said, and, turning to his compatriots seated on his right, added, "this is Ezekial McIlroy and Edward Fontana. We're deputy U.S. marshals out of Yankton, Dakota Territory. We were in the area when we heard about the Red River Gang tearing through your town the other day. We're here to bring them to justice."

Smiling, very pleased with himself, he glanced around the table, as if waiting for applause. The old people watched him dully. One of the checker players wrinkled his nose and shook his head, shakily lifting his coffee to his lips. Two withered ladies whispered in each other's ears.

Prophet stared at the three young men in their boiled shirts and brushed vests and blemished faces, barely able to keep from laughing. So these were the lawmen they'd sent after the Red River Gang? Inwardly, Prophet shook his head. Hell would freeze over and the devil would have icicles in his beard before these three even got close to taking down that bunch.

"You boys done anted up for a whole pack of trouble when you signed up to take down the Red River Gang," Prophet warned.

Flushing, the three took exception with being called "boys." Their eyes fell to Prophet and set up like pudding.

"We know exactly who and what we're up against, Mr. Prophet," the red-haired deputy McIlroy announced self-righteously. "We've studied all the paper we could find on this gang."

"Have you ever met up with any of 'em?"

"No, but we didn't have to, to know who and what they are," said Edward Fontana, a short, sandy-haired lad. "They're lead by Handsome Dave Duvall and his number-one henchman, Dayton Flowers. Both spent time in Arizona's Yuma Prison, where they met, and together they've robbed stage coaches and banks across the West for the past six years. They kill flagrantly and with apparent glee, and often torture their victims. They're also kidnappers and rape—"

"That'll be enough business talk now, gentlemen," Cordelia announced as she strode into the room with a platter of bacon and a bowl of fried potatoes. When she'd set the food on the table, she folded her hands before her and turned to one of the checker players. "Floyd, would you mind saying grace this morning, please?"

No more was said on the topic, but over breakfast, the three deputies eyed Prophet derisively, taking his measure again and again and never appearing to like the tally. Keeping the peace, Prophet merely grinned and forked potatoes into his mouth.

When he'd finished eating, he took his coffee cup out to the porch. As he knew they would, the deputies followed him. They lined up before him, glaring down icily under the broad brims of their hats, their black boots polished to high shines. The sandy-haired Fontana was smoking a slim cheroot. Prophet glimpsed Montgomery's badge peaking out from behind his vest.

When they didn't speak, Prophet looked around and said affably, "Looks like it's gonna make a nice one today. This far north, you never know what kind o' weather the good Lord's gonna bless us with."

Montgomery's eyes remained frigid. "Last night we learned from Mrs. Ryan's helper, a Miss Annabelle, that you rescued a girl back from the gang over in Wahpeton." His voice was friendly enough, but Prophet could tell it was a strain for him. "We appreciate that, Mr. Prophet. From now on, however, we respectfully request that you stay out of this affair. It's our job now to bring the Red River Gang to justice."

Prophet poked his hat back from his forehead and gazed

up at the deputies troubledly. "You boys know where they are and where they're headed?"

"We have reason to believe they're headed for Fargo, and then Grand Forks," McIlroy said, his red hair catching the morning sun beneath his snuff-colored hat. "They'll rob a bank in Fargo, one in Grand Forks, then head to Canada. That's been their pattern, once every year for the past three years."

Montgomery added, "Then no one will see them again for another six months, when they'll show up farther west, heading south and starting their vicious, rampaging arc all over again, starting with the gold camps in Wyoming."

Prophet nodded, admiring their knowledge of the gang. It was one thing to gather information, however, and another to bring down a small army of badmen.

"Maybe I should throw in with you b—" He stopped himself, cracked a smile. "Marshals."

In unison, all three shook their heads. "You have bounty hunter written all over you, Prophet," Montgomery growled.

"And we don't cotton to bounty hunters," Fontana added, wrinkling his slender nose as though detecting dog droppings.

"So stay out of it, Mr. Prophet," McIlroy warned. "If we see you or hear of you out there, within twenty square miles of us, we'll arrest you for interfering with the duties of federal law enforcers."

Prophet studied them with an incredulous frown. "You boys sure take yourselves serious," he said, raking his eyes across their fancy six-shooters prominently displayed and secured to their thighs with leather thongs. Then he raised his hands and dropped them to his knees. "But have it your way."

"That'll be all, Mr. Prophet," Montgomery said, as though dismissing him. But it was they who turned and headed back into the boarding house.

They reappeared five minutes later, carrying rifles, war bags, and bedrolls. They didn't so much as glance at Prophet as they crossed the porch, descended the steps, and filed off toward the livery barn for their horses.

Cordelia stepped outside and gazed after them for several seconds before turning to Prophet, who'd finished his coffee and was smoking a cigarette, his right boot hiked on his left knee, hat tipped back on his head.

"Do they have any chance at all, Lou?"

"Yeah," Prophet said with a sigh. "But a very slim one. How's the girl?"

"Still sleeping. She's pretty beat up. She'll probably sleep the rest of the day and maybe even tomorrow. I dread her waking up and having to tell her that both her parents are dead."

Prophet looked around to see if anyone was watching, then reached out and took Cordelia's hand in his, caressed her tender skin with his thumb.

She dropped her eyes to him and offered a fragile smile. Her words were not fragile at all, however, when she said, "Make them pay for what they did here, Lou. I'm normally a Christian kind of woman, but what they did here wasn't Christian, and they should be treated accordingly. I know those boys with badges can't do it, so you'll have to do it. You're the only one."

"I know," Prophet said, nodding.

"Do you think you can, Lou? Do you think you can get all of them?"

"I think so." With a certain little farm girl's help, he thought with a grim light in his eyes.

He stubbed out his cigarette, stood, and hugged Cordelia tightly, then went inside for his gear. When he came back carrying his shotgun and rifle, Cordelia was still standing on the porch.

"Will you be back?"

Prophet grinned. "I have to come back. I left a pile of dirty clothes on the floor up in my room."

He looked around cautiously again, then kissed her full on the lips, gave her a wink, and walked off the porch and around back to the carriage shed.

When he'd rigged out Mean and Ugly, he rode the horse south to Main Street. He stopped on a corner by the barbershop when he saw the three deputy marshals leading their saddled mounts down the livery barn's ramp. Looking serious and businesslike, the three lads adjusted their stirrups, double-checked their cinches, donned their cream dusters, and tightened the chin straps so their hats wouldn't fly off their heads. Exchanging official nods, they mounted up and gigged their horses eastward, primly ignoring the dogs that ran out to bark at their horses.

Again remembering the dangerous officers in charge of his ill-fated company during the War, Prophet shook his head, glanced around, and gigged the line-back dun to the gunsmith shop up the street to his left. When he'd bought a good supply of shells for his shotgun, rifle, and Peace-maker, he headed over to the barbershop. Getting a shave and a haircut would kill enough time for those three badge-toting younkers to get a safe distance ahead of him. He didn't want to see them any worse than they wanted to see him. They were the very picture of meat headed for the grinder, and they gave him the willies.

He tied Mean and Ugly to the hitch rack before the barbershop and stepped inside. He walked out forty-five minutes later not only shaved and trimmed but bathed, as well. It had turned out the barber, trying to drum up business again after the renegades had given the town a bad name, was running a special, and the bath had cost him only one extra dime.

"I'd say I smelled some better than you, Mean and

Ugly," Prophet told the horse as he gathered the reins from the rack. "What do you think about that?"

He'd just stepped off the boardwalk when a shot rang out, tearing Prophet's hat from his head.

14

PROPHET CROUCHED AS he drew his pistol, holding out his left hand so his fiddle-footed horse wouldn't trample him. Tossing his gaze across the street, he saw smoke dispersing in the air over a feed trough.

Prophet fired twice at the trough, then, releasing Mean's reins, he pivoted to his right, ran back onto the boardwalk, and crouched behind a barrel someone had cut in half and filled with petunias.

The pistol across the street cracked again, the slugs plunking into the barrel. Certain that members of the Red River Gang had tracked him from Wahpeton, Prophet stretched his arm around the right side of the barrel but held his fire when he saw the gunman dart up from behind the trough and disappear around the corner of the millinery shop.

Only one man?

Prophet hesitated, knowing it could be a trap. If he followed the gunman, he might run straight into the rest of the gang waiting for him in an alley. But his legs had already taken him halfway across the street before his mind decided to go ahead and chase the son of a bitch.

He pressed his back to the front of the millinery store, and slid a cautious gaze around the corner. One man, a stout hombre in a floppy hat and suspenders, was mounting a dust-gray horse waiting for him in the alley. Vaguely surprised to not see more men with drawn weapons, Prophet bolted around the corner as the man gigged the agitated mount southward, and fired off three ineffectual shots at the retreating figure.

Prophet paused to stare at the dwindling horseman befuddledly. Something about the man's homespun clothes, crude gear, and heavy-footed horse told the bounty hunter he was not a member of the Red River Gang. But if he was not, then who was he, and why in the hell was he trying to kill Prophet?

Prophet ran back for his horse, but Ugly was not where he'd left him. He cursed again, ran down the side street, and found the dun standing by a trash heap in the alley, his bridle reins hanging, an owly look in his eyes.

"Easy, Mean—damnit," Prophet groused, walking slowly up to the perturbed mount in spite of his need to hurry. "Don't act like you never heard gunshots before, you old crank."

When he got close, the horse sidled away, but Prophet lunged for the reins, grabbing them, and jumped into the leather. A moment later he was following the gunman's path south, tracing a meandering trail around shanties and log cabins. He stopped at the school, where children paused in their play to regard him curiously.

"A man just gallop through here?" he asked, suddenly unsure of the gunman's trail.

A boy in highwater coveralls lifted his arm and pointed southeast. "He crossed the river through there! Wolf chased him!"

"Much obliged!"

Prophet had no idea who Wolf was, but he found out

a minute later, when a big, black sheepdog loped toward him from the south, tongue hanging. The dog paused and hunkered low in a patch of high grass, watching Prophet gallop toward him. As Prophet passed, the dog leapt at Mean and Ugly's hocks, snarling, but was too tuckered to give chase.

Prophet crossed the shallow river and climbed the sparsely wooded rise on the other side. Raking his gaze around, he saw a rider cresting a hill in the middle distance, heading southeast at a lumbering gallop.

Prophet heeled Ugly after him, and when he'd ridden a good mile, he topped a high hill on the other side of a brushy creek. Looking eastward, he saw dust lingering in the still morning air, but he did not see the rider. Apparently, the man had ridden over the next rise east. If he held true to his speed and course, about now he should be climbing the next, higher hill beyond.

But he wasn't.

Prophet turned Mean and Ugly back down to the creek bottom and tied the horse to a tree. Looping the shotgun around his neck and holding it out before him, he followed the base of the hill southward. When he came to a cleft in the hill, he followed it east.

On the other side of the hill, he paused, looking around. Several trees and boulders provided good cover. A horse blew somewhere nearby, and Prophet crouched, quickening his gaze. Seeing nothing, he moved farther east, staying low in the brush and looking northward up the ravine.

He stopped when he saw the gray horse tied to a tree about fifty yards before him.

Prophet sucked his teeth, wary. Was there really only one man, or was that how it was supposed to look? Was he supposed to creep up on a man placed as a decoy while others crept up on Prophet from behind?

Chewing his cheek, Prophet gazed around with cautious

eyes, and peeled the Richards's hammers back, ready to start blasting at the first sign of trouble. Stepping eastward, he came upon a thin game trail hugging the east side of the ravine, and followed its meandering path north through shrubs and bramble.

Birds cried and gophers chattered in the grass.

When he came to a cottonwood, Prophet stopped suddenly.

About forty feet before him, the gunman crouched behind a mossy boulder, keeping his eyes and rifle trained on the western ridge of the hill looming up before him. He was waiting for Prophet to come galloping down that hill and into his rifle fire—lights out, that's all she wrote. Fiddler, start the music.

Crouching, holding the shotgun chest-high, Prophet started toward the man. His foot cracked a branch, and the man swung toward him, eyes widening, face coloring up like a sunset.

"Stop!" Prophet warned.

When the man didn't check the arc of the rifle, Prophet tripped his right trigger, and the Richards jumped with the explosion of spewing buckshot. The gunman fired once, the slug smacking into the tree behind Prophet. As the buckshot took him through his middle, he flew back against the rock and dropped his rifle. He stood there a moment and lowered his chin to stare down at his open belly, losing his hat in the process. He looked at Prophet, stumbled forward snarling, then fell to his knees, breathing hard and making high-pitched sobbing sounds.

"Goddamnit!" Prophet groused. "I told you to stop!"

"Y-you blasted me . . . ye . . . snake."

"You're the one layin' for me in the grass," Prophet reminded the man as he stepped forward, lowering the Richards, and glancing around to make sure they were alone.

"Who the hell are you?" Prophet asked, crouching

down and removing the six-shooter from the man's holster. He had wavy brown hair and a broad, pitted nose. Half his left ear was gone, leaving an ugly mess of scar tissue—the result of a knife fight, no doubt.

"I'm Carlton Mack," the man groaned, turning onto his shoulder, his face bunched with pain. "You shot my brother, Benny, and brung him here for the bounty, you no-good"—the man cried out in pain—*"bounty hunter!"*

Prophet stared down at the man wearily, lining up his thoughts. Then he remembered that Benny Mack was one of the two men he'd killed in the Johnson Lake Roadhouse, prior to traveling to Luther Falls. The corners of his eyes creased with surprise.

"You're Benny Mack's brother?"

"C-came t-ta . . . kill you . . . you son . . . of a *bitch!*"

With that, the man expired, his head dropping, his mask of pain flattening out and relaxing, tongue drooping. His eyes remained open, sightlessly studying the ants that were already moving in to investigate the gift of carnage fallen here as if from the sky.

"You goddamn fool," Prophet snarled.

On one hand, he was relieved that the man had no connection to the Red River Gang. On the other, he felt chagrined by the fact that a family member of one of his quarry had come gunning for him. Not that it hadn't happened before, and not that it wouldn't happen again.

He just didn't like it. There were too many ways to get killed at this job.

He didn't bother burying the man. The brush wolves and the bears in these parts would only dig him up in a few hours, anyway. Besides, he didn't have time. He had the Red River Gang to hunt.

Moodily, he took the man's guns and walked over to his horse tethered to the oak. He slid the rifle into the saddle boot and dropped the six-shooter in a saddlebag, then led the horse over to Mean and Ugly.

A minute later, he was heading back for Luther Falls, trailing the dust-gray for delivery to the school. No doubt one of those younguns on the playground could use a good saddle horse.

An hour earlier, Tom Taber and Billy Silver were sitting before the lumberyard across from the livery barn, smoking and trying to look as inconspicuous as possible, given this was a good Lutheran town and the two gang members not only had sidewinder written all over them, but one was Indian and the other white.

And, of course, there was the little matter of their raid a few days back.

Neither man worried about any of that, however. The town was without its sheriff, and thus these pious folks of Luther Falls were babes in the woods, without threat and defenseless—except for the man who'd taken the girl out of the Wahpeton saloon, that was. That's who Taber and Silver were watching for now, believing he'd sooner or later show himself around the livery barn. They'd recognize him easy enough. A rough-hewn character like that, clad in trail garb, would stand out in a porridge-and-raisin village like this one.

Taber was talking in a desultory way to Silver about the pony drip his brother had died of last month. "Went plumb wild, and even shot a whore, though she wasn't the one who gave it to him—" Taber stopped, noticing that Silver was staring eastward down the street, where three men were walking along the boardwalk, headed this way on the other side of Main.

"Well, well," Taber said under his breath. "Now who in the hell you s'pose they are?"

"One, he's got a badge," Silver said in his guttural Indian-English.

"Badge?" Taber squinted his eyes to see better. Sure enough, when the trio stepped out from under an awning, something pinned to one of the men's vests winked in the sun. "Well, I'll be damned."

The three men marched like proud soldiers home on leave, tipping their hats to the ladies, their jaws straight, the brims of their hats pulled low over their eyes. Their black boots shone like obsidian, and the guns tied on their hips appeared well-chosen and -tended.

As they approached the livery barn, Taber said, "Greenhorns with badges is what they are." He waited for Silver to say something, but the tight-lipped Sioux just stared, his muddy eyes glinting with kill lust. He got that look every time he saw a badge or soldier blue.

"You s'pose one of them nabbed the girl?" Taber said, not expecting a reply. Around Silver, you did a lot of talking to yourself.

He was surprised when the Indian offered a slight shrug. Even more surprised to hear, "We know why they're here," in that flat, low, menacing tone of Silver's.

Taber spat, snorted, and poked his cloth cap up on his pale, bald head. He chuckled at Silver's laconicism, contrasting it with the war whoops the Indian had given last night when, half smashed on rye, he'd gone upstairs in the saloon.

"We sure do," Taber said. "Well now, I reckon we see what direction they're headed . . . and follow 'em." He looked at Silver, who'd stood and was moving toward the lumberyard's main building behind them. "Hey, where you goin'?"

"Gonna use a grindstone . . . sharpen my knife."

Silver was returning from the lumberyard and inspecting his freshly sharpened knife blade when the three lawmen descended the livery barn's ramp, two leading duns, the third, a tall black stallion.

"Here we go," Taber said.

Silver stood beside Taber and watched the three men trot their horses out of town.

Taber and Silver walked to their own mounts tied to the hitch rack around the corner, and climbed into the leather. They moved deliberately, not in any hurry. They didn't want the lawmen to know they were being trailed.

An hour later, when they were about eight miles northwest of Luther Falls, Taber glanced at Silver, forming a gap-toothed grin. "What do you say, Billy? Circle around 'em, set up an ambush?"

The Indian didn't say anything. He just gigged his horse to the right of the oxcart trail they were following and spurred him into a gallop.

"Well, goddamnit . . . wait for me, ye crazy Injun!"

15

UNDER NORMAL CIRCUMSTANCES, Prophet would have turned Carlton Mack's possessions over to the local law. But since the sheriff was dead and the office hadn't yet been filled, Prophet stopped at the school and gave the horse to a scrawny lad with a club foot. He gave the rifle and pistol to the two oldest boys, then turned to leave, offering a wink to the pretty teacher, whose spelling lesson he'd interrupted and who regarded him with a wistful glimmer beneath mock-stern brows.

He gigged Mean and Ugly north of town, giving the horse his head, for he wanted to make it to Fargo before dark. Following the fresh hoof prints in one of the several oxcart trails that lead out of Luther Falls, he'd traveled about eight miles when he stopped suddenly, hearing gunfire.

Pricking his ears and gazing across the prairie before him, he could tell the shots originated from dead ahead. His first thought was of a stage holdup, but scouring the ground with his eyes, he saw no fresh tracks of the kind made by steel-rimmed wheels. There were the light, neat tracks of a slow-moving farm wagon, and those of several horses. But no stage. The shots weren't those of hunters, either, for there were too many rounds fired too quickly, with a definite air of anger and aggression.

Curious and cautious, Prophet gigged his horse ahead, scowling over the line-back's ears. At length, several smoke puffs appeared above the tawny grass straight ahead of him. He moved Ugly to the right of the trail, heading due north, splashing through a slough. After a couple hundred yards, he swung west again, intending to stay outside of firing range.

When he figured he was close enough to the shooters to glass them without getting shot, he dismounted, grabbed his field glasses, and peered southwest. Focusing the instrument, he brought two groups of shooters out of the prairie. One was hunkered down in the trees lining a stream bed. The other lay about fifty yards straight east of the stream, on the trail meandering across the naked prairie, with not a tree or rock for cover.

The second group appeared to involve three men firing over the tops of their dead horses. Two were spread about ten yards apart. The third lay about twenty yards behind and north.

Watching for several minutes, Prophet concluded there were two men in the trees, and that they must have bushwhacked the other three. One of the three appeared to lie dead behind his dead horse. As Prophet watched, another took a bullet in his shoulder and slumped down behind his saddle. As the man twisted around to lie on his side, the sun winked off something on his shirt.

Prophet glassed the man thoroughly, and cursed. Sure enough, it was deputy Montgomery. The other two were Fontana and McIlroy. What was left of them, that was. Whoever was in the trees—and who else could it be but members of the Red River Gang?—had drygulched them. McIlroy was the only deputy still returning fire, with only his six-shooter. It appeared his horse had fallen on his rifle.

It wouldn't be long before he ran out of shells or the two in the trees surrounded him and turned him into a sieve. . . .

"Kids," Prophet groused, replacing the glasses in his saddlebags.

Mounting up, he rode another hundred yards north, so the men in the trees wouldn't see him, then swung back west. Riding hard, he splashed across the stream and traced a broad arc around the two drygulchers in the trees. When he figured he was about a half mile straight west of the drygulchers, he found what passed for a hollow in this godforsaken pancake land, and hobbled his horse.

Then he grabbed his rifle and began running back toward the stream defined by the line of gray trees chaperoning it across the prairie. He didn't run far, however, for gopher holes had pitted the ground, threatening a broken ankle.

Walking fast, with an eye on the trees, from which sporadic gunfire still resounded, he made the grove and crouched behind a box elder, staring westward through the branches. As he looked around through the shady grove, he realized the gunfire had stopped. From far ahead came the wan sound of laughter.

Clutching his rifle before him, Prophet made his way through the trees, ducking under branches and trying as best he could to avoid those on the ground. When the light at the other side of the trees grew more distinct between the trunks and branches, he paused, looking around warily, to make sure a trap had not been set for him. One or both of the drygulchers could have seen him when he'd ridden in from the east. Savvy to his plan, they could be waiting for him, having done away with all three deputies.

Then more laughter rose from dead ahead, negating the speculation. Prophet heard what sounded like an Indian war whoop, rippling cold reticence along his spine and pricking the hair between his shoulder blades. Moving quickly forward, he came to the edge of the woods, then crouched behind the bole of a tree and stared out on the prairie beyond.

The three dead horses lay fifty yards out. Deputy Fontana lay with the horse farthest on Prophet's right, both dead. But near the middle horse, all hell was taking place.

One of the deputies—Montgomery, it appeared—was on his knees. His shoulder and arm were covered with blood. His hat was off, and his face was bloody as well, as though he'd been slashed with a knife. A short, stocky, dark-skinned man with long black hair was dancing some bizarre Indian dance around him, screeching and hooting like a devil.

About twenty yards to the north, a big white man in a buffalo coat and wool cap was jerking Deputy McIlroy to his knees and pistol-whipping the lad. The deputy's face was a dark-red oval, except for his teeth, which glistened whitely through a grimace.

"There you go, marshal-boy—how's that one feel?" the big man bellowed as he let McIlroy have it again with his pistol barrel.

McIlroy gave a cry as he fell sideways. Then the big man reached down and, grabbing his shirt collar, jerked him back to his knees.

Meanwhile, the Indian was still howling and dancing around Montgomery, who knelt in the grass with his head lolling back on his shoulders.

Cursing under his breath, Prophet raised his rifle to his shoulder. He planted the bead on the big man, but just as he did so, the man bent suddenly and jerked McIlroy to his feet again, placing the deputy between Prophet and himself.

His effort thwarted, Prophet winced and dropped his rifle barrel. He turned to the Indian, hoping for a better shot.

He had not yet brought the rifle to his shoulder when the Indian suddenly lunged at Montgomery, straddling the deputy's back and jerking the deputy's head up with a fistful of hair. With two quick, smooth motions, he ran the blade of a big knife across the young deputy's throat, then scalped the lad, blood flying as though splashed from a barrel.

Dead, the deputy slumped to the ground while the Indian raised the lad's bloody scalp in the air, giving a shrill, red-faced victory shriek.

His face bunching with exasperation, Prophet planted his rifle bead on the Indian's foread, muttering, "Why, you murdering son of a bitch!" and pulled the trigger. The Indian gave a start and shuffled backward, his hand coming down and releasing the scalp. His other hand rose to his face, weakly searching for the neat hole Prophet had drilled through his cheek, just below his left eye. Then the savage shuffled farther backward, stumbled, and fell on his ass with a grunt.

Prophet turned the rifle on the other man, whose head was whipping around in shock, trying to figure out who had shot his compadre. He clutched young McIlroy before him, shieldlike, so Prophet couldn't get a decent shot.

The man backed up, a fistful of the sagging deputy's collar in his hand, and stared savagely at Prophet, whom he'd picked out of the trees at the edge of the grove. Bringing his pistol to the deputy's head, he shouted, "I'll kill him!"

Prophet knew he would. He also knew he didn't have any time to spare. He brought the gun up, trying to find a shot that wouldn't take out young McIlroy. But then the young deputy gave a sudden yell, and plunged to his knees, leaving the big man open.

Prophet fired once, taking the man through the chest. He jacked and fired again, drilling another hole through the man's throat, then another through his head. Wailing and shooting his pistol in the air, the man backed up and fell to his knees. He fired one more shot into the ground, then sighed heavily and collapsed on his face.

Prophet lowered the Winchester and stepped out of the trees, looking carefully around to make sure no more gunmen were about. When he was relatively sure the two drygulchers had acted alone, he walked over to McIlroy, who cursed and sobbed as he climbed unsteadily to his feet. His face was bruised and bloody from the pistol-whipping, and his sweat-soaked, orange hair lay matted to his head. Confused and unnerved, he scoured the ground with his eyes as though looking for something, muttering curses all the while.

"Easy, son," Prophet said.

The lad whipped his head around, looking at Prophet as though startled. Finding the bounty hunter, the red-haired deputy's blue eyes narrowed with recognition. "You."

"Sit down. You need tendin'."

"Those sons o' bitches killed my partners." He resumed his reckless search, nearly stumbling over the hooves of his fallen horse.

When he found what he was looking for, he stooped to retrieve his silver-plated Colt "Storekeeper" six-shooter. Straightening, he aimed the short-barreled pistol at the dead man on the ground and tried to fire, but the gun was empty. The lad sobbed hoarsely from deep in his chest, big tears rolling down his blood-smeared, freckled cheeks.

"Here," Prophet said, offering his own Peacemaker butt first.

The deputy took the gun and fired three rounds into the big man's forehead. Then he walked over and emptied the gun into the Indian. He backed up three steps, gazing at the carnage all around him—at his fallen comrades—and dropped to his knees, his face chalky and expressionless. His head hung, his chin to his chest.

He looked so much like a war-addled soldier that Prophet wanted to weep. Instead, he found a canteen that hadn't been smashed by a fallen horse, and dropped it beside the lad. "Here you go, son. Have you some water. I'm gonna fetch my horse, find one for you, and be back in a few minutes."

The deputy did not reply.

Prophet walked back through the trees, retrieved Mean and Ugly, then found the gang-members' two horses tethered in the trees, and returned to the scene of the slaughter. McIlroy was swabbing his face with a handkerchief he'd soaked from the canteen. Flies whirred around the blood-soaked bodies of the dead men and horses.

"You can ride one of these two horses," he told the deputy. "We'll lay your friends over the other and take them to Fargo, ship them back to Yankton on the train."

Grimly, the young man nodded. He glanced at Montgomery, winced, appeared about to tear up again, then checked himself, and resumed swabbing his face from the canteen. Meanwhile, Prophet hefted the dead men over the back of an Appaloosa, covered them with the outlaws' bedrolls, and secured them with rope.

When he was finished, he offered the reins of the second outlaw horse, a mouse-brown gelding, to McIlroy, who climbed wearily to his feet and silently accepted. Just as silently, he climbed into the saddle, grunting as though, in the last hour, he'd aged fifty years and grown a ton.

Prophet in the lead and trailing the pack horse, they headed northwest on the oxcart trail, and the wily bounty hunter kept his eyes skinned for another possible ambush. He doubted it would happen—if the gang leader had sent more than two men after him or the marshals or whoever in hell they were after, they all would more than likely have been at the stream—but it was better to err on the side of caution.

They rode for nearly a half hour before the deputy said,

"Thanks for your help back there, Mr. Prophet." He'd gigged his horse up beside the bounty hunter and looked at him sincerely. Both his eyes were swollen, but the cuts had dried.

Prophet nodded. "I take it they took you by surprise from those trees?"

"We didn't have a chance," the deputy said grimly.

They'd have had a chance if they'd kept their eyes better peeled, but they were young and inexperienced, and that's what happened when you sent three younkers out after cutthroats like the Red River bunch. But Prophet didn't give voice to such thoughts.

"It's all right, son," he said instead. "We'll get your face sewed up by a sawbones, and you can head back to Yankton with your comrades."

His jaw set hard as a steel rail, the deputy said, "I'm not going back to Yankton until I've completed my business here . . . or died trying."

"That ain't wise."

"You going after them?"

"Yes."

"Then I'll ride with you."

Prophet wagged his head. "Nope."

The deputy flashed an irritated look at him. "Because of how we treated you back at the Ryan place?"

Prophet chuckled and shook his head. "Son, I've been treated worse by better than you!"

"Well what's the problem, then?"

"I work alone, that's all."

16

"DAVE, ME AND Sully are easin' back. We can't take this heat and dust."

Handsome Dave Duvall turned to the short, wiry man who'd ridden up beside him in the pack heading north for Fargo. Duvall laughed. "Eddie, you look as green as Kentucky. How much o' that bull piss you swill, anyway?"

"I musta downed at least a bottle my ownself," Eddie Leach complained. "I just can't ride no more for a while. Me an' Matt, we're gonna throw down somewhere and sleep it off. We'll meet up with yous at Cora's later tonight or early tomorrow."

"Well, if you don't, you're gonna be out one hell of a poke," Duvall warned.

"We'll be there, Dave," Leach said, wincing at the blacksmith hammer working with fierce abandon at the tender nerves in his brain.

He reined his horse out from the pack, letting the group canter past him on the trail. Several of the men, nearly as sick as he from all the forty-rod they'd swilled the night before and had been unable to sleep off like they'd planned, sneered at him and cursed, their faces pallid and, in several cases, the green-yellow of a stormy summer sky. But they were tough hombres, as tough as Leach had ever seen. They'd probably stomp some more again tonight.

Just the thought of it made Leach's bowels roll and his head throb mercilessly. He used to think he could keep up with these boys, but maybe he couldn't. Maybe it was time to try some other group without quite so much vim and vinegar, so many reprobates fresh from federal lockups.

But, then again, Leach had never had so much fun terrorizing folks, smashing into homes and looting trunks and mattresses, raping women and girls, beating and shooting men. He'd even run a man through with a pitchfork! Then there was this girl he'd whipped to death with his belt, just after he'd . . .

Leach shook his head. No, he'd never known what fun was until he'd joined up with Dave and the boys. He guessed he could no more give out on the gang than a child could give up candy. But boy, oh boy, did he need to grind his heels in now and sleep off some of that redeye!

He gigged his horse back on the trail, where Matt Sully stood beside his mount, bent over, hands on his knees, heaving as though hacking up his innards.

"You find him?" Leach asked.

Sully lifted his waxen face and growled, "Who?"

"That Ralph you keep calling for."

Leach smiled in spite of his swirling bowels and throbbing eyeballs. But when Sully barfed again, the green bile from his tormented guts splatting on the grassy turf, Leach lost his own cookies—or whatever was left in there—down the side of his saddle.

"Goddamnit!" he groused. "Look what you made me do to my stirrup!"

The tall, greasy-haired Sully donned his battered, rain-stained hat, and legged it over his saddle, hunkering over his horn as though chilled. "Come on," he rasped. "Let's head for that tree yonder . . . get some shut-eye."

Spatting the foul taste from his mouth, Leach followed Sully toward a large cottonwood poking up in the west. It was the only landmark out here, and the only tree they'd seen since crossing a creek about five miles back. This flat land was all stirrup-high grass and sky, and Leach vaguely wondered how, on a cloudy day, you ever knew which direction you were headed.

Bees buzzed and the hot sun beat down, making Leach's head thunder even worse. He was glad when he and Sully finally made the cottonwood, which offered sizable shade on the south side of its trunk. The wind in its leaves made a cool, fresh sound, sporadically distracting Leach from his misery.

The outlaw tore the leather from his horse in a daze. When he'd hobbled the animal beside Sully's, he grabbed his bedroll, spread it out beside the tree, lay carefully down on his back, crossed his arms over his chest, and tipped his hat over his eyes.

Sully did likewise, and both men were sound asleep in minutes.

A half hour later, Leach opened his eyes and lifted his head. He looked around at the sun-washed grass. "What was that?"

He looked at Sully, who lay on his side, sweating, his eyes pinched shut, his lips moving as he dreamed.

"Hey, Sully," Leach said, nudging the other man's arm.

Sully opened his eyes angrily. "Leave me alone, god-damnit!"

"Didn't you hear it?"

"Hear what?"

"I don't know—that's what I'm askin' you."

Sully grunted with exasperation, then closed his eyes

and repositioned his head on his saddle. "Shut up and let me sleep. I know one thing—I'm goin' back to Wahpeton first chance I get, and I'm gonna make that apron guzzle a whole bottle of his own busthead . . . see how he likes it."

With that, Sully fell back asleep.

Leach looked around again. Only the sound of the wind in the cottonwood and grass broke the quiet. Occasionally a fly buzzed and one of the horses tore at the grass or snorted, but that was all. Finally deciding that he must have dreamed the sound that had awakened him, Leach eased his still-aching head back onto his saddle, and closed his eyes.

But then he heard it again—a sound like a girl singing far off in the distance. Leach couldn't make out the words, but it sounded like a song a child might sing on a playground. It owned a haunting, dirgelike quality, and it came and went on the breeze.

"Damn it all!" he groused.

He looked around again, shielding his eyes against the afternoon sun with his hand, blinking against the drum throbbing within his skull. All he saw were the horses and the wind-ruffled grass. Finally, with another curse, he gained his feet and scoured the distance in a full circle with his eyes. He expected to see a farm somewhere along the horizon, where kids might be playing.

But nothing . . .

What the hell . . . ?

He was about to sit back down when heard the keening sound again. Swinging around, he looked to his right and saw a tree way off in the distance. It had to be a half mile away, all alone amidst the tawny, sunburned grass.

The singing, if that was what you'd call it, seemed to originate from over near the other tree.

Leach swung his gaze back to Sully, who slept with his eyebrows rumpled and a heavy sheen of sweat above his mouth. No use trying to wake him. He'd just curse some more and go back to sleep. But there was no way Leach could relax, not hearing that damn ghost sing her damn song in his ear, just loud enough to give him the willies.

Who in the hell was she, anyway? *Where* in the hell was she?

Wrapping his gunbelt around his waist and cinching the buckle, he started walking toward the other tree, which appeared a thin shadow from this distance. Every once in a while, just when he was about to turn back, he heard the girl's high, sonorous voice. She seemed to be calling to him, beckoning him toward the cottonwood growing slowly on the horizon, all alone in the sea of ruffling, shadow-swept grass.

When Leach was within fifty yards of the cottonwood, which looked like a mirror image of the one he and Sully had chosen for their naps, he stopped. A black horse stood beneath the tree, its reins tied to the trunk. The horse nickered when it saw Leach, and twitched its ears. The horse blew and shook its head, watching Leach warily.

Leach scowled, peeling his lips back from his teeth. "Now what in the hell . . ."

He saw something hanging from the branch above the horse. Unable to make out what it was from this distance, he walked forward several more steps. He stopped again, feeling something wet and cool skitter along his spine.

What hung from the branch above the horse was a noose. A hangman's noose . . . swaying in the wind. . . .

Suddenly, a figure stepped out from behind the tree. Leach's heart jumped into his throat, and he reached for his six-shooter, but stopped when he heard a hammer ratchet back.

"Uh-uh," the girl said.

Leach froze, lifted his head to look at her. She was, indeed, a girl—a fair-faced, blue-eyed blonde, hay-colored hair ruffling in the wind. She held a silver-plated revolver on him. Had him dead to rights, too.

Leach screwed up his face at her, befuddled. "What . . . what you doin' out here, Missy?"

"Waitin' for you, sir."

"Me?"

"Yeah, you." She raised the gun higher, then moved her head to one side a little, indicating the noose. "That's for you."

"Me?" Leach smiled nervously. He suddenly wondered if this were a joke the gang was pulling on him, to razz him about his hangover. But who was this girl? Where in the hell had they found her . . . ?

No. Couldn't be.

"You murdered my family," the girl said tightly, her pretty eyes squinting mean. "You played a part in it . . . I remember you. I remember your face from your dodger, too, Eddie Leach."

At the sound of his name, Leach's face flattened out, and his eyes gained a fearful cast. "What are you talking about, girl?"

"I'm talking about Roseville, Nebraska. Last year, about this same time. A little farm on Pebble Creek. My mother and father. My two sisters and my brother. You killed 'em all after you savaged my mother and sisters."

Leach was amazed at how steady she held the gun while she spoke with such passion. The barrel was aimed directly at his heart. He was trying to think back to a year ago, trying to remember a place called Roseville.

The girl read his mind. "Oh, you won't remember it, I'm sure, Mr. Leach," she said, her voice heavy with sarcasm. "I'm sure there are far too many such atrocities in your history to remember just one family on Pebble Creek. Just take it from me—you were there. You and the others in your gang took my family away from me forever, and now you're gonna pay for it. Climb up on that horse and put your head through that noose."

Leach could barely feel his hangover anymore, barely register the throbbing in his brain. Fear had overcome him. Fear and exasperation that this little snot-nosed girl thought she could get by with such a thing.

Anger flattening his eyes, he snarled, "I . . . I ain't climbin' up on no horse . . . and I ain't stickin' my neck through no noose, Little Miss."

"You'll die now, then."

She closed one eye, sighting down the barrel.

He threw up his hands. "Wait, wait, wait!" he cried. "Wait a minute now. You don't wanna do this."

"I'm going to give you to the count of three," the girl said. "Then I'm going to sink one forty-five-caliber slug through your lung and leave you to choke to death on your own blood."

Gazing at her with astonishment, Eddie Leach realized she would do exactly what she'd promised.

"And if you call out to your friend," she added, again reading his mind, "the last word will not have died from your lips before I've killed you deader than a widow's husband."

His voice gaining a beseeching tone, he said, "Well, what good's it gonna do me to get on that horse? You're gonna kill me one way or another!"

"It will give you several more precious seconds to breathe the air and reflect on your life. Maybe even a minute or two. We humans do cling to life so, when the chips are down. Seconds can feel like hours."

"Jesus God, kid, you're one crazy little bitch!"

Her voice remained maddeningly level. "It's your choice. You can die slowly now, choking on your own bodily fluids, or you can have the few extra minutes it takes you to climb into the saddle and tighten the noose around your neck." She licked her lips, inclined her head slightly, and gazed down the barrel at his chest. "I'm going to start counting now. When I get to three, I'm going to shoot you in your right lung."

She stared at him.

"One, two—"

"All right, all right!" Leach cried, flabbergasted, his head pounding now even harder than before.

He was stuck between a rock and a hard place. There was no way out. All he could do was hope that some miracle happened between now and the moment he stuck his head through that noose.

Matt Sully heard the yell and opened his eyes. Slowly, he sat up and looked around.

"Hey, Leach?"

Eddie Leach was nowhere in sight.

"Who in the hell yelled?" Sully asked himself, wincing against the throbbing in his head.

He was sure it was a yell he'd heard. A loud one, coming from a long way off. And, come to think of it, the voice had sounded like Leach's. Was that why Sully's heart was pounding?

Sully stood, grunting, and shielded his eyes against the bright sun, scanning the grassy terrain around him.

"Leach?" he yelled.

He yelled it several times. There was no more reply than the breeze rustling the cottonwood and the nicker of Leach's horse standing with Sully's nearby.

Sully saw the tree standing in the direction from which he thought the yell had come. Corroborating his assumption was a silvery trail of bent grass leading that way. Hitching his gun belt on his hips, Sully began following the path toward the tree.

When he was about a hundred yards from the tree, Sully stopped. Something appeared to be hanging from it. Something long and shaped like a body.

Frowning curiously, feeling a sluggish reticence nip at

his already seared bowels, Sully drew his revolver and resumed walking toward the tree. The closer he got, the more reticent and fearful and cautious he became.

Approaching the tree, he stared up at the body with wide-eyed horror and indignation. "Leach?" he whispered.

His mind swirled and wheeled and tumbled back over itself. Was he dreaming? Was Eddie Leach really hanging there from that tree, his neck stretched a good foot, out here in the middle of nowhere?

Who? Why? How?

Sully heard feet crackle grass behind him, but before he could wheel around, he felt the cold steel of a pistol barrel jammed against his neck. He froze, bile flooding him, his knees turning to glue.

"Kneel," came a girl's voice.

"Wha . . . wha . . . ?"

"Kneel down."

"Why . . . who . . . ?"

"Kneel down!"

The man knelt down. Louisa Bonaventure snugged her silver-plated revolver up to the back of his head and fired two bullets through his skull. Then she wheeled, holstered her revolver, and walked away through the grass.

Behind her, Sully's body tipped onto its side. Eddie Leach moved gently at the end of his rope.

17

DRYING DISHES IN the kitchen of her brothel three miles south of Fargo, Cora Ames looked out the window into the backyard, and shook her head. The two French girls were running around bare-breasted again, while several of Cora's other girls hung the wash on the lines strung between the cottonwoods along the Wild Rice River.

All the girls were dressed skimpily, in wrappers and pantaloons and such, their hair uncombed or in curlers, but those two French girls just loved to waltz around naked as the day they were born.

Frowning, Cora opened the outside door and yelled, "Babette, Joelle! You're going to catch your death of cold runnin' around like that! I declare, have some sense!"

The girls ceased their nymphlike frolic in the high, green grass, and turned to regard Cora beseechingly. "Oh, please, Cora!" Joelle cried. "We have been bundled up all winter. It feels so good"—the auburn-haired waif with big brown eyes sensuously cupped her tiny breasts in her hands and rolled her head to one side—"to have the air against our skin!"

"I'll give you something against your skin if you catch
colds and can't work!" Cora replied with several angry
shakes of her small, plump fist. "Now put some clothes
on and help the other girls hang the wash!"

"Oh, Cora!" Joelle complained.

"Don't 'Oh Cora,' me, girl. Just do as you're told!"

"Oui, Madame," Babette said, crestfallen, as she and
Joelle reluctantly headed for the brightly colored wrappers
they'd tossed on a tree stump.

Sighing with dismay—those two were going to be the
death of her yet!—Cora returned to the kitchen. As she
set the plate she'd been drying in the cupboard over the
sink, a girl's voice sounded from the parlor.

"Miss Cora—riders!"

Cora checked the clock above the cupboard. It was only
four o'clock—too early for the hands from the bonanza
farm over west. Those boys would be planting their wheat
and potatoes until sunset. The cowboys from the nearby
ranch were tied up with calving.

Frowning, Cora set down her towel and walked into the
parlor, where the rawboned but pretty German girl, Guida,
was sitting on the red plush sofa, absently stroking the
kitten in her lap while she read an illustrated newspaper,
moving her lips to sound out the English which still befuddled her. Marci, an orphan from Illinois, stood before
the window, barefoot and in a Chinese kimono—a gift
from a railroad man. She had a dust rag in her hand and
a sleeping cap on her head.

Turning to Cora curiously, she said, "A whole pack of
men on horses . . ."

Cora sidled up to the girl and gazed out the window.
Sure enough, a band of riders was pounding down the
road from the west, heading this way. When the men had
moved close enough for Cora to get a look at the two lead
riders, her stomach tossed and sweat popped out on her
lip.

"Girls," she said without moving her eyes from the window, "fetch the others and go upstairs."

"Huh—what?" Marci said, bewildered.

"Do as I say," Cora said. "Stay there until I tell you it's safe."

Guida said from the sofa, "Miss Cora, what is wrong . . . ?"

"Just do as I say!" Cora snapped, a slight trill in her voice.

Both girls jumped and hurried from the room. When Cora heard the back door close, she moved stiffly to the foyer, her slippered feet heavy with fear, and stepped onto the porch, closing the door behind her. She walked to the porch steps and stopped beside the sign nailed to an awning beam, which read COWBOYS AND FARMERS—SCRAPE THE DUNG FROM YOUR BOOTS BEFORE ENTERING.

She adjusted her gray flannel wrapper over her giant bosom and folded her arms over her chest, trying to keep from shaking. Every vein in her body filled with dread as she watched the ragtag team of hard-featured horsemen canter into the yard, scattering chickens. They reined up before the porch, dust billowing, horses blowing and shaking their bridles and bits.

"Hello, Miss Cora!" Handsome Dave Duvall greeted the woman exuberantly, checking his mount down before the tie rail. "We're back!"

Cora Ames set her jaw to hide her fear as she stared back at the handsome rake in his dusty black frock coat, string tie, and black hat. With his piercing gray-green eyes, dimpled chin, and brushy, upturned mustaches, he was indeed a handsome devil. But a devil he was nonetheless, and the worst Cora Ames had ever laid eyes on.

As her eyes skidded apprehensively between Duvall and Dayton Flowers, equally as bad, she wished she still had the big Indian, Leonard Two Horses, riding shotgun around the place.

Finding her tongue at last, she said, "Dave Duvall, you and your men are not wanted here."

Duvall frowned. "Huh?"

"In light of what happened during your last visit, I'll have to ask you to leave."

"Leave?"

The puzzled frown still etched on his whiskered, handsome face, Duvall turned to his partner. Flowers sat beside Duvall on a skewbald horse lathered with sweat and peppered with dust and weeds.

Flowers was as ugly as Duvall was handsome, with his long, horsey face, red-rimmed hound-dog eyes, and long, greasy hair hanging straight down from his frayed bowler. His pallid, large-pored skin was pitted and scarred, and a brown, teardrop-shaped birthmark resided to the left of his hooked nose, a black hair curling out of it. The sight of the man made Cora weak with revulsion and horror, and it was a hell of a job to not show it.

Flowers returned Duvall's look with a grin, and shrugged.

Duvall turned back to the madam holding her ground on the porch. "Cora, I don't have the foggiest idea what you're talkin' about."

"Your boys tore up my house, Dave. They like to burned the place to the ground, and . . . and then there . . . there was what you did to Vivian. . . ."

Flowers looked at Duvall, wrinkling his bushy brows. "Vivian? Who in the hell's Vivian?"

It was Duvall's turn to shrug.

"She's the one whose toe you bit off!" Cora fairly yelled, angry now as she remembered the poor girl screaming and bleeding as she stumbled down the stairs. Vivian had long ago limped off with a horse buyer from Glendive, Montana, but the memory of that night would haunt Cora forever.

Chuckles rose from the motley group sweating behind

Duvall and Flowers. Like a sheepish child, Dave shrugged and grinned and shook his head.

Finally, he said over his shoulder, "Boys, take your horses to the corral. Miss Ames here just needs her feathers smoothed a little is all. Her and me'll confer privately, and I'm sure we'll have this little misunderstandin' straightened out in no time."

As the others headed, snickering, for the dilapidated corral near the buggy shed, Duvall climbed out of his saddle and tossed his reins to Flowers. Then he turned to Cora, smiled, and removed his hat. Still grinning, he slapped the hat against his thigh, billowing dust, and shook his head as though at a joke that tickled him no end.

"Yeah, that was some night," Duvall said through a chuckle. "But if memory serves, I apologized for that, Miss Cora."

"You can't apologize for biting a girl's toe off, Dave! Go away and take your crew with you. You're not wanted here."

Dave looked at the short, squat woman, her brown hair piled and fastened with barrettes atop her head. The smile faded from his lips. "If memory serves, I gave her twenty dollars and a watch. A gold watch with a picture of Mary Lincoln inside!"

"The watch wasn't no toe, Dave. And the twenty dollars ain't the goin' rate for toes, neither."

"You don't have the right spirit, Cora. Forgive and forget—that's the Christian spirit."

"What would you know about anything Christian, Dave?"

Duvall grinned again sheepishly. "You got me there, Cora." Slowly, he climbed the steps.

Cora shook her head. "No, Dave. This is my place. I order you off the premises."

He kept coming. She took two shuffling steps backward, her chubby face mottled with anger.

"Let's go inside and talk about it, Cora."

"No! I—"

Duvall opened the door, grabbed Cora's arm, and shoved her inside. She grabbed the coat tree, nearly upending it, to keep from falling.

Her voice was small and tight, and her lips trembled. "Dave . . . please . . . I can't have you eatin' limbs off my girls!"

Dave smiled again, as affable as a boy at a church picnic. Then, before Cora could comprehend what was happening, he balled his right fist and punched her in the stomach—hard.

Cora bent over with a deep "Uggh!" as her breath exploded from her lungs. She dropped to her knees, wheezing as she fought for air.

"Ah, Cora, now look what you made me do!" Duvall exclaimed, dropping to a knee and lowering his head to peer into her face.

She rasped, grunted, and coughed.

Smoothing a lock of hair from her face, Duvall said with mock tenderness, "Now, I wouldn't have had to do that, Cora, if you'd have shown me some proper respect. I mean, I don't see no cause to speak to me in front of my men like you just did. No sir, not after all the money and gifts I've bestowed upon you and your girls."

Duvall paused, gave his head a grieved shake. "Now, I'm sorry if I injured little Vivian, but like I said, I done apologized for that. Why, I even gave the girl a gold watch with a picture of Mary Lincoln on the lid!"

He caressed Cora's face gently with the back of his hand. "Now, don't you think I should be forgiven one teeny-weeny little indiscretion that happened when I was drunk on your booze pret' near a year ago?"

Trembling and regaining her wind, Cora lifted her head and stared at him coldly.

"Don't you think so, Cora?" Dave asked her again in an innocent little boy's voice.

Cora swallowed and panted, holding her aching stomach. Sweat streaked her forehead and cheeks, and her face was as pale as death. She swallowed again, ran her tongue across her lower lip, and said something inaudible.

Turning his ear, Duvall said, "What's that, Cora? I couldn't hear you."

Giving a shallow sigh, Cora said weakly, "I said . . . p-please . . . don't do nothin' . . . nothin' crazy, D-Dave. . . ."

"Cora, Cora, Cora," Dave said, as if deeply chagrined. "I would never." He grinned and gently helped her to her feet. "And just to show you how good I can be, I'm gonna let you be the first one to escort me upstairs."

He turned her around, slapped her ample rump, and shoved her down the foyer. "What do you say to that, Cora, old girl!"

18

AN HOUR AND a half later, Louisa rode along the wagon trail the Red River Gang had followed north of Wahpeton, on the west side of the north-flowing Red River. She reined up when, about an hour before sundown, she came to the point where the gang had turned westward onto a shaggy two-track showing the recent semi-circular gouts made by shod hooves.

Now, why would they head west when Fargo was another three or four miles north?

Then she saw the crude sign someone had kicked into the grass where the two trails intersected. Riding over and gazing down at the pink lettering on an arrow-shaped board, she read: CORA'S PLACE—1 MILE.

Louisa pursed her lips and nodded knowingly. A brothel. Figures. She had a mind to camp nearby, see if she couldn't carve a few more cadavers out of the gang later tonight.

She turned it over in her head and decided not to push her luck. After hers and Prophet's raid on their party last night, they might be perked for trouble. She'd continue on to Fargo and try to pinpoint the havoc they'd planned for the next river hamlet north on the north-flowing Red.

She'd learned from a conversation she'd overheard between two gang members draining their bladders outside the saloon in Wahpeton that the gang had been planning a job in Fargo for the past several weeks. From the way the men had talked, it sounded like a big takedown, involving "enough loot to set 'em up for several years down in old Mexico with two or three senoritas apiece."

Gigging her horse northward along the trail, Louisa thought it over. What kind of job could be that big in Fargo? A bank? An assay office? An express terminal? A hotel?

She'd heard Fargo was a growing river port. Maybe it had something to do with riverboats and gambling and such. . . .

Whatever it was, she smelled the town a good while before she actually saw it, for a stiff north breeze commenced blowing before sunset, sending southward the pungent smell of privies and charred trash heaps. It was a familiar smell and one reason why Louisa avoided most population centers, especially boomtowns. They smelled bad, they looked bad, and most of the people populating them were the very epitome of bad—pimps, painted ladies, confidence men, gamblers, and gunmen.

As she neared the town, farms with sod houses and fenced pastures gave way to sod-and-log shanties, tar-paper hovels, and makeshift canvas affairs clustered along the shiny new railroad line on its high, black bed. A wide, muddy street called Broadway appeared to be the town's hub, and Louisa halted her horse between the railroad tracks and a loading dock, watching in amazement as men of all shapes, sizes, colors, and creeds mucked through the ankle-deep mud-and-dung between the milled lumber establishments fronting Broadway.

She'd never seen such a concoction of white men, red, black, and yellow, or heard so many different languages yelled, laughed, and spoken in low tones over cigars on the nearby mercantile stoop.

A gun barked, and Louisa jumped, instinctively grabbing for the Colt beneath her skirt. She stopped when, turning toward the report, she saw three men coaxing two mules pulling a wagon heaped with barbed-wire spools and seed sacks out of the mud behind a post-and-wire shop. One of the men—a tall, burly fellow in coveralls and smoking a pipe—held a Civil War–model pistol in the air. He yelled something and fired the big iron again, and the mules jerked the heavy wagon out of the mire, the men around the wagon shouting and laughing with unrestrained exuberance.

Two of the men clapped each other on the back and walked into a nearby saloon. The big man with the gun tossed the revolver under the wagon seat, then climbed aboard. He grabbed the reins off the brake and hee-hawed the mules into the street, pulling to a halt before Louisa. Only then did she realize she must have been staring with eyes large as 'dobe dollars, amazed at such a place, half frightened out of her wits. She felt as though she'd landed on a foreign continent.

"Help you, Little Miss?" the big man called through a chip-toothed grin. The accent was either Dutch or Scotch—Louisa wasn't sure which.

She was shocked into fearful silence before thinking of a question. "Uh . . . is there a feed barn hereabouts?"

The big man jerked a thumb over his shoulder.

"The Associated's down that way, and McMurphy's place is down t'other." He looked her up and down as he sucked on his pipe. "You all alone, Little Miss?"

Louisa hesitated, startled momentarily by several Sons of Han crossing the street before her in black pajamas and tassled hats. "Uh," she hemmed, "uh . . . no, sir. I'm waiting for my brother—my brother and my father. They're bringing a wagon to town."

The big man nodded. "I see, then. Sure. Might want to wait for them over by the notions shop, Miss. The sun's going down, and ole Broadway, she gets a little rough come nightfall." He gave her a wink and a nod and slapped the reins against the broad backs of the mules, who jerked their heads up and lumbered westward along the rails glistening silver and mauve as the sun slipped bleeding into the sod.

Keeping one hand close to the revolver beneath her skirt, Louisa neck-reined the Morgan toward the river, soon wishing she'd gone the other way. Just about every building down here sported a sign announcing a saloon or tavern. Painted ladies leaned against awning posts in their frilly, low-cut dresses, net stockings, and feathered hats. Some wore boas and smoked cheroots. All watched Louisa pass on her Morgan with wistful slants of their heavily made-up eyes.

Louisa glanced away from one such marvel of chintzy exhibitionism only to see another between two buildings, bent over a wood pile with her skirts pulled up, laughing while a grunting man banged away at her from behind. In the past year, Louisa had been to a lot of places throughout the West, but she'd never seen anyplace like this, and she felt a mute, black dread swath her very soul.

This was the last town she'd ever visit—at least in Dakota. She might even set a match to it on her way out; it was going to burn sometime, one way or another.

"What are you staring at, Missy—you want him next?"

Louisa stiffened when she realized not only that she'd stopped the Morgan to stare at the copulating couple in awe, but that the whore was speaking to her, in Irish-accented English.

"No thank you," she said primly, kicking the Morgan down the street as the whore's cackle echoed behind her and her face heated like a skillet.

The livery barn sat dangerously close to the Red River, which had flooded a half-dozen establishments along its banks. She negotiated with the dark, wiry little man who ran the place for the stabling and feeding of the Morgan, then asked if she could stay there, too.

"What, with your horse?" the man asked, blinking.

"Yes, sir."

He looked her up and down in much the way the big man with the wagon had done. "You don't want to stay here, Miss." He looked around, scowling. "This is a barn."

"I know it's a barn, sir. But I'd like to stay with my horse, if you please. I'll share his stall and keep to myself. I don't drink or use tobacco."

The little man regarded her again, skeptically. "Are you all alone, Miss?"

She sighed, tired of all the questions she had to contend with everywhere she went. Tiring of all the lies and excuses she'd had to concoct to detract attention from herself, a young woman alone, she said with an air of great impatience, "Yes—is that a crime?"

"No, it's not a crime, Miss, but . . . it might not be safe here for a girl. I go home at eight-thirty. I have a half-breed who mans the office, but . . . there's strange men about, Miss."

"I know that, sir, but I assure you I can take care of myself. I won't be any trouble. You won't hear a peep out of me, and I'll tend my horse myself."

The man shrugged and looked at her sadly, piteously. The look annoyed her. Louisa Bonaventure could take being yelled at and cussed and even threatened bodily, but pity was something with which she could not, would not, contend. Wishing she'd gone ahead and told the lie about meeting her father and brother here, she said, "How much more do you need to house me along with my horse, sir?"

"Nothin'," the man said after brief pause. "You can stay with your horse for nothin' extra." Shrugging, he appraised her and the Morgan one more time, then turned away, grabbed a pitch fork, and headed out the double doors to the paddock.

Louisa wheeled to the Morgan and, annoyed without fully realizing why, stripped the tack from the horse, groomed him, and filled his trough with fresh oats. When she'd lugged in a pail of water from the well and filled the Morgan's water trough, she froze suddenly and dropped her head. Her heart wrenched and tears spilled out from her tightly shut eyes.

Silently, she sobbed, though she didn't know why. She suspected it was the piteous looks the man with the wagon had given her, which was then equaled in sympathy by the dusky-skinned stableman. In their eyes, she saw the reflection of how she was: alone and pitiable.

She, Louisa Bonaventure, daughter of Kyle and Marie Bonaventure, sister to James, Elsie, and Donna, was alone.

She was an orphan, with no home whatsoever. With no friends or family or prospects for happiness. All she had in this cruel, barren world were the clothes on her back and her horse and her quest for the gundogs who'd murdered her family. That's all that kept her eating and sleeping and breathing and going. . . .

For nearly a year now, she'd tried to keep her mind clear of everything but the Red River Gang. For the most part, and aside from occasional nightmares that plucked her, sweaty but chilled, from deep sleep, she'd accomplished the feat. But now, suddenly, in this dank barn in this sleazy town amidst lost souls rutting like pigs in alleys, she thought of her house and her family and her sisters' taunts and grins and their two-mile rides to school on the old spotted pony their father had received in trade from transient Indians.

She thought of the kitchen where she'd worked each day, helping her mother prepare meals. She thought of the old, chipped percolator she'd never given much thought to when she was still on the farm. She thought of the lilacs that grew thick by the cellar their father had dug, and how they'd perfumed the whole barnyard for one wonderful week every June.

She thought of their windmill and corral and the place by the spring where Elsie had seen the snake. She thought of the hills and the river and the deer that came out at twilight to forage the creek banks for bluestem and grama. How soft and ethereal they'd looked, with the rosy sun on their coats and on the tawny weeds around them.

She thought of her bed and heirlooms she'd brought from their old place in Vermont, and of the way Donna would grin big whenever she talked about the neighbor boys, the Thompsons, over on Buffalo Head Creek, not far from town.

She thought of the chickens and the pigs and the two milch cows and her father's old work wagon that kept falling apart and of how in the summer his big arms were always nearly black from the sun but above his sleeves they were powder white, and so was the line above his forehead covered by his hat.

Her father . . . Kyle Bonaventure. She'd loved him. She'd loved her mother. She'd loved her sisters, though they'd often made her so angry she'd screamed. She'd loved her brother in spite of his teasing her about Buck Thompson, and she'd always secretly wished she'd been a boy like James—a boy all the girls liked and followed around at church picnics by the creek.

Rushing in like a haze over all the memories was the smoke from the fire the Red River Gang had set, and the sounds of the screams, her father yelling, "No! No! No!" while the gang members laughed and chased her mother and her sisters . . . like it was all just a game . . . a playground game . . . and all the while James lay dead in the yard, his head scarlet with blood . . . clubbed down and trampled and shot like a dog in his own yard. . . .

And then Donna was carried kicking and screaming . . . No! . . . into the weeds where they'd played when they were smaller . . . down by the creek . . . where two days later, when Louisa had come out from hiding, she'd found her . . .

"No! No! No!"

Louisa lifted her head and looked around the stable, half expecting to find herself in the weeds behind the house, where she'd hidden when, returning from selling eggs at the Miller farm, she'd seen the riders attacking her family, burning the house and barn and shooting their livestock.

She looked around now, realizing she'd been lying on her side in the stable, her knees to her chest, arms over her head, tears washing over her face as she'd fought the memories like Indians screaming down a hill. The Morgan watched her, frightened and pricking his ears. He kicked the partition, jarring Louisa to her senses.

Her muscles relaxed, and she crawled to her knees, feeling foolish, washed-out and weak.

She hadn't cried since it had happened. She'd felt little emotion whatever, only a deep, muted anger, like a coal vein smoldering deep within the earth.

And a quiet resolve for vengeance.

But never outright sadness. The emotion frightened her, for it was the one thing that could sap her strength and derail her plans. She had to be as tough and as fearless as Handsome Dave Duvall. Only then could she have the strength to hunt him to the very ends of the earth if she had to.

Feeling self-conscious, she stood and looked around, wiping the tears from her cheeks with her hands. She was alone in the barn, but she heard two men talking and laughing near the open paddock doors. Distant wagons squawked. Men called, and dogs barked.

Louisa looked around the barn once more, seeing only thickening shadows and stabled riding stock, several buggies lining the outer walls, tack hanging from joists. Several nearby horses had craned their necks to watch her with a caution similar to the Morgan's.

"Don't worry," she said softly. "It was just a little tumble I took there." She chuckled and looked at the hay at her feet. "Must've . . . must've stepped in some dung and lost my footing."

She patted the Morgan and whispered reassuringly in his ear. The horse sniffed her suspiciously, then, encouraged, lowered its head and went back to work on the oats.

Knowing she couldn't stay here alone in this darkening barn, Louisa brushed the hay from her hair, donned her floppy hat, and headed for the front doors. She felt doubt rear its ugly head again, however, when she wondered where she'd go or what she'd do.

She needed to eat, but where? She didn't know the town, and it was getting dark. Not that she was afraid, but she didn't want to draw attention to herself by having to shoot someone bent on assailing a young lady all alone in a perdition like Fargo.

Then she remembered Prophet, and she felt heartened. The big, rangy bounty hunter with the self-assured twinkle in his eyes and that sapsucker grin on his face was really the only thing she had by the way of a friend. In spite of her distrust of people in general and men in particular, she found herself looking forward to seeing him again.

Besides, they had a common goal. Working together to reach that goal made sense.

He'd be here soon. She had to watch for him. . . .

19

WITH HER QUEST for Prophet in mind, Louisa stepped through the door and looked up and down the dark street lit here and there by saloon lights. Piano music clattered tinnily in both directions, and an approaching train gave a deafening hoot.

Louisa turned to the stableman in the paddock. He was hammering a shoe on a horse's hoof by lantern light, a quirley jutting from between his lips. A stout man in a muddy duck coat watched, a tin cup in his hand. They were talking softly.

"Excuse me?" she hailed the men, clearing the frog from her throat. "By which route would a man coming from Luther Falls enter Fargo?"

The stableman looked at his friend conspiratorially, then at Louisa. Something in his manner was different from before, and then she saw the whiskey bottle standing on a bench.

The stableman dropped the horse's hoof and straightened, turning to face her. He took the tin cup from the other man, who was also looking in Louisa's direction, a faint grin stretching his mouth.

"You got a man comin', Missy?" the stableman said. "I thought you was all alone." He took a quick drink from the cup.

"I've a . . . business associate on the way," Louisa said. "So I guess no, sir, I'm technically not alone. Now would you answer my question, please?"

She didn't like the smoldering gazes directed at her. The lantern buried the men's eyes in shadows, but Louisa felt the stares raking her body, undressing and ogling her. She been accustomed to such looks from men since practically her thirteenth birthday, for she'd filled out well, and there had been a time she'd been flattered by such attention. No longer. She knew the dark side of it now. It was one of the reasons she'd avoided the cesspools of humanity known as frontier towns. For there, men lurked, waiting and watching for somewhere to poke their prods, like these men here, their lust stirred from the sips they'd been taking from the cup.

All men were louts and hardcases underneath, and when they smiled at a girl or showed her sympathy, it was the smile of a snake in the grass, intended only to weaken and disarm. They had to be watched—all of them. None were to be trusted. Not even her friend, Lou Prophet, she reminded herself.

The stableman sipped from his cup again, made a rasping sound, and said, "A man comin' from Luther Falls would no doubt ride in from the east on Main. That's the street over yonder, paralleling the Great Northern rails." He stared at her again, tipping his head slightly to the side.

"Just one more question," she said, despite the discomfort she felt in the presence of these two. "Is there a safe place to eat on Main Street?"

"There ain't no safe place in Fargo after dark, Little Miss," the stableman said while his friend stood silently at his side, shorter and stouter and weaving ever so slightly.

"You might try the Chinaman's," the other man said in a deep, thick rasp. He pointed with one short arm. "It's beside the old express office, one block that way, and one block that way."

"Much obliged," Louisa said, bowing her head slightly, and walking off in the direction the man had pointed.

Behind her, the stableman said something she couldn't hear, in a humorous, conspiratorial tone. She'd be sleeping lightly tonight, with her .45 in her hand.

Walking briskly and avoiding the leering gazes and indecent proposals muttered by the drunken dregs of male humanity loitering upon the boardwalks outside the saloons, Louisa found the Chinaman's place, Hung Yick's Food, beside the boarded-up express office. She ordered the pork special with sauerkraut and ate sitting at a corner table at the back of the room, pleased that she was the only customer and that the Chinaman and his pudgy son were either too ignorant of English or too busy cleaning up for closing to engage her in conversation.

While she ate, she kept a constant eye on the street for Prophet. Not seeing him, she finished her meal, paid for it, and quietly left, resuming her brisk, chin-up pace back to the livery barn.

She'd have to wait for daylight to find Prophet. Remnants of her bout with terror and loneliness lingered, and she wanted very much to see the sly frontiersman with his easy ways and humorous eyes—in spite of knowing that, as a man, he would eventually disappoint her—but she knew now that it wasn't to be. He'd probably get to town late tonight and shack up with the first whore he ran into.

Denying a vague feeling of jealousy, she approached the barn looming darkly against the starry sky. She opened the small door and stepped inside, smelling the

ammonia, and felt around for the lantern she'd seen earlier
on a post.

"Hello, Little Miss."

She stopped and gave a sharp intake of breath, startled.
The voice had come from her right. Turning that way, she
saw only a vague shadow before a small, sashed window
violet with starlight. She'd recognized the stableman's
voice, thick with drink.

"Would you light a lamp, please?" she said. "It's dark
in here."

She could hear the man breathing sharply through his
nose. He seemed to be hesitating. "You said you'd pay
extra . . . you know . . . for housing ye here tonight."

Oh, cripes!

"Will fifty cents do?" she asked with disgust.

"I thought we could work it out another way."

Louisa stared through the darkness between them, not
so much frightened as revolted. "Are you married, sir?"

Another pause during which she could hear him
breathe. "What . . . what's that got to do with it?"

She gave a caustic chuff. "I'll give you fifty cents. Take
it or leave it."

"Nah," the man said. She heard him move closer.

"Stay away from me," she said.

"Listen, Little Miss, I just want one tiny little favor,
that's all. Then I'll leave ye alone, see?"

"Stop where you are, Mister. I'm warning you."

He was close enough to her now that she could smell
the sharp tang of the sour mash whiskey on his breath.

"Just one little favor, Miss . . ."

Holding her ground, Louisa reached for her six-shooter
through the fold in her skirt. Raising it and ratcheting back
the hammer, she said with disgust, " 'Pears you're in a
tolerable stampede to get to hell, sir."

Just when she was about to fire, a voice sounded outside. "Louisa?" Short pause. "Louisa Bonny-venture—you in there?"

It was Prophet's Southern drawl. Louisa's heart quickened.

"I'm in here, Lou!"

The small door beside the large ones opened, and for just a second, the outline of a big man in a flat-crowned hat was silhouetted against the more luminous night outside. He stepped to the side, instinctively avoiding targeting himself, and said, "Well, why in the hell don't you have a lamp fired?"

"You'll have to ask my friend that question."

A phosphor flared in Prophet's hand. He raised it, shedding a gaunt, flickering glow over Louisa, who saw that the stableman had gone. She heard him shuffling around in the tack room—doing what, she had no idea.

Prophet looked around, then at Louisa. "What friend?"

She'd never been so happy to see a man before in her life. She could have run to him and hugged him. Retaining control, she merely holstered her revolver and shrugged. "He must have had some other business to tend to. How did you know I was here?"

"I saw you pass on the street awhile ago. Me and the deputy were at the undertaker's. I got my horse and followed you." He looked around again, the heavy brows under the crown of his weathered hat puckered in a frown. "What the hell's goin' on?"

"The proprietor of the barn and myself were just discussing terms for sheltering the Morgan and myself."

"In the dark?" Prophet had found the lamp on the post. He raised the window and lit the wick.

"Well, after he'd had his fill of the devil's bile, it seems he decided he wanted—"

A loud throat-clearing sounded from the tack room, and the stableman appeared, tucking his shirt in his pants. His face was drawn and flushed.

"Now just wait a minute here, Little Miss—I was just funnin' ye, see?" He was gazing impatiently at Prophet. "Who might you be and what in the hell do you want?"

Prophet's eyes dropped to the man's open fly. Instantly knowing the score, he jerked a wry look at Louisa, then back to the stableman. He chuckled and shook his head. "Name's Prophet. I'd like to stable my horse for the night, and if your fly was a barn door, amigo, all the horses would be headin' for the Dutch clover by now."

Louisa snickered. The man looked down, winced, and turned away as he buttoned his fly.

Prophet opened the big doors, led Mean and Ugly inside, and told the man to stable the horse with plenty of oats and water, gave him the customary warning about the horse's predilection for biting and kicking when bored, and turned to Louisa.

"Come on."

"Where we going?" she asked, following him northward on Broadway.

"I'm gonna locate the biggest damn steak and bottle of whiskey I can find this time of the night in this backwater hellhole, and you're gonna tell me what we're doin' here."

"I already ate," Louisa said, jogging to keep up with Prophet's long-legged stride.

"I'll buy you a sarsaparilla."

They walked through ankle-deep mud toward a long tent paralleling the railroad tracks. The tent was lit from within, and the smell of charred beef issued through a tin stovepipe. The silhouettes of reveling men danced behind the canvas.

Louisa said, "Who's the deputy you mentioned, and what were you two doing at an undertaker's?"

Prophet did not reply. Following him into the tent, Louisa stopped by the door and looked around at the dozen or so tables occupied with big, dark, hard-looking men in coveralls and stovepipe boots. They were rail-

roaders, she knew, of just about every nationality you
could think of, including Chinamen and Negroes. Probably just getting off the day shift or about to start the night
shift. In spite of the grease and sweat stench of the men,
the smell of the steaks being grilled over barrels at the
back of the tent was heavenly.

Several men looked at her with surprise and their customary, automatic lust. Wrinkling her nose, Louisa hurried toward Prophet, who'd gotten in line with a tin plate.
She followed him, feeling the eyes of the crowd on her.
When Prophet had a big T-bone on his plate, smothered
with potatoes and onions, he turned to her.

"Sure you don't want a steak?"

When she shook her head, he ordered a shot of whiskey
and a mug of beer from a wiry, apron-clad Chinaman
tending the keg.

"You have sarsaparilla?" he asked the apron.

The Chinese looked at him, too puzzled to frown.

Prophet turned to Louisa. "I don't think they have sarsaparilla. You'll have to have a beer."

"I don't like beer."

"It ain't American not to like beer," he said. To the
Chinaman, he nodded. "Give her a beer."

They found an unoccupied bench and sat at a table.
Prophet wasted no time throwing back the whiskey, then
plunking the empty glass down and sawing into the T-
bone draped across his plate, buried in the greasy potatoes
and fried onions.

Louisa sipped her beer and made a face. Licking the
foam from her mouth, she said, "Leave it to men to like
such a putrid concoction."

"What's that?" Prophet said with his mouth full.

Louisa sipped the brew again, not liking the taste any
better but not minding the headiness it instantly offered.
She admonished herself to go slow, however. She certainly didn't want to become one of the boisterous apes

rousting about the tent, many of whom still watched her, glassy-eyed. One such gent caught her eye, stuck his fat, wet tongue out, and ran it slowly along his mustachioed upper lip.

Louisa rolled her eyes and looked away.

"Shoot," Prophet said between forkloads of food, oblivious to the stares Louisa was getting.

"Huh?" she said, taking another dainty sip of her beer.

"Tell me what in the hell we're doin' here."

Above the din, she told him about the Red River Gang's plans for a raid on Fargo.

"So what are they plannin' to hit?" Prophet asked.

"I don't know," Louisa replied, glancing around the room, absently wondering why God—if there was a God, which she'd seriously come to doubt—had ever come up with the idea for men. "I figured we'd find that out once we got here."

"Any ideas?"

"I got in too late to see much—much of any importance, that is. They must be gonna hit a bank or something. I can't think of anything else here. As a matter of fact, I can't think of any reason why anyone would want to come to a town-sized privy like this. Why, if I had my druthers and access to a good wagonload of dynamite, I'd . . ."

"All right, Miss Bonny-venture—thanks for the commentary. These boys may not look like much at the moment, but they're what built this country. They and others like 'em. Breakin' their backs while their rich employers back East rake in millions while swilling Eye-talian wine and eating duck ala whatever."

"No wonder everything's going to hell in a hand basket. Anyway, tell me about the deputy and the undertaker's."

Prophet told her about the three deputy marshals two of the Red River Gang ambushed between Luther Falls and Fargo, and how only one survived.

"His name's McIlroy, and we hauled the other two here to town and dropped them off at the undertaker's before reporting the whole bloody mess to the sheriff. The bodies will ship back to Yankton when the undertaker's done with them—along with McIlroy, I hope. He's still in shock over the whole thing, and he was too young to be sent here, anyway. They all were. I'd like to find the senior marshal that sent them, and thrash the living daylights out of the son of a bitch."

"Where's the deputy now?"

Prophet swallowed a mouthful and washed it down with a long swig of beer. "We parted at the undertaker's. I hope it's the last I've seen of him. I think he headed for a sawbones to get his face cleaned and sewn."

"Did you tell the sheriff about the gang?"

"I told him they were in the area. He just shook his head, turned a little peaked, and said he'd put a few more deputies on the streets. I'll talk to him again in the morning. Maybe he has some idea about what the gang might have targeted here in town."

Prophet forked more steak in his mouth and looked at Louisa, who sat staring at her beer, a third of which was gone. Her cheeks were flushed.

"Grows on you, don't it?"

"It's awful. I'm just drinking it to be polite."

"Your manners are right impeccable. How was your trip up from Wahpeton?"

Louisa shrugged and grinned wistfully. "Lovely. And the gang has dwindled by two more."

Prophet looked at her with his jaw hanging. "How in the hell . . . ?"

"A lady doesn't give away her secrets."

Prophet sighed, shook his head, finished the last couple bites of food, and drained his beer in a single gulp. "Come on," he said with a belch, wiping his mouth with his sleeve. "Let's get the hell out of here."

"Wait—I haven't finished my beer."

Prophet got another beer and finished it about the same time Louisa finished hers. Then they got up—Louisa a little unsteadily—and left the tent.

"Where we goin', anyway?" Louisa asked him.

"I got a hotel."

"I don't waste money on hotels. I'm sleepin' with my horse."

"You're not sleeping with your horse. Besides that, you need a bath. You smell as bad as I do. Come on." He tugged on her arm, but she resisted.

"Wait—I need my saddlebags."

Prophet looked at her, frowning. "I reckon you do," he grumbled. "All right . . ."

When they'd retrieved her saddlebags from the livery barn, where a mild-mannered half-breed Indian sat playing solitaire in the office, they headed for the hotel Prophet had checked into after riding into town earlier.

They were taking a shortcut between two clapboarded warehouses when two figures appeared at the end of the alley. From their dark outlines, they were big men, and they were holding something in their arms—either guns or clubs.

"Uh-oh," Prophet said.

"I don't think we should have taken your shortcut," Louisa grumbled.

"I don't, either. In fact, I think I've changed my mind." Prophet turned around and froze. "Shit," he rasped, seeing two more figures at the alley mouth.

They were walking this way.

"Throw down your guns and knife, buddy," a man called from before them. His accent was distinctly Irish.

"And no one gets hurt. All we want is the pretty little lass at your side."

"Now you've done it," Louisa snapped at Prophet. "I'd have been a lot better off with my horse!"

20

READING LOUISA'S MIND, Prophet grabbed her arm. "Keep your pistol holstered. They have us dead to rights."

"The hell they do!"

"Do as I say!"

Prophet watched the two men approach in the darkness. Light glanced off something in the arms of the man on the left. Probably a shotgun. The other man tapped a club in his open left palm.

Turning around, Prophet watched the other two approach—big, burly types in overalls and smelling like breweries. Railroad men fueled by forty-rod and out for some fun. Prophet thought he recognized them from the food tent.

"Drop that knife and pistol in the dirt, laddie," one of them ordered. He was aiming what looked like a snub-nosed, small-caliber pistol at Prophet's solar plexus. Now he clicked the hammer back, and the bounty hunter's stomach tensed. He winced as he removed his bowie and Colt and stooped to set them on the ground.

"Listen, boys," he said, straightening, "you don't want to mess with this girl. She's not as innocent as she looks."

"She not, eh?" one of the railroaders said, this one in a German accent. "Maybe she give goot time, then, no?" He chuckled. "Rolf—I think thiss girl give goot time in the repair shop, no?"

"Ah, she's a fine little lassie, Peder," agreed the Irishman, reaching to brush a lock of hair from Louisa's face. "Yessir!" Turning to Prophet, he said, "We're just gonna tap ye on the head now, laddie, nice and sweet-like. You won't feel a thing till mornin'."

Out of the corner of his eye, Prophet saw the man with the shotgun move up on him from behind. As Prophet crouched to duck the blow, he heard an anguished cry followed by two sharp pistol cracks. The commotion distracted the man with the shotgun enough that the butt of the sawed-off weapon merely grazed the back of Prophet's head.

Ignoring the gunfire for the moment, Prophet swung his leg up sideways, and funneled all his strength into a solid kick to the shotgunner's groin, effectively immobilizing the man. As he turned around, two more pistol shots sounded—these from a larger-caliber revolver, setting his ears to ringing painfully, the smell of cordite burning his nostrils. He saw another of the big railroaders stumble back against the building, grunting and bringing his hands to his chest.

Heart thudding and adrenaline coursing, Prophet jerked left. Louisa stood beside him, her silver-plated Colt extended straight out before her, aimed at the railroader who'd just collapsed against the building. Smoke swirled around her head and curled from the Colt's five-inch barrel.

The man muttered something. Louisa fired again. The man's head dropped and he said nothing more.

Hearing the sound of retreating feet behind him,

Prophet turned around and saw the fourth railroader running off down the alley, fading in the darkness. He reappeared in the dull light at the alley's end, turned, and disappeared.

The man Prophet had kicked cursed and groaned, hands to his crotch, while he rolled face-down on the ground.

Prophet turned back to Louisa, who was turning her gun on the Irishman, who now lay on his back in the middle of the alley, blood gushing from a long, deep gash in his neck. He blinked his eyes rapidly and worked his mouth, making weird, wet, guttural sounds. His pocket pistol lay beside him. Prophet figured the first two slugs he'd heard had come from the Irishman, fired involuntarily after Louisa had cut his throat.

"Jesus Christ, girl," Prophet said, awestruck. After all he'd seen her do, he now realized he still had no idea what she was capable of.

"No one touches me unless I say," she said mildly to the dying Irishman. Raising the gun to the man's head and thumbing back the hammer, she added, "And I rarely say."

"Easy, easy," Prophet said, shoving her gun down. "He's good as dead, and we've made enough noise the way it is. Let's get out of here before we have to explain all this to the sheriff." He stooped to retrieve his Colt and started down the alley. "Come on."

When he didn't hear her running behind him, he stopped and turned. She was on her knees, looking suddenly, uncharacteristically weary.

Running back to her, Prophet knelt down. "What's the matter, girl?"

She gave a heavy sigh. "I feel faint . . . all of a sudden. . . ."

"Probably all the beer and excitement. You'll be all right in a minute. I'll take your saddlebags."

He reached for the bags she'd draped over her shoulder.

She stopped him with, "No—that ain't it. I always feel
faint when I see my own blood."

"Huh?"

She took Prophet's arm and heaved herself standing,
then stooped to place a hand on her calf. "Think I took a
ricochet from the Irishman's peashooter," she said.

Prophet frowned with concern. "Where?"

"Here."

"How bad is it?"

"I don't know, but"—she swooned like a Southern
belle—"I think I'm gonna faint."

"Oh, Jesus!" Prophet carped, catching her.

He picked her up, saddlebags and all, in his arms, and
ran clumsily down the alley. The man he'd groined spat
behind him, "You goddamn . . . sons'bitches . . . ye fight
yella!"

Prophet was amazed at how light the girl seemed at
first, considering all her sass and firepower. Her saddlebags dangling off his left arm felt heavier than she herself.
The whole package, however, became more cumbersome
the farther he ran, looking for his hotel, which he seemed
to have misplaced. He was considering setting Louisa and
her cargo down for a breather when he finally saw the
place—a modest, two-story building with a café on the
first floor and a handful of rented rooms on the second.

"It's more money for two," announced the cranky old
bat behind the front desk, scowling over the cream-
colored poodle sitting on the counter. The dog growled
through its teeth at the big, clumsy newcomer stumbling
through the lobby door with a comatose girl in his arms.

"I'll pay up in the morning," Prophet said, heading for
the narrow, winding stairs behind the desk.

"You'll pay now!" chirped the shrew, jutting a crooked
finger at a hand-lettered sign requiring all payments in
advance.

"Go diddle yourself!"

Aside from the poodle's single yip, that was the end of
the conversation, for Prophet had made the landing and
was starting up the second flight of stairs, fumbling his
way through the darkness. The old biddy was too cheap
to keep a lantern lit in the hall, so he had to count the
doors on the left before finding his own.

Grappling in his pocket for the key which he was glad
he hadn't turned over to the biddy before leaving, he got
the door open, stepped inside, and lay Louisa gently down
on the bed. Not having heard a peep out of her for several
minutes, he was worried she was dead.

Quickly, he kicked the door closed, got a lantern lit,
and set it on the rickety table beside the lumpy, slanting
bed, upon which Louisa lay on her hat, which had tumbled down her back, hanging by its cord. Her hair was in
her face and her skin looked pale.

"Louisa," Prophet gently called, leaning down to listen
to her heart. "Louisa, you all right, girl?"

He listened for several seconds, not sure if what he was
hearing was her heart or something else. Worried she'd
taken more than one bullet and was teetering on death's
doorstep, he headed for the door in search of a doctor.

He'd just opened the door and was heading into the
hall when Louisa sighed behind him.

He turned.

She sighed again, and mumbled something.

Prophet went to her, leaned over the bed, took her delicate chin in his hand, and gently moved her head from
side to side. "Louisa? You all right?"

Her eyelids fluttered open. Her mouth opened and she
took a deep draught of air. "Oh, God . . . what happened?"

"You passed out. Tell me where you're hurt."

"My leg . . ."

"Just your leg?"

"I think so. . . ."

Prophet ran his eyes down her body, looking for more

wounds. "Sure you're not hit somewhere else?"

"No—just my leg." She lifted her head to look at her leg, made a face, turned pale again, and made a gagging sound. "Ah, God! I can't . . . I never been able to stand the sight of blood."

Prophet looked at her skeptically. "What?"

She rested her head back on the pillow. "Never could stand it."

Still scowling, Prophet moved to her ankle, lifted her skirt up until he saw the blood staining her pantaloons. He began separating her stockings from her pantaloons, and she said, "No!"

"I gotta get that wound cleaned and see if the bullet's still in there!"

She made another gagging sound and turned her head to the side, ready to vomit.

"Get a grip on yourself now, girl," he admonished, rolling the pantaloons up her leg. "I'm not gonna hurt you, and I'm not lookin' for a thrill, for Chrissakes. I'm just gonna see how bad you're hit."

"The bullet"—she gagged again and coughed—"the bullet ain't in there; I can't feel it. Th-the bullet just creased my calf."

In a moment, Prophet saw that it was true. The slug had made a small neat furrow along her calf, drilling just deep enough to make it look worse than it was. Finding it hard to reconcile her reaction—he'd thought she was dead!—to the superficiality of the wound, he put his head close to her naked leg, carefully scrutinizing the wound.

"Sure enough, it's just a graze!" Prophet looked at her frowning, then broke out in laughter. "It's just a graze! What in the hell you makin' such a big fuss about?"

"I told you," she said tightly, angry now, staring up at the ceiling, "I can't stand the sight of blood."

"Your own blood, you mean."

"Yes, mine."

Prophet guffawed. ". . . Because you sure as hell don't mind the sight of others' blood . . . !" He sat down on the bed beside her and threw his head back with laughter, until someone from below hit the floor several times with something hard.

He covered his mouth, squealing and wheezing, until he finally settled down, chuckling, and turned to her, wagging his head. "Girl, you take the cake, you know that?"

"I'm glad you're so amused, Mr. Prophet."

He chuckled again, as relieved she wasn't seriously hurt as he was amused by her. In spite of her off-putting idiosyncracies, or maybe because of them, he'd taken a shine to this girl. Mystified and appalled by her, he knew the world would be a duller place without her.

Finally, he stood and poured water from the pitcher on the washstand into the basin, and found a clean cloth in his saddlebags. He brought the basin and the rag to the bed, soaked the rag, and began dabbing at the girl's bloody calf.

"Don't you go lookin' at my leg now," Louisa scolded. Her voice was still tight, as though she was doing everything she could do distract herself from the idea of her own blood.

"Now, how am I supposed to clean your leg if I don't look at it?"

"Well, just don't look at any more of it than you have to."

"Too late," Prophet quipped. He grinned. "Already took me a good, long look, and that's one pretty leg you got here, Miss Bonny-venture. I bet more than one boy set store by you back home."

When she did not reply, Prophet looked up at her. She lay still, still staring at the ceiling, but her eyes were shiny, and a single tear rolled down her left cheek.

Prophet frowned. "What's the mat—?" he stopped, realizing what it was. He'd mentioned home.

He started dabbing at the blood again, letting several minutes pass before asking, "Want to tell me about it?"

She swallowed and shook her head. Her voice was phlegmy when she said, "Uh-uh."

That was all she said, and Prophet said nothing more, either, as he finished cleaning the wound with whiskey from his saddlebags, and wrapped it with a clean cloth.

"There you are—good as new," he said, getting up from the bed and returning the basin to the stand. "You can bear to look at it now. It's got a nice white cloth on it."

She sat up, scooted up against the headboard, and looked down at her leg. Glancing at Prophet sheepishly, she said, "Obliged."

"De nada."

"Sorry I passed out."

Prophet shrugged. "I've had women faint on me before." He smiled as he rinsed his rag in the basin. "Just not one quite like you."

"I reckon I better see about getting my own room." She moved to get off the bed.

"The biddy's done turned in. She closes at nine, and it's past nine now. You'll have to sleep here tonight. Don't worry, I'm too tired to maul you."

Louisa looked at him warily, then carefully scooted back against the headboard, adjusting her skirts over her legs and lacing her fingers in her lap. "That isn't right."

"What—my not mauling you, or our sharing the same room?"

"You know what I mean, Mr. Prophet."

"Hey, just cause I seen your leg doesn't mean you have to start calling me Mr. Prophet." He pegged his hat and shell belt, then held his quart bottle of Tennessee rye up to the light. Noting the liquid's level, he sat in the barrel chair by the window, set the whiskey on the floor between his feet, and fished his makings sack from his shirt pocket.

Louisa watched him. "You gonna smoke and drink now?"

He looked at her dully. "Is that all right?"

"You can open the window for the smoke, but what if the drinkin' turns you into a savage?"

Prophet snorted and went to work on the quirley. "Don't worry—I'm well aware of that knife and six-shooter you're packin' under your skirt."

There was a pause while Prophet finished building his smoke and cracked the window. He lit the cigarette, picked up the bottle, corked it, and took a swig. Balancing the bottle on his knee with one hand, he smoked the quirley with the other.

He frowned at her staring at him. "How does that work, anyway?" he said, exhaling a long plume of smoke.

"What?"

"How are you carryin' that knife and gun under your skirt? Don't worry—I ain't gettin' fresh. Just curious about your armaments, is all."

Louisa shrugged. "I got a gunbelt on under my skirt. I cut slits in the skirt so I can retrieve the gun or the knife pronto. The poncho covers the bulges."

"Where did you get such an outfit?"

"What—the gunbelt and knife? Stole 'em off the first man I killed."

"A Red River Ganger?"

"Yep. Killed him with my pa's twenty-gauge I fished out of the barn's ashes. Then I took the outlaw's weapons and his horse—the Morgan was his, too, the poor horse—and I camped for a month in the Nations, and practiced my shootin' and knife-throwin'. Pa was right handy with both, since he'd fought in the Indian Wars, and I'd picked up a few tricks over the years. I could shoot faster and straighter than my brother, James."

Prophet stared at her, took a sip from the bottle, then

stared at her again. Frowning, he asked, "What are you gonna do, Louisa, when all this is over?"

She stared at the wall straight off the end of the bed, thinking. Then she slid her eyes back to Prophet. "I don't know. What are you gonna do?"

"More o' the same. I do it for a living."

A faint smile pulled at her full, pink lips. "Well, then, maybe I will, too."

Prophet finished his cigarette, then built and smoked another while he sipped the whiskey. Finally, he flicked the cigarette stub out the window and held the bottle up to the light, scrutinizing the whiskey line. He took a final sip, corked the bottle, and returned it to his saddlebags.

"Well, I reckon," he sighed, stretching. He kicked out of his boots and started unbuttoning his shirt.

"What are you doing?"

"I'm comin' to bed."

"I told you the whiskey would turn you into a savage."

Prophet looked around, thoughtful. "I don't feel so damn savage."

"You mean you're just gonna sleep?"

"What else would I do?"

"Ravage me."

Prophet chuckled. "I done told you, I ain't in the ravagin' mood."

"I thought all men wanted to ravage virgins."

He was peeling off his denims but stopped and looked at her under his brows. "You a virgin?"

"Of course. I ain't married, am I?"

Prophet snorted and kicked off his jeans, leaving them bunched on the floor. "Figures."

Prophet emptied the wash basin in the thunder mug under the bed, then refilled it from the pitcher and splashed water in his face. When he'd dried himself on the towel hanging on the stand, he stretched again, scratched his hairy chest through his union suit, and headed for the other side of the bed.

He crawled in, groaning and tired, and fluffed his pillow. Then he lay back, drew the quilt and sheet up, yawned, and closed his eyes.

After a minute, Louisa said quietly in the silent room, "You can if you want to. I mean, I mind, of course, but I reckon all men need it, so . . . since we're workin' together and all."

He turned to her. "I can what?"

She turned to him, blinking and looking annoyed. "Ravage me."

"I'm too tired to ravage a virgin tonight. Maybe some other time. Now go to sleep, and don't forget to blow the lamp out."

Stunned and incensed but not quite knowing why, Louisa stared at him lying there with his big, muscled arms crossed over his broad, hairy chest which pulled the threadbare union suit taut across his rounded shoulders.

"Fine, then," she said, finally.

She got out of bed, stomped over to the light, blew it out, stomped back to bed, and crawled under the covers.

"Fine."

21

THE NEXT MORNING, Louisa woke with a start and reached for her revolver, but it was not where she normally kept it when she slept, in the holster looped around her saddle horn. Not only that, but she wasn't sleeping on her saddle, which she'd done nearly every night since hitting the vengeance trail.

She was in Prophet's hotel room.

Remembering that she'd looped her shell belt and holster around the bedpost after returning from the privy during the night, she grabbed the weapon from the holster and thumbed back the hammer as she tossed a quick glance to her left and saw that Prophet was gone, his covers thrown back.

The knock sounded again.

She turned to the door, aiming the revolver. "Who is it?" she snapped.

A muffled voice sounded behind the door.

Scowling sleepily, Louisa threw back the blankets, brushed her hair from her eyes, and headed for the door, gun extended, wincing at the burn in her right calf.

"Who is it?" she repeated impatiently.

"Bath water, ma'am."

Louisa thought it over for several seconds; she hadn't survived this long being gullible. Finally, she turned the key in the lock and cracked the door. In the hall, a black boy of about eight or nine stood holding a bucket of steaming water. A white towel thrown over his shoulder, the boy stared up at her wide-eyed. When he saw the gun Louisa had poked through the crack, his eyes widened even more, and he shuffled back with a start.

"Don't shoot me, missy! The gen'leman tol' me to bring ya up some bath water at seven o'clock sharp!"

"He did, did he?" Louisa said dryly, knowing the boy meant Prophet.

"Yes'm. He give me two bits. Said to tell you he'd meet you at eight-thirty at Hung Yick's café for breakfast."

"Did he say where he'd be till then?"

"No'm."

Louisa glanced up and down the hall, then stepped back, drawing the door wide. The boy entered the room, set the steaming bucket on the braided rug beside the bed, hung the towel on a wall hook, grabbed the thunder mug by its handle, and brushed past Louisa on his way back out, eyeing her warily.

When he was gone, Louisa closed the door, sheathed her revolver, and regarded the steaming pail. She hadn't had an indoor sponge bath in a long, long time. In spite of being slightly miffed by the bounty hunter's presumption, she was grateful for the hot water. It would indeed feel good to have a bath.

The bounty hunter.

Where in the hell was Prophet, anyway? He must have dressed and slipped off without a sound, for Louisa prided herself on waking at the rustle of a pine cone falling a hundred yards away.

That bed must've been more comfortable than she'd

first thought. Or had she felt safer and thus more able to relax, with him near . . . ?

She repressed the idea, for this was no time to start setting store by some down-at-heel bounty man. But as she stripped out of the dusty clothes she'd slept in and began sponging her naked body with warm water from the pail, avoiding her bandaged calf, she couldn't help thinking of him . . . the easy way he carried himself . . . that rueful glimmer in his eyes . . . those big arms straining the seams of his threadbare union suit. He'd shown gentleness and sensitivity, odd for a man, when he'd cleaned her wound last night.

He did seem different, didn't he . . . than most of the other men she'd come to know and hate . . . ?

When Louisa had finished her slow, luxurious sponge bath, and dressed, she saw by her timepiece that she still had forty-five minutes before she had to meet Prophet at the Chinaman's place. Deciding to spend the time riding around town looking for the Red River Gang's target, she left the hotel, ignoring the spiteful stare of the old biddy at the front desk, and headed for the livery barn.

She rigged up the Morgan and left her payment in the office, pleased that the drunk stableman was nowhere to be found, and walked the horse up and down Broadway. She found three banks and an express office, but none looked like they'd provide a gang of venal cutthroats with the kind of stake she'd heard discussed in Wahpeton.

She'd just crossed to the south side of the Northern Pacific tracks when she heard a train whistle, and turned to see a locomotive panting into Fargo. A big bruiser of a beast, it was, throwing black smoke and cinders every which way, filling the air with its burning-coal stench, and making the ground tremble under the Morgan's feet.

Chuff! chuff! chuff! it coughed as it slowed, brakes squealing and couplings crashing. Trains were still new enough to this region that they still attracted admiring stares from people on the street, Louisa saw as she glanced around. But in the faces of two old men with gray mustaches perched on the mercantile's loading dock, she thought she saw something more than just mild esteem.

She followed the men's bright, wistful gazes back to the train, which was moving about five miles per hour now as the locomotive approached the water tank beyond the depot. She frowned, surprised to see that this was no ordinary passenger train with weathered gray cars cramped with gaunt-faced immigrants in homespun clothes and squawking chickens and boisterous children hanging out the windows.

In fact, this was no immigrant train at all.

Eminently grand, this one included five passenger cars, a Pullman sleeper, and two stock cars between the coal tender and the caboose. The passenger cars were a rich mauve with yellow trim. Brass fittings and lanterns gleamed in the climbing prairie sun. All the windows were nearly twice the size as on any ordinary train, and behind the sparkling glass most of the cars were as uncluttered as Mexican ballrooms.

At the rear of each passenger car, there was an open bay area enclosed by brass rails trimmed in striped bunting fluttering in the breeze. In one such open-air vestibule, ladies dressed like queens in crinoline and lace sat holding multicolored parasols over their feathered hats. In the bay area of the car directly behind the one that carried the ladies, portly gentlemen in silk top hats, derbies, and camel-hair frocks stood or sat, smoking stogies as they regarded Fargo with expressions of mild amusement. Several held goblets on their knees. One man wearing a big, Texas-style hat with the brim pinned up on one side, said something with a supercilious grin and a grand gesture indicating the street before them. The others roared.

Soon the men's car passed beyond Louisa, screeching to a halt before the depot. Stopping before her was the second of the two stock cars, and peering through the slats she saw horses. Thoroughbreds and Arabians, all.

The Morgan twitched its nose at the stock car from within which whinnies and nickers issued along with the smell of horse dung and alfalfa. As she stared at the car, Louisa's heart began beating resolutely against her sternum. Adrenaline spurted in her veins. And then her heart was picking up until her face grew hot and her blood was fairly racing.

Twisting back in her saddle, she looked around the street. Then she reined the Morgan around and spurred him over to the mercantile, where the two old townsmen still sat under the awning drinking soda water from bottles.

"Excuse me, gentlemen, but can you tell me who's on that train?"

"Don't you read the papers, young lady?" the man on the left said with twinkling, washed-out eyes. "Why, that's the Duke of Dunston-Abbey! He's the one in the Texas hat—ha! ha!"

"Who's the Duke of Dunston-Abbey?"

The old man shrugged and glanced at his friend puffing on a corncob pipe. The second man said, "Some Britisher, they say. Part o' some big syndicate that has ranches all over the West. He's headin' to Montany with his wife the duchess and some o' their Britisher pals. 'Parently he just bought a brand-new ranch for the little woman. Her birthday's coming up, don't ye know. Hee-hee-hee!"

"Blast it, Foley!" the first man said, turning sharply to his friend. "My birthday's comin' up, an' no one bought me a ranch in ole Montany!"

The men slapped their thighs and cackled like geese. Frowning, her heart throbbing in her temples, Louisa reined the Morgan back into the street, walking the horse toward the depot as she studied the train grandly shining in the sunlight. Several workers spoke loudly as they swung the spout from the stilted water tank over the locomotive, and dropped a lever.

The ladies and gentlemen from the train were disembarking as though from a gala, and the red-suited porters in billed caps were helping them down the steps, bowing to each in turn with nervous grins. As Louisa reined her horse before one of the several hitching racks before the red brick station, she watched the man in the Texas-style hat.

The Duke of Dunston-Abbey was a large man with flowing auburn locks and a mustache whose ends swung around to meet his brushy muttonchops. He was pale with freckles, a double chin, and small, steel-rimmed spectacles perched on his nose. The cream Stetson matched the fringed deer-hide coat hanging past his hips. From the perfect tailoring, Louisa could tell the coat had been sewn and purchased in an Eastern shop, for nothing so impeccable would be found west of St. Louis.

The man rose up on the balls of his feet and crossed his arms on his broad chest as he spoke loudly and with supreme arrogance to the men gathered around him—men who laughed loudly and nodded vigorously at everything the duke said. Apparently, the men and the ladies twittering under the parasols in the shade of the depot overhang were just stretching their legs while the water tank filled, and would be off again in a few minutes.

Studying both groups from the Morgan's saddle, Louisa wondered how much money was on that train. Why, in the pockets of the men and in the purses of the ladies milling on the platform there had to be more than Louisa would ever see in her life! And when you took into account what was probably stowed away in the luggage and added it to the worth of the horses . . . damn!

Certain she had discovered what had attracted the Red River Gang to Fargo, Louisa whipped her head around, searching for signs of a possible attack. The gang could be anywhere, waiting for just the right moment.

Or would they wait until the train had steamed out of town a ways, beyond the immediate help of the law?

Deciding the latter was probably the most likely course of the gang's action, Louisa looked around again, this time for Prophet. She saw no sign of him—only several townsfolk, children and dogs included, gathering for a look at the Duke and Duchess of Dunston-Abbey. By now, Prophet was probably waiting for her at the Chinaman's place.

Deciding something had to be done and done soon, Louisa climbed down from the Morgan, tied him to the hitch rack, and made her way toward the Duke still holding court on the brick platform with his entourage.

When she was about thirty feet from the group, a brute in a black suit and bowler suddenly stepped in front of her, blocking her way. Holding up his huge hands, palms out, he said, "Hold on, there, Miss. Where do you think you're going?" It was the first British accent Louisa had heard close up, and the novelty of it shocked her.

"Huh? What?"

"Where on earth do you think you're going?"

"I have to speak to the duke."

"You have to speak to the duke?" The brute chuckled. "Yes, well . . . I don't think so."

"Please, I have to—"

"Run along now, Miss. That's a good girl."

"Listen," Louisa said, trying to peer around the brute's wide frame to catch the duke's eye, "this train is going to be attacked by the Red River Gang!"

"Huh? What? Attack? The duke's *trine?*"

"Yes, the train," Louisa said, trying futilely to push past the brute whom, she noticed, wore a Colt Lightning in a shoulder rig under his open frock. "Please let me speak to the duke."

The brute was about to say something when a man

spoke behind him. "McDormand, do keep these people back, won't you?"

The brute half turned, glancing around at several scruffy-looking townsmen crowding onto the platform for a closer look at the duke and his fancy train.

"Yes sir, right away, sir," the brute said with a tense smile.

He turned to Louisa and sighed peevishly. Putting his hands on her arms and shoving her back toward the station house, he said, "All right, Miss, I'm not joking around now. Get back and stay back or I'll throw you in leg irons."

He gave her one last, resolute shove, then turned and jogged out ahead of the crowd of curious townsfolk, flinging his arms out from his sides to usher them back. Another brute made his way over from the other end of the station house to help, and soon they had the crowd shuffling backward toward the street.

Looking up and down the platform, Louisa saw two more bodyguards stationed along the train, facing the street. Both were big men with bulges under their jackets, and while they looked capable enough, unless there were at least ten more of them on the train, there weren't enough of them to foil the Red River Gang's imminent raid.

Louisa shifted her eyes between the duke and his entourage and the group of women chattering to her left, under the station house's overhanging roof. The engine sputtered and sighed, sending jets of steam skittering over the cobbles.

Louisa was obviously not going to be able to talk to the duke, and even if she did, she wouldn't be taken seriously. No one took a lone girl in farm clothes seriously. So what she had to do, she decided, was somehow get aboard the train.

Why she needed to be aboard the train, she wasn't sure.

It was just an irresistible impulse and, before she knew what she was doing, she was wandering northward along the track, strolling along the platform toward the engine, whistling and gazing about her with mindless fascination— just a country girl admiring the duke's fancy train.

As she approached the first bodyguard down this way, she gave him a big smile and strolled on past. She gave the second bodyguard the same nonthreatening smile, pretending to be merely amazed by the big train. Since she wasn't doing anything to rile the duke or duchess, the bodyguard just nodded at her amiably and let her go.

She wandered on around the engine, past the men in bib overalls filling the boiler, and down the other side of the train, flicking coal cinders from her poncho. When she was about halfway down the train's length, a voice rose from the other side.

"All aboard, please! All aboard, please, gentlemen and ladies!"

Alone on this side of the platform, Louisa quickened her pace and began searching for a spot to board one of the cars. Since the passenger cars were fairly open, she knew boarding one of them without being noticed by the embarking passengers would be impossible.

Boarding the sleeper was out of the question, too, for steel doors sealed this side of the vestibule.

As she jogged, stumbling along the cinder apron, the locomotive gave a high-pitched whistle. The couplings clattered and the cars screeched as the steel drivers began grinding, the wheels turning, and the cars began moving north down the rails.

Louisa stopped, panting, and studied the train as it moved past her, picking up speed. Coal smoke choked her. Her hat whipped off her head and hung down her back by its cord.

"Damn oh damn oh damn!"

The stock cars pounded by, whipping her with a breeze rife with ammonia and hay.

"Oh, come on, damn you. Come on!" she pleaded, looking for anything to grab onto.

Here comes the red caboose. Her last chance.

In desperation, she leapt for the rail on the caboose's vestibule, and grabbed it with both hands. Half running, half hanging from the rail, she got her feet up on the dimpled iron platform, and climbed. . . .

22

IT WAS PAST eight-thirty before Prophet had the Chinaman's place in sight.

He'd spent about a half hour visiting with the Cass County sheriff, but to no avail. The portly lawman, who seemed a bit too dull-witted for the job, could offer no clue as to what the Red River Gang might be targeting in Fargo. He figured it was either one of the banks or the express office or—Prophet had had to suppress a snort at this—the ladies' millinery on Third Street.

"Mrs. Norman does a right smart business!" the man had exclaimed after seeing the doubt in Prophet's eyes. "Why, ladies from as far away as Grand Forks come here to buy her hats!"

"Maybe you'd better post a deputy at each of the banks, anyway—just to be on the safe side," Prophet had said as he'd opened the office door to leave.

The sheriff stood, his jowls coloring and shaking with anger. "I will do that, but I don't like your attitude, young man. And I don't appreciate being told what to do by a lowly bounty man!"

The sheriff had said more, but Prophet hadn't heard it, because he'd already closed the door behind him and was making his way up the street to check out the banks.

Now, having checked them and deciding two of the three were possibilities, if slim ones, he pushed through the door of Hung Yick's, looking around for Louisa. The place was busy with shop workers and railroad men, but Prophet didn't see Louisa.

Glancing at the clock on the wall, he frowned. It was five minutes past eight-thirty. Had the black boy at the hotel forgotten to tell her about breakfast?

Deciding to go ahead and order—maybe she'd show up late; she was a woman, after all—he headed for one of the two empty tables at the back. He paused when he saw the red-haired deputy McIlroy, sitting at a table in the corner, a half-empty plate and papers before him. He was writing on one of the papers and didn't look up.

Prophet strode that way. "Mind if I sit down?"

McIlroy looked up, and Prophet winced. The man's face had swollen around the stitches a doctor had sewn, and just looking at it made Prophet's own face ache.

"Help yourself," the deputy said, nodding at one of the three vacant chairs at the oil cloth–covered table.

Prophet sat down and regarded the deputy, who held his pen out before him in both hands as though studying it. He was a broken man, Prophet saw. He felt sorry for the lad. It wasn't easy being young in the West, even when you weren't wearing a badge.

"Writin' up reports to bring back to your boss?" Prophet asked when a girl had brought him coffee and taken his order.

"To send back to him," McIlroy corrected.

"I see," Prophet said with a slow nod, sipping his coffee. "You're sendin' the bodies back alone."

"That's right, Mr. Prophet. I came here to do a job, and I aim to finish it."

In spite of his doubt about the young man's ability to bring the Red River boys to justice, Prophet had to admire McIlroy's spleen.

"I can understand the notion," he said. "You have any help coming?"

"I've requested four more deputies. I doubt I'll get anymore than one, two at the most. Most of the men are needed in the Black Hills and in the northwestern part of the Territory, where the Sioux are on the rampage."

When Prophet didn't say anything, McIlroy said, "Have you come up with the reason the gang is headed to Fargo?"

"No," Prophet said with a sigh. "Not a thing." He was looking around for Louisa. Not seeing her and growing concerned, he turned to McIlroy. "What about you? You come up with any ideas?"

"Just this," the young man said, slipping a newspaper out from under the report he'd been writing. He dropped the paper before Prophet, who frowned down at the first page, reading the twenty-point headline: ROYAL TRAIN TO STOP IN FARGO. Below it, in slightly smaller letters: "Duke and Duchess of Dunston-Abbey Bound for the Duchess's Birthday Ranch in Montana." Between that and the article there was one more subheading: "Many Prominent Britishers on Board Birthday Train!"

"Holy shit," Prophet mumbled, scanning the lengthy article. "When's this train gettin' to town, any—?" He stopped and stared at the red-haired deputy. "This mornin'."

"You thinking that's their target?"

"I haven't seen anything more likely." Prophet thought of something. "I seen a train pullin' into town about twenty minutes ago. You don't s'pose that was the one, do you?"

"I think it says in the article there that it's due in around eleven."

"They could've been ahead of schedule."

"A train? *Ahead* of schedule?"

McIlroy hadn't completed his last sentence before Prophet had bounded out of his chair and headed for the door, weaving around the tables.

"Well, wait for me, damnit!" the deputy exclaimed as he hurriedly shoveled his papers into a cowhide valise, dropped some coins on the table, and followed Prophet out the door.

Outside, the bounty hunter turned left and ran toward the railroad tracks paralleling Main Street. When he'd passed a lumber yard, he looked westward down the shiny, new rails, and scowled. A red caboose was diminishing in the distance, dwindling darkly, swallowed by prairie and crowned with coal smoke. The faraway whistle sounded forlorn.

Prophet cursed and ran across the rails, angling over to the red brick station house. Several people had gathered there and were staring westward down the tracks.

"Please tell me that wasn't the duke's train," he told a pleasant-faced gentleman in a minister's collar and floppy black hat.

"Why, sure it was!" the minister said with a mild grin. "Got to see the duke close up, too—at least, as close up as his muscle men would let us get. I wanted to offer a prayer, but don't you s'pose—?"

"It said in the paper he wasn't due in till eleven!" Prophet groused.

"They made better time than they expected comin' out of Minneapolis," said a man dressed in a blue coat and uniform hat staring westward.

"You the station agent?" Prophet asked the man.

"That's right."

"Where's the train stoppin' next?"

"Oh, they won't be stoppin' again till Jamestown for water."

"Any way to get a message to them between here and there?"

The agent beetled his heavy, salt-and-pepper brows at Prophet, peering at him sharply. "Only way would be to telegraph the station in Valley City, then signal the train to stop. But—"

"How far is Valley City?"

"Pret' near seventy miles. Say, who are you, anyway, and why would you wanna—?"

"Never mind," Prophet said, staring thoughtfully down the rails. The caboose had diminished to a small, black dot, and then it faded altogether.

Behind the bounty hunter, McIlroy approached running, gripping his valise in his right hand, his frock coat winging out behind him. Breathless, he asked, "Was that it? Was that the duke's train?"

The station agent was eyeing them both suspiciously. "Say, why in the hell are you two so damn interested in the duke's train?"

"It's about to be robbed," Prophet said.

McIlroy cleared his throat and judiciously added, "Well, at least, it's a distinct possibility. We don't know that for sure."

"Yeah, we do," Prophet groused.

Wheeling and heading south for the livery barn and his horse, he stopped suddenly and turned to his right. Tethered before the station house was Louisa's black Morgan. Curious, Prophet walked over to the horse, then raked his gaze in a full circle around the station.

He called her name, but it was a wasted breath. She was nowhere near. She'd been here, though. That was obvious.

McIlroy approached, frowning. "What's with the horse?"

"Belongs to a friend of mine."

"Oh, yeah? Well, where is he?"

"She's on the train." As Prophet said it, he knew it was true. She'd seen the duke's train pull into town, realized the train was the Red River Gang's next target, and some-how got her sneaky self aboard.

Prophet chuckled without humor, shaking his head. Running a big, brown paw across his face, he said, "Damn, girl . . . you're gonna get yourself killed yet."

"Your friend aboard the train is a woman?" McIlroy was thoroughly befuddled. "I don't understand."

Prophet looked at him seriously. "All you need to un-derstand, Deputy, is that train is gonna be robbed by the Red River Gang. And they won't just rob it, either. They'll probably butcher everyone onboard. You best run and inform the sheriff."

"Where are you going?"

Prophet had untied the Morgan's reins from the hitch rack and was jogging toward the livery barn, the Morgan following at a canter. "Where the hell do you think I'm goin'? I'm gonna get my horse and follow the train!"

Louisa climbed over the rail at the end of the caboose and stood peering at the town dwindling before her, the flat, virtually treeless prairie rushing in on both sides. Glancing behind her, she saw the door into the caboose. There was a window in the door, and she crouched, backing up to the wall beside the door so she wouldn't be seen by the man or men inside.

She dropped to her butt to avoid the wind swirling un-der the roof's slight overhang, and bit her lower lip. Okay, she was aboard the train. Now what was she going to do?

For starters, she decided, she'd try to make her way to the passenger cars and look for the Duke. If she could only get past his brutes and talk to him, she might be able to convince him the train was headed for hell with a cap-ital H. If not, well, she'd tried. . . .

There wasn't much the Brit could do to her except have

her expelled from the train at the next water stop—if they made it that far, that was. She doubted the man, arrogant as he'd appeared on the station platform in Fargo, was haughty enough to have her removed while the train was still moving.

The worst that could possibly happen was that the gang would murder her when they murdered the others. But by God, she'd die triggering her trusty six-shooter, and she wouldn't die alone!

Now, to get to the passenger cars . . .

Looking up, she saw the metal rungs climbing the caboose's rear wall. Standing unsteadily as the train rocked and swayed, clattering over the rail seams, she grabbed the lowest rung, and climbed. When she poked her head over the roof, she was pleased to see a catwalk stretching from the caboose all the way to the locomotive, traversing every car.

But when she'd hoisted herself onto the roof, she realized getting to the duke's car wasn't going to be as easy as it had first appeared. There was nothing to hold onto, and when she tried to stand, with the train rushing forward at a good twenty miles per hour and rocking and swaying this way and that, jerking over the seams, she nearly lost her balance and flew over the side.

Deciding crawling was the safest strategy, she got down on her hands and knees and began putting one hand before each knee. When she came to the front of the caboose, she climbed down the ladder, crossed the vestibule, and began climbing the first of the two stock cars. Crawling into the wind was getting easier now, and before long she was nearing the end of the second stock car, and hearing voices raised in jovial laughter.

She was approaching the duke's car.

"What . . . who the hell is that?" inquired one of the Brits as Louisa descended the ladder on the stock car's front wall.

When she'd stepped onto the vestibule, she turned to the covey of well-dressed gents smoking stogies and standing about the open bay of the duke's natty car. Several were holding shotguns with richly gleaming stocks. Some were polishing the guns with white cloths while others thumbed wads into the chambers—apparently about to start pot-shooting birds along the right-of-way.

All froze, however, and turned wide-eyed, astonished looks at the girl who'd just appeared before them dressed in a plain gray skirt and brown poncho, her long hair tussled by the wind, her hat hanging down her back by the cord around her neck. Her face was flushed, her eyes red from windburn.

The breeze tussling the red locks hanging down from his Texas hat, the duke edged forward, scowling and rolling his half-smoked stogie to the right side of his mouth. "Who are you?" he said, with a slight, emphatic pause between each word.

Louisa was about to answer but stopped when what sounded like an explosion from somewhere ahead of the train lifted on the wind. It was followed by the high-pitched shriek of the train's brakes, throwing Louisa and the duke's party off their feet.

Louisa was vaguely aware of being tossed like a doll over several overstuffed chairs and into a wall before everything went black.

23

PROPHET RODE HARD for several miles before he halted Mean and Ugly, dismounted the exhausted beast, and mounted Louisa's Morgan, which he'd been leading by its bridle reins. Then he rode hard for another several miles before topping the rise and spying the train halted on the tracks below, puffs of black coal smoke issuing from its funnel-shaped stack.

He'd heard the dynamite explosion followed by the flat cracks of pistol and rifle fire a good twenty minutes before, and he'd tried to keep from imagining what had been happening aboard that train in the meantime. He knew the dynamite had been used to blow up the tracks and cause the engineer to stop the train. He could guess what the pistol fire was all about.

Now he produced his field glasses and did a quick scan of the train, which sat a hundred yards west, its engine sighing and panting like a steel dinosaur taking a respite from battle. Several bodies littered the grade amidst well-dressed men running around aimlessly. The Red River Gang, it appeared, had already gotten what they'd been after, and left.

Leading Mean and Ugly, Prophet gigged the Morgan down the hill. He was about fifty yards from the train when he noticed several of the well-dressed gents, who were no doubt from the duke's entourage, form a scraggly line and raise shotguns to their shoulders. They stood there, shoulder-to-shoulder, looking like a small, portly, out-of-uniform regiment waiting for Prophet to get within bird gun range.

Scowling and impatient, Prophet reached into his saddlebags for a white handkerchief. He tied the handkerchief to the barrel of his Winchester, and held the gun high as he rode slowly toward the train, hoping one of the Britishers looking dazed and disheveled didn't go ahead and shoot him anyway.

The men kept the butts of their shotguns snugged against their shoulders and watched him critically, but no one fired.

"Easy," Prophet said. "I'm here to help."

The Britishers appeared to believe him. Two of the four shotguns went down, and the other two men relaxed considerably.

"Are you a policeman?" a man in blood-streaked, snow-white muttonchops inquired.

"Something like that," Prophet said, casting his gaze about the train, half appraising the damage, half looking for Louisa. Five men lay dead along the tracks, three of the bodies covered with blankets. Up near the engine, another was being tended by a man and a woman.

"What happened here?" Prophet asked the Brits.

One dropped his shotgun to his side, wiped a stream of blood from his lip—they all appeared to have been roughed up some if not pistol-whipped a lot—and said, "Bandits attacked us. They stopped the train. They—"

"They took the duchess!"

"Took her?" Prophet said. "Why?"

"They're holding her for ransom," another man carped, patting his mussed hair down.

"They got all our money and valuables, shot the duke's bodyguards, and took the duchess!"

Prophet was still glancing around for Louisa. He heard women crying aboard one of the passenger cars, but there was no sign of Louisa.

"Where's the duke?" Prophet asked, turning his head back to the men standing before him.

"He went after them," the man with the muttonchops said with a shake of his head. "He and Senator Dawson. Imagine that. On foot."

"On foot?"

"Yes. They released our horses from the stock car and scattered them to the four winds. The duke took after the ruffians with only his Wimbley twelve-gauge. Senator Dawson went after him."

"The duke was addled by the clubbing they gave him," another man added.

"Yes, that explains it. Poor man. He and the duchess have only been married a year, don't you know? Poor man. What a ghastly place, the West. What do you suppose lay in store for the duchess now? So close to her twenty-third birthday . . ."

Prophet declined to answer that question. They might keep her alive long enough to pick up the ransom money, but she might not want to live that long. . . .

Thoughts of the duchess's fate pointed Prophet's concern back to Louisa. "Any of you men see a blond-headed girl aboard? She'd have been wearing a gray skirt and a brown poncho."

The man with the muttonchops blinked his eyes at Prophet puzzledly. "Well, yes . . . yes . . . the girl who climbed down from the stock car." His voice was breathy with wonder. "Who on earth was she?"

Prophet's heart picked up its beat. "Was?" he exclaimed, whipping his head around the dead lying along the train. "Where the hell is she?"

"They took her, too. Her and Harrington's poor, sweet niece."

"Yes, they took the young, pretty ones—poor dears," the man called Harrington said, wagging his head and mopping at his sweaty forehead with a silk handkerchief. "Oh, my dear sweat Evelyn," the man complained, turning his gaze northward though the stalled train impeded his view. "Packed off with the duchess . . ."

"Shit!" Prophet swore.

He couldn't help feeling more concerned for Louisa than for anyone else out here. He sympathized with the duchess and Harrington's niece, but they were mostly just spoiled Brits to him—haughty English fops buying up pieces of the West for their sporting forays. He'd seen others like them, attended by vice-presidents or wealthy senators, shooting game from their private Pullman cars while the ladies sipped tea from China.

Prophet gigged the Morgan up to the engine, where a uniformed man was being tended by an older woman in a torn, dusty gown and a ruddy-skinned, wizened gent with a wide tie pierced with a diamond stick pin. Probably two of the duke and duchess's attendants, Prophet thought.

"Are you the engineer?" the bounty hunter asked the uniformed man.

The man nodded, glancing up from his bullet-pierced arm. "You the law?"

"No, but they should be on their way soon. You and your crew sit tight. I'm going after the gang."

The man sized up Prophet, then said, "Well, they shouldn't be hard to follow. They headed northwest, and they had three women with 'em. They kidnapped the duchess for ransom, don't you know?" The engineer swore, apologized to the lady wrapping his arm, and returned his gaze to Prophet. "They're also pullin' a wagon."

"A wagon?"

"Yeah, they took a wagon off the train to carry all the booty they stole. You know, trinkets and jewels and coins and whatnot. . . ."

"Good," Prophet said, meaning he was glad the gang had a wagon to slow them down. With both his horses tired out from the ride from Fargo, he wouldn't be able to follow them with any speed. In fact, he'd have to give both mounts at least a fifteen-minute breather before pursuing the gang at all.

With that consideration in mind, he gigged the Morgan around the panting engine, to the other side of the train. Dismounting, he tied the horses to one of the passenger cars, filled his hat from his canteen, and fed the water first to the Morgan, then to Mean and Ugly, who'd been studying the black horse with derision.

When both horses were watered, Prophet donned his hat and looked around for the Red River Gang's tracks. They weren't hard to find, even in the tough prairie sod: A dozen horses and one wagon heading northwest.

Heading for what? Did they have a hideout that way? If so, and if Prophet could penetrate it, would he be able to rescue Louisa and the two British women?

One man against a small army?

Prophet sighed and shook his head, but the urge to get moving made him itch all over. He had to give the horses another few minutes of rest, however. Louisa and the British gals were good as dead if his horses gave out. They probably were, anyway, but Prophet figured if he could follow them to their destination, the women would at least have a chance. . . .

He thought of Louisa. How had they ever gotten her subdued? They must have practically killed her, because that would be the only way she would have gone along for their ride. Unless she'd gone willingly . . .

Prophet wouldn't have put it past her. She was just determined and careless enough to get herself killed.

When Prophet felt the horses had rested enough, he mounted Mean and Ugly and headed off along the tracks of the Red River Gang, leading Louisa's Morgan. He'd ridden only about twenty minutes or so, cantering and walking the horses so he wouldn't play them out, when he turned to see a rooster tail of dust lifting in the distance toward the train.

Wondering who that could be, he kept the horses to a fast walk, letting the rider catch up to him. When he turned again ten minutes later, the rider had come within seventy yards. He, too, was leading another horse, a feisty roan.

"Well, now, what in the hell?" Prophet carped to himself, yanking his dun to a halt and staring back at the approaching, redheaded McIlroy in a snuff-colored Stetson.

"What did you think I was going to do—sit around in a warm bath in Bismarck?" the young man said as he approached, reading the disdain in Prophet's expression. "I'm a deputy U.S. marshal, for chrissakes. This is more my business than yours, Mr. Prophet."

Knowing there was no point arguing about McIlroy's presence and intention of tracking the gang, Prophet said, "Did you get the story from the Brits?"

"That they have the Duchess and two other women? Yep. I told the sheriff about your suspicions before I left Fargo, so he and his deputies should be along shortly. I doubt they'll be much help, though. We're nearly to the Cass County line, the end of their jurisdiction."

"Good," Prophet said. "We don't need anymore dust kicked up back here than we already got."

Annoyed and confounded, McIlroy's brows wrinkled

and his freckled face flushed. "If you had your druthers, you'd really rather track them alone?"

"If I had my druthers I'd track them with a handful of hand-picked military scouts or a couple regiments from the U.S. cavalry armed with cannons—preferably from a Southern battalion. Anything less, I'd just as soon go it alone. Nothing personal, but you're just too green."

With that, Prophet neck-reined Ugly around and continued riding at a fast canter.

McIlroy caught up to him and said, "I think you judged me too quickly, Prophet, on the basis of one mistake. I don't need to ask you for another chance, because I'm the one in authority here. But because you're the one with more experience, and because I for one don't want to track these men alone, I am asking you to give me one more shot at proving myself."

Prophet looked at the deputy, who did not look at him but rode face forward, stiff-backed in his saddle. Around his mouth and eyes, his face looked like rotten beef. He didn't have to be here, Prophet thought. He could be on the train back to Yankton with the bodies of his friends. You had to give him something for his pluck, anyway.

"Okay, okay," Prophet said, and turned forward in his saddle.

Staring northwest, he frowned. Something had moved ahead of them.

"You see that?" he asked the deputy.

"Yep. Two men afoot."

"Oh, shit," Prophet said, knowing who it was.

"What?" McIlroy said, reaching for his sidearm.

"Keep it holstered."

The two men were walking about fifty feet apart, one behind the other. The first man was tall and portly and carrying a shotgun, thick auburn locks bouncing on his shoulders. The second was tall and slender and wearing a black suit and coat, a fat necktie flopping back on his shoulder. He was bald. Both men were hatless.

Prophet and McIlroy approached the second man first. Looking exhausted, he was yelling at the first man, "Duke! Duke! You must stop! We've no horses and there are *Indians* about!"

The first man, the duke, yelled something without turning around and kept walking, almost marching, his shotgun barrel resting on his shoulder.

The sound of Prophet's and McIlroy's horses turned the second man around, fear etched in the senator's long, flushed face adorned with a gray spade beard. "Oh! Who . . . what . . . ?"

"It's all right, Senator," Prophet said. "We're friendly. We're after the hombres who took the duchess. What in the hell are you two doing out here afoot?"

Prophet and McIlroy had halted their horses before the senator, who bent over with his hands on his knees, trying to catch his breath. He looked like he was about to expire.

"We . . . he," the senator said, glancing at the duke who had stopped and turned toward Prophet and McIlroy, his brows crumpled with curiosity. "He wanted to go after the savages who kidnapped his wife. I just . . . I ran along to try to get him to stop. They'd kill him for sure, and . . ."

"Oh, button your mouth, Andrew!" the duke bellowed, walking quickly toward Prophet with his bird gun still on his shoulder. "You just came because I promised to invest in that beef-packing plant of yours in Deadwood Gulch, and you thought you had to make a show of fetching my wife or I'd pull out of the deal!"

"No!" the senator rasped. "I came to fetch *you* back, Duke. What on earth do you think you can do afoot, except get yourself scalped by Indians?"

The duke marched up to the senator, brought his shotgun down off his shoulder, grabbed it by the gold-plated receiver and forearm, and swung the stock soundly against the senator's head. With a shocked cry, the senator went down like a windmill toppled by lightning, arms flying.

"Never could stand a coward," the duke said in his limey accent. "Couldn't stand 'em in Delhi, and I can't stand 'em here."

"Damn," Prophet intoned with a wince, staring down at the idle senator. "You're like to have killed him!"

"Who are you?"

Prophet turned to the duke, who was eyeing Prophet and the deputy suspiciously. Before the bounty hunter could say anything, McIlroy said, "I'm Ezekiel McIlroy, U.S. deputy marshal out of Yankton, Dakota Territory. I've been tracking the Red River Gang for some time, and—"

"I need your extra horse," the duke said matter-of-factly, heading for the roan the deputy had tied to the tail of his black.

McIlroy glanced at Prophet, who shook his head vehemently.

"Uh . . . I don't think so, sir," the deputy said, trotting his horses in a wide half-circle around the determined royal.

Red-faced with exasperation, the duke aimed his bird gun at the deputy. "I want your extra horse. I need him to fetch the duchess. I'd pay you for the animal and your trouble, but that gang of hellions took everything I had on my person. Turn the animal loose, I say. Turn him loose!"

"If we're gonna get your wife back, we need all four horses," Prophet said. "Now put that cannon away, ye crazy limey!"

"Put that gun away, Mister," the deputy intoned. "I told you who I am, and if you mess with me further, I'll be obligated to arrest you."

"My wife is young and beautiful," the duke persisted. "If those men have their way with her, I'll . . . well, I cannot let that happen, you see. My god! She's the duchess!

My bride! A virgin until the night of our wedding! Now turn that horse loose, or I'll shoot you where you sit!"

Prophet ground his spurs into Ugly's flanks, and the horse bolted forward, hammering the duke with a well-muscled shoulder. The duke cried out as his shotgun lifted, booming skyward, and fell face down under Ugly's hooves.

"Come on, Deputy!" Prophet called to McIlroy. "We're burnin' daylight!"

Caught off guard by Prophet's maneuver, McIlroy stared dazed at the trampled, cursing Brit. Seeing Prophet galloping westward without looking back, McIlroy spurred his own horse after the bounty hunter.

When he caught up to Prophet, he said, "Shouldn't we see if he's seriously hurt?"

As if in reply, a boom lifted on the wind behind them. Both men turned to see the duke lowering his shotgun from his shoulder as powder smoke puffed around his head. He yelled something as he breeched the gun to re-load.

To McIlroy, Prophet said, "You go ahead if you want, but he looks all right to me!"

Then he lowered his head and spurred Ugly northwest at a sod-churning run.

24

"OH, NO! OH, God! For the love of the crown, help me! Help us all! We're going to perish, certainly!"

With her hands tied behind her and her ankles tied before her in the bouncing wagon box, Louisa turned to the woman who'd been yelling and sobbing off and on since they'd been taken from the train a good half hour before.

"Be quiet," Louisa warned the duchess. "You're giving me a headache."

"Ohhhhh!" the duchess sobbed, her head between her upraised knees.

She was tied as Louisa was, and, like Louisa, sat with her back against the driver's box, facing the wagon's rear. With her rich, brown tresses hanging down from the once-taut coils piled atop her aristocratic head, and her blue silk gown torn and soiled, she didn't look much like a duchess anymore.

She lifted her head, turning to Louisa with her tear-streaked face beseechingly. "I'm going to die! Don't you see? They're going to kill us all, and I'll never see my dukey or little Timmy or Mum or Poppa or Gran—ever again! *Ev-er!*"

"Don't worry. They're not gonna kill us for a while yet," Louisa said under her breath, regarding the dull-eyed men plodding along behind the wagon. "They're gonna have plenty of fun with us first—you can bet the pot on that."

"Ohhhhh!"

Louisa's flip tone belied her fear, the shudders that leapfrogged her spine every two minutes or so. Her hands and feet were bound, and she was in the firm, deadly grasp of the gang who'd murdered and ravaged her family. They were all about her, in fact—Handsome Dave Duvall and Dayton Flowers included, heading up the pack before the wagon.

What, oh what, had ever made her board that train!

Louisa turned her head away from the shrieking duchess, and saw the other woman the gang had kidnapped, sitting on Louisa's left. Slightly younger than the duchess—probably Louisa's age—the young woman had passed out again, and her head lolled back on her shoulders. Little ringlets of flaxen-blond hair hung to her small, powder-white breasts only partially concealed by her dainty pink gown. Her delicate, small-boned face was drawn and pale and dust-layered, and her fine jaw bounced slightly with the wagon.

Louisa was glad the girl was unconscious. She couldn't have endured the screams of both women at once.

Looking around again, Louisa regarded the dusty riders surrounding the wagon—a hawkish, mean, ugly, unshaven lot of gun toughs. The Red River Gang they were, and this was the first time Louisa had seen them all together up close.

They rode their saddles with lazy arrogance, slouching, smoking, and squinting against the dust and the westering sun, confident in their villainy. It was their aim, Louisa knew from what she'd overheard in their conversation with the duke earlier, to hold the duchess for ransom, until the duke could come up with fifty thousand dollars.

Where and when the duke was supposed to make the drop, Louisa hadn't heard; she'd been too far from the men and still woozy from the braining she'd taken when the train had stopped so suddenly following the explosion that had ripped up the rails.

The part about the drop didn't matter, anyway. Louisa knew that either she or the Red River Gang would be turned toe down long before any of that occurred. She still had her gun under her skirt, as well as her knife. None of the gang members had thought to check the pretty little girl with the honey-blond hair for hideout weapons. As soon as one or more of them tried to ravage her as they'd ravaged her mother and sisters, Louisa would make them damn sorry they hadn't been more cautious.

She turned to her left and saw that one of the dust-soaked riders was staring at her, a lewd light in his eyes.

"What are you looking at?" she asked him haughtily, covering her fear with a taut upper lip.

"You, sweet girl."

"You're not my type, sir, nor me yours."

To the man riding beside him, he said, "This one here's not only perty, but she's got spunk. Did you hear how she said that?" The man lifted his chin and scrunched his eyes. " 'You're not my type, sir, nor me yours.' " He slapped his thigh and guffawed.

"Yeah, I saw. I like the duchess, myself. I don't know why we took this one when we had all those rich Englishers to choose from."

" 'Cause this one was pertier than them Englishers, and cause she tried to knock Dayton's block off when he grabbed her out o' that car. Ha! Ha! How could anyone resist a girl like that!"

"I like the duchess myself," the second man repeated, wiping his mouth with his shirt cuff. He looked at the girl to Louisa's left. "And this girl here—her titties are about to jiggle out of that little dress she's wearin'—like little white pears!"

"What the hell are you two doin'?" Handsome Dave Duvall asked, slowing his horse to let the wagon catch up to him. When he was riding even with the box, between the other two gang members, he said, "I told you boys to leave these girls alone."

"Ah, come on, Dave," the first man said. "We're just lookin'! Besides that, I don't see no harm in havin' some fun."

"If I turned you boys loose on these women now, they'd be dead before nightfall. Besides that, I don't want any of you ever touching the duchess, understand? Her husband ain't gonna pay the ransom to get her back if she's defiled."

"Okay, Dave," the second man said. "But what about these other two? I mean, we brought them along for the fun of it, didn't we?"

"That's right, Grogan," Duvall said with a grin. "And you can have all the fun you want with 'em tonight, after we reach the cabins. In the meantime, we're gonna ride like hell, understand?"

"You think someone's followin' us, Dave?"

"Doubt it, but it's always better to be safe than sorry, now isn't it, Chess?"

"I reckon," Chess allowed.

Duvall gave the two men a wink and turned to Louisa with a thoughtful frown. "Who in the hell are you, anyway, honey? What were you doin' on that train with all those uppity Englishers?"

Thinking fast, Louisa said, "I . . . I was hired to help the cook. You know, to peel potatoes and serve coffee and such. Please, mister, won't you let me go?" She lowered her head and feigned a sob, not a difficult job under the circumstances. "I'm so frightened."

Duvall sidled his horse to the wagon, nudging Grogan

out of his way. Keeping pace with the bouncing contraption, he smiled lustily at Louisa, reached down, and took her chin in his hand. He baldly appraised the two bulges in her tunic, then stared into her eyes, grinning with only his mouth. His gaze was dark, his cheeks coloring slightly. A wintery chill sent a shiver the length of her body. The duchess leapt into another crying jag, and Duvall, wincing at the ear-piercing shrieks, straightened in his saddle and galloped back up to the front of the pack.

Grogan snickered and turned to Louisa. "Just better hope he don't go for your toes, Miss—that's all I got to say!"

Grogan elbowed the man called Chess, adding, "Poor Cora Ames. Ha! That poor woman's gonna be walkin' with a limp till the day she meets St. Pete. Ha! Ha!"

He and Chess shared another round of laughter, then gradually turned their attention to cigarette-building. When they'd drifted off, Louisa looked behind her and over the riders following the wagon. She hoped she'd see a sign of Prophet back there, but all she saw was more of this godforsaken prairie, creased here and there with shallow ravines and studded with occasional cottonwoods.

Had the bounty hunter found her horse at the train station in Fargo, and realized her ploy? She didn't know. Even if he had found the horse, it didn't mean he'd guessed she'd hopped the duke's train. But she hoped so. If not, she was all alone out here, with only the single Colt on her hip and the bowie knife on her belt—against twelve of the owliest-looking savages she'd ever laid eyes on.

And then there was Handsome Dave Duvall, as square-jawed handsome as he was evil.

The hell of it was, she didn't think she'd have done such a thing unless she'd known she had Prophet to back her up. Maybe she'd been better off back when she was depending only on herself. . . .

Maybe it was better if she always just rode alone. . . .

One thing she knew for sure, though—if she was going under the green, she was damn sure going to take a handful of the Red River Gang with her.

She rested her head on her knees and tried squirming into a more comfortable position. But there was no such thing as comfortable when your wrists were tied behind your back, your ankles were tied before you, and you were riding a wagon straight to hell. . . .

25

IN SPITE OF the wagon's constant jarring and pounding, Louisa fell into a doze. She snapped out of it when the buckboard suddenly stopped. She jerked her head up, looking around.

Night had fallen. They were in a hollow in the hills through which a stream or a river coursed, through tall cottonwoods silhouetted against a pale, rising moon.

Bringing her gaze lower, she saw what looked like a lean-to attached to a log corral. To her left, she saw a sod cabin with an extension made from milled lumber. It was a dark, rambling place that smelled of dank earth and rotten wood and mouse droppings, and Louisa shrank from it like she would a dungeon tended by ogres.

"We're home, my lovelies," came a voice out of the darkness. A figure moved toward the wagon, and Louisa recognized Dave Duvall. "Time to dismount and enter our humble abode. Admittedly, it isn't much, but then, we don't get many visitors out here." He chuckled, pleased with himself.

Louisa saw that the other men were dismounting their

horses, ripping the tack from the animals, and turning them into the corral. They moved slowly as though weary from the hard ride.

As for herself, Louisa wasn't sure she could move. Her butt and legs were numb, the small of her back felt as though a nail had been driven through it, and what hadn't gone to sleep ached from all the jarring. In addition, her face was badly wind- and sunburned, and her eyes were full of grit.

She nudged the duchess, who'd fallen asleep against Louisa's arm. The other girl was curled up in the corner between the driver's box and the left sideboard. The duchess gave a startled grunt and lifted her head.

"What is it . . . oh . . . no!"

Several men, including Dayton Flowers, had now gathered around the wagon—dark figures moving wearily but with lascivious grins bunching their cheeks and bringing snickers up from their throats. Louisa's temples throbbed with fear, and her throat was dry. She tried to stand, but fell back against the driver's box.

"I can't," she said.

"Day, help the ladies," Duvall said.

"Be my pleasure, Dave!" Flowers replied, climbing heavily into the wagon box with a witch's cackle. Ignoring the women on either side of her, he went right for Louisa, bent down, grabbed Louisa's arm, and brusquely tossed her over his shoulder, as though she were nothing but a sack of seed corn.

Her back cried out, feeling as though it would surely snap like dry kindling, but Louisa ignored it, more worried the man would feel the holstered gun on her hip. Fortunately, he'd thrown her over his left shoulder, so the gun was away from him. Her bowie, however, was on her right hip, and another problem altogether.

As he turned and jumped off the wagon, Dayton Flowers laughed again, patted her bottom, and said, "Dave, I like this country girl. Her bottom feels nice and so do her titties. I call dibs on this one."

He headed for the cabin, and as he walked across the yard and mounted the stoop, Louisa felt as though her bones were being ground to powder. She grunted and sighed with the pain, and Flowers seemed to enjoy it. He patted her bottom again, and when he stepped into the dark, musty cabin, where the smell of mice was so strong it nearly took Louisa's breath away, he twirled in a circle several times, stumbling and almost falling.

Louisa cried out and Flowers laughed. Then he stumbled toward the back of the place, kicked open a door, stooped through the low opening, and tossed Louisa onto a narrow bed that reeked of mildew. Her head hit the feeble, straw tick mattress hard, bouncing off the wood-slatted frame beneath, and the pain was so intense she saw red for several seconds.

Suddenly, as she blinked her eyes, trying to see something in the black room, she was aware of Dayton Flowers kneeling beside her. She could smell the rancid sweat of the man, hear his labored breathing and his chuckles.

"Let me see what you got here, little miss," he said, brusquely reaching down the neck of her tunic and blouse and roughly fondling her breasts. His coarse hands scraped her and chafed her, and she set her jaws against the pain, fighting the tears she felt welling from her eyes.

She wanted to beg him to stop but would not, could not let herself do that. She wouldn't give him the satisfaction of knowing how terrified she'd become.

He stopped, finally, and removed his hands, when another man shuffled through the doorway, grunting as though carrying something heavy.

"Day, where should I put the queen of England here?" The man's voice was loud and harsh in the quiet room.

"Just throw her anywhere. There's only one bed, and

I've given it to the country girl with the nice teats. The queen can slum it with the mice."

"Okay," the other man said.

There was a loud thump and a scream as the duchess was dropped on the floor. She began bawling then and did not stop when another man banged his head on the low doorway and cursed savagely as something else hit the floor with a thump and a female scream. That must have been the other girl. She gave several more loud, fervent screams, and as the floorboards jumped and rattled, Louisa figured that the man who'd banged his head on the door frame was kicking the girl into the room, cursing all the while.

Above the cries of the women, Dayton Flowers said, "We'll be back for some fun later on. First, we're gonna get us some grub and rest. You girls might wanna tidy up a bit for the menfolk."

He and the other two men laughed and chuckled and jabbed each other mockingly, then went out and slammed the door.

Dust and what sounded like mud chunks sifted down from the rafters. Wings beat over Louisa's head, and she heard a bird's frightened chirps. Lifting her head to see the window in the wall about ten feet off the end of her cot, she saw the wing-flapping silhouette of the bird as it tried to make its way through a broken pane. With a screech and a rattle of glass, it was gone, its exasperated cries diminishing as it fled this hellish hollow.

Envying the bird, Louisa lay back on the cot, the pain in the back of her head slowly subsiding. Ignoring the weeping of the other two women and the growing cacophony of the men entering and beginning to make themselves at home in the cabin's main room, she tried to get her fear under control enough to figure out a plan.

There was a window in the wall before her. She could tell by the moonlight slanting into the room from behind

her that there must have been a window back there, as
well.

Escape routes, they were—if she could get her arms
and feet untied. . . .

She jumped when a gun barked in the other room. She
tensed, her heart leaping and pounding painfully against
her breastbone. The gun barked again, and she held her
breath, listening.

"Damn!" a man cried, laughing. "Did you see that? A
skunk!"

"Did you get it, Dave?"

"Think I nicked it before he got out through that hole
there." Boots scuffled and chairs scraped the floor. Duvall's voice again: "Millen, get some boards from the
lean-to, and cover that hole. Fuckin' skunks!"

The main door opened and closed, and the voices settled to a low din. Shortly, pots and pans clattered, and the
smell of a cook fire filtered into the tiny room in which
Louisa lay on the cot, listening and thinking, trying to
wriggle her wrists free of the rope binding them together
behind her back.

If she could only free her hands, she could untie the
other two women and they could flee through one of the
windows. At the very least, she'd have access to the revolver still secured to the holster on her hip. . . .

For an hour, she worked at wiggling her hands free of
the ropes, her shoulders and arms aching with the effort,
her back and neck going numb. Finally, she had the rope
loose enough to slip the knuckles of her right hand
through. She'd just accomplished the maneuver when
boots pounded suddenly, and the door opened.

"Hello, girls," Handsome Dave Duvall said, standing in
the open doorway, silhouetted against the lighted main
room behind him.

Louisa froze, shuddering. She'd freed her hands from
the ropes but she knew she didn't have time to go for her

revolver. She might—might!—get off one shot, but only one. She'd be dead soon after.

"We had us a little bet," Duvall said. "Dayton here won. He'll be taking you out to the lean-to, Little Miss. Me, I'm gonna stay right here"—he swung a bull's-eye lantern around from behind him, holding it high before him, lighting the cramped room—"and have me a little fun with the little English girl . . . while the duchess watches. Hee-hee-hee."

Suddenly, he stepped back and sideways, and Dayton Flowers stepped around him and into the room. Giving a whoop, Flowers bent down and pulled Louisa over his shoulder and carried her through the door. Pretending her hands were still tied, Louisa hung down Flowers's sweat-damp back, glancing around at the men sitting around the room, drinking whiskey and smoking and grinning at her.

If she couldn't get away from Dayton Flowers, she'd have to endure each one of them, in turn, for the next several hours. The thought was as raw as the image of her dying mother and sisters, and she turned her mind away from it and toward the hope that once she was outside, she could somehow escape Dayton Flowers, and run away to seek help for the other women.

Flowers was across the room and on the stoop in three or four long strides. He stepped off the stoop, stumbling from drink, and headed across the dark yard to the lean-to. Once inside, he bent down, and Louisa fell off his shoulder into the hay. It was a soft landing, and she lay there, staring up at Flowers towering over her, breathing hard and balling his fists.

Soft, white moonlight angled through the sashed window to his left, limning the side of his face and shoulder. Finally, he doffed his hat, tossed it aside, and unbuckled his gunbelt.

"We're gonna have us a good time out here, sweet girl. Yes, sir—just you an' me." His voice was breathy with lust; Louisa could smell the fetid odor of whiskey on his breath. Combined with his sweat stench, it was enough to make her retch.

As he hurriedly undressed, kicking off his boots, Louisa snaked her free left hand out from under her—slowly, carefully, so Flowers wouldn't detect her movement. She wiggled the hand through the slit in the left side of her skirt, but stopped suddenly, clipping a horrified grunt when she realized her knife scabbard was empty!

The knife must have fallen out, fallen through the slit in her skirt, when Flowers had been carrying her across the yard.

Damn! Now she had no choice but to use her gun, which she could feel was still there in its holster, despite the fact of its noise.

She'd fished it out of its holster and through the skirt slit just in time, shoving the Colt into the hay only a few inches to her right, away from the moonlight, her hand remaining on the grips. Flowers had just ripped out of his underwear, tossing the garment aside, and turned to her nude, silhouetted against the window, the moonlight laying a sheen across the sweat-slick hair curling off his chest, left arm, and thigh.

Rubbing his hands together briskly, he said, "Now ole Dayton's gonna show you a time you won't soon forget!"

His knees bent as he stooped toward her. She removed the gun from the hay, aimed it straight at the dark center of his chest, and pulled the trigger.

The gun jumped and barked, the flames lighting up the lean-to for a split wink and filling the air with powder smoke. Flowers gave a jerk and a low grunt, and froze. He grunted again and sagged to his knees.

"Wha—what the hell?" He lowered his chin to look at his chest. "What the hell? You shot me?"

"Think I'd let a greasy polecat like you grunt around between my legs?" Louisa castigated the man as she

scrambled to her feet, her muscles and legs moving slug-
gishly, painfully, and ran to the door.

Leaving Flowers to die, resisting the urge to finish him
with another shot to the head, she flung open the squeaky
lean-to door and cut a look at the cabin. The other men
had heard the shot and were already spilling onto the
stoop, guns drawn and yelling.

Louisa's face flushed with panic and grief. Oh god, oh
no . . . *jeepers!*

She ran around the lean-to and into the woods behind,
hearing the men behind her calling for Dayton. Her gun
in her hand, she jumped deadfalls and wove between cottonwood trees and rocks, pushed through spiky bramble,
making her way toward the river murmuring in its bed
only a few yards away.

If she could get into the water, she might have a chance.

"Hey, you guys," a man's voice boomed behind her. "I
can hear her in the brush back here. Come on!"

She ran harder, but she knew it wasn't fast enough. Her
legs and feet were still cramped from the wagon ride, the
muscles sluggish and jittery. Behind her, the men's yelling
grew louder and louder, and then she was hearing brush
thrashing and twigs snapping under pounding feet.

"Girl! I know you're back here! You're gonna die,
girl!"

It was Dave Duvall, his voice high-pitched with lunatic
exasperation. It turned Louisa's knees even weaker, and
they almost buckled. But then she pushed through another
bramble patch and saw the river winking silver in the
moonlight.

She made for it and started across, her heart sinking
when she saw it was not deep enough to carry her downstream. In fact, it barely covered her ankles!

She ran as hard and fast as she could, sliding on rocks
and tripping over snags. Behind her, the sound of pounding boots grew louder, until she knew at least one of the

gang members was closing. She was certain of it when she heard Dave Duvall.

"You can run but you can't hide, girl!"

His voice was so loud and filled with such belligerence it made her eardrums shudder and her breath catch in her throat. He gave a whoop, and then she heard him splashing across the creek.

Realizing she couldn't escape him, she stopped and turned, clawing her revolver out of her skirt. She raised it, aimed at Duvall's tall, dark, running figure outlined by the moonlight, and fired twice. As she did, Duvall gave a mocking whoop and dove to his left, dodging both shots, which made wet spanging noises as they ricocheted off half-submerged stones.

He drew his own gun and fired quickly, the slug whistling past Louisa's ear. Giving a cry, she wheeled, almost falling in the creek, and ran up the opposite bank, bulling through shrubs, which caught on her clothes, catching and tearing them, yanking her hair.

When she'd run several more yards, she waited until she saw Duvall again—a quickly moving shadow amidst the shrubs—and fired three quick rounds. Not waiting to see if she'd hit her mark, she turned and ran through the trees. Suddenly, the ground gave way beneath her—she'd come to an old creek bed—and she fell hard and rolled to the creek's rocky, brushy bottom, losing her gun in the process.

"Oh . . . *no*. . . . !" she cried, knowing that without the gun she had no chance at all.

Ignoring her scrapes and scratches, she ran her hands over the dark rocks, feeling for the revolver. She stopped when a rock tumbled down the slope behind her, and she heard breathing sounds. Turning slowly, she saw Duvall standing on the bank, both hands hanging at his sides, his silver-plated Colt winking in the moonlight.

After what seemed like hours, he blew a ragged sigh and said in a low, menacing voice, "That wasn't nice, killin' Dayton. That wasn't nice atall."

26

TO LOUISA'S SURPRISE, and partly to her chagrin, Duvall did not kill her.

Instead, he leapt down the bank, grabbed her painfully by the arm and half-dragged her up the bank, back across the creek and through the trees, summoning his men. Louisa cried out against Duvall's excruciating grip and against the pain in her knees and shins scraping along the ground.

Most of the men were already in the cabin yard when Duvall and Louisa got there. Others were filtering back through the trees behind the lean-to. One man came out of the lean-to and said grimly. "Dayton—he's deader'n a doornail, Dave."

Duvall dragged Louisa to the cabin. He opened the door and heaved her inside. She flew across the floor and landed in a heap at the base of the square-hewn center post.

The red-faced, wide-eyed Duvall followed her in, his men seeping in around him, and jerked his finger at Louisa angrily. "You're gonna pay for that, Little Miss! You hear me? You're gonna pay for that!"

"Here . . . I'll finish her right now," said one of the men, walking up to Louisa and drawing his gun.

"No!" Duvall said. "That's too easy. Way too damn easy!"

He stared at Louisa for a long time as she huddled against the center post, wishing he'd end it once and for all, knowing he wouldn't . . . knowing she'd be alive a lot longer tonight than she'd want to be. She stared back at him and was vaguely surprised at his scrutiny, as though he were seeing her for the first time.

His men stood around him. Several had rolled and lighted fresh cigarettes; others were pouring drinks or tipping back bottles, glowering at the pretty little killer in torn clothes on the floor. They all shuttled their gazes to Duvall, awaiting his next move. The air was heavy with the stench of their smoke, breath, and sweat.

"Say, boys," the gang leader finally said, curiously thoughtful. "Have we seen this girl somewhere before?"

Several glanced at him, wonderingly.

"What's that, boss?" one of them said, clearing his throat.

Duvall's eyes lingered on Louisa, whose heart was beginning to pound even harder. "Have we seen this little girl . . . this innocent little girl . . . somewhere before?"

There was a pause filled with the quiet sounds of the gang's breathing and smoking.

"Not sure what you mean, boss," another man said from behind a cloud of cigarette smoke. "I've never seen her before."

"Well, I think I have," Duvall said. "Sure . . . I've seen her. I've seen her several times in some o' the towns we pulled through. Don't you boys remember seein' an innocent little blonde in a brown poncho and ridin' a black horse. A Morgan horse, like the one Giff McQueen stole from that breeder down in Arkansas?"

Another pause. All eyes were on Louisa now.

"Just sittin' Giff's horse here an' there, waitin' on street corners or sittin' on steps or lounging around on loafers' benches in front of mercantiles an' such . . ."

"What are you sayin', Dave?" one of the men asked him, frowning.

"I'm sayin' this girl's been trailin' us for a long time now. Layin' for us. Any of you ever wonder why none of the gang that broke off from us never showed up again?"

Duvall looked around at the faces surrounding him and Louisa, a bemused grin pulling at his wide mouth, his lantern jaw set like a blacksmith's sledge.

"What about Norall and McQueen? Jimmy Dahl and Fred Barnes? What about Leach and Sully? They were just gonna take 'em a little snoozer south of Fargo. Did they ever show up at Cora's?"

Duvall looked around the room, at the faces regarding him with faintly quizzical eyes. Cigarette smoke puffed and webbed under the low rafters through which the sod roof bowed.

"Guess we just figured they sorta got sidetracked, kinda," someone said.

Duvall returned his gaze to Louisa, who stared at him bleach-faced, her chest rising and falling as she breathed, terror-gripped.

"Yeah, I guess that's what I figured," Duvall said mildly.

Anger shouldering past her fear, Louisa licked her lips and said, "You bastards murdered my family. You raped my momma and sisters. You killed my pa and my brother James." Her eyes pinched and her face flushed as she added, "I vowed to kill you all—to murder you all and send you all to hell where you belong with the devil! And I got a good many of you, too. More than I can count on one hand, at least, and that's something. Lou Prophet will get the rest of you. He'll gun you down or watch you hang. Either way, you're wolf bait—every single one of you greasy sons of bitches!"

Her heart was hammering now, and she wanted to charge them, to go out screaming, with blood on her lips and fingernails. But her legs simply wouldn't work.

Duvall watched her dully. "Who's Lou Prophet?"

"You'll know soon enough," Louisa spat. "You mangy dog!"

She heaved a deep sigh and rolled her eyes around, taking in all the faces staring at her, the men suddenly realizing they'd not only been duped, but duped by a girl. Embarrassment mixed with exasperation smoldered far back in their coal-dark eyes, the lines in their foreheads smoothed out with half-formed plans for retribution.

The silence was broken by laughter. Louisa swung her gaze back to Duvall, who was bent over and laughing so hard he appeared as though he were about to drop to the floor. He lifted his knee and slapped it, then danced a little jig, twirling around and lifting his laughing mouth to the rafters, guffawing as though at the most hilarious story he'd heard in a month of Sundays.

He fell silent as quickly as he'd become hysterical, then twirled toward Louisa. He jerked her up by her neck, backhanded her once hard, then slapped her with his open palm. Her head whipped from side to side, her hair flying, but Duvall kept her from falling by clutching her poncho and shoving her back against the center post.

He hit her thrice more, and as she slipped into semiconsciousness, her head pounding and sparks flying behind her closed eyelids, he flung her through the crowd of men and onto the eating table on the other side of the cook stove.

"Here you go, girl," Duvall said, unbuttoning his pants. "Have you a little taste o' what your momma and sisters had, courtesy of Dave Duvall's Red River Gang!"

Suddenly there was a loud, splintering bang, as though

someone had kicked in the door. It was followed by a
barrage of gunfire so loud it shut out all the rest of the
world and set Louisa's ears to tolling like bells. There
were two cannon-like booms, as though from a double-
barrel shotgun; on the heels of the booms, a rifle cut loose,
the shooter jacking and firing, jacking and firing, his
ejected cartridges making a steely clatter beneath the near-
continuous roar of his gun.

Louisa's eyes were squeezed shut, but she was aware
of someone jerking her off the table by her arm, of being
thrown over a broad shoulder, of hanging down a tall
man's back as he hustled her out the door, where the
shooting from within the cabin was quieter, the air cooler
and minus the suffocating smell of gunpowder.

She was lifted onto a saddle and held there while a man
mounted behind her. He was breathing heavily, and
Louisa could feel the heat from his body and sense his
excitement.

"Come on, Deputy!" Lou Prophet yelled above
Louisa's head, as his horse fiddle-footed and kicked, ready
to gallop. "Let's ride like hell, boy!"

They were off at a lunge, riding hard, and Louisa's eyes
fluttered open. She could see the hilly, moonlit landscape
sliding past, interrupted here and there with trees and
boulders. The horse's pounding hooves made her head
and body ache, but when all the pieces of the last few
minutes arranged themselves in her brain, she felt lighter
somehow, and welcomed back to the living.

"L-Lou?" she said, turning her head to his wide, sweating chest behind her.

"Just hold tight, girl. We have some hotfootin' to do!"

She clamped her hands on the saddle horn and lowered
her head over the horse's bouncing mane, hearing the big
horse puffing and snorting as it galloped, feeling the chill
night breeze in her hair.

She was alive. . . .

The Red River Gang hadn't killed her. . . .

Prophet had come for her, like she'd known he would. She wasn't sure how much time had passed before the horse slowed suddenly, nudging her up over its head.

"Hoah! Hooooo," Prophet yelled.

He turned Mean and Ugly around. Louisa opened her eyes and saw they'd been trailing her Morgan. A rider appear out of the darkness, the moon behind him, lighting his shoulders. She recoiled and gave a shudder.

"It's okay, it's okay," Prophet told her, placing a placating hand on her arm. "This is Deputy McIlroy. He was the one doin' the shootin' while I got you out of the cabin." Prophet turned to the slender man, a few inches shorter than himself. "You hit?"

The man was so breathless, he only wagged his head. It was several seconds before he said, "No . . . I ain't hit . . . but they were startin' to open up on us. Barely made it out. That was pure-dee craziness, Prophet. There was pret' near a dozen men in that cabin."

"How many you think we hit?"

"Well, you hit at least two with that scattergun of yours—turned 'em to blood an' mush before any of them even knew they had company." The deputy couldn't help an anxiety-relieving laugh. "Jesus Christ! Then I laid out five or six with my Winchester." He wagged his head. "Must've got at least that many before they started shootin' back."

The deputy removed his hat, slapped it against his thigh, and shook his head like a runaway horse. "Jesus Christ, Prophet—that was pure-dee crazy!"

"Well, we got Miss Bonny-venture out of there, anyway," Prophet said. "How you doin', girl?"

"Much better, Lou," Louisa managed. It was true. In spite of her scrapes and scratches and the bruises welling on her face, she'd never felt so good in her life. "I knew you'd get them, Lou! I knew you'd lay them out like the mangy dogs they were!"

"Well, they ain't all dead," Prophet said with a sigh. "And the two Brits are still back there. I s'pect the gang's feelin' right surly 'bout now, too. They're probably headin' our way—what's left of 'em."

"What are we gonna do?" McIlroy said. "These horses are exhausted."

"I reckon we'll take care of the rest of the gang," Prophet said wistfully, gigging his horse over to a low hill on the east side of the two-track trail they'd been following. "Then we'll go back for the two English women. You stay over there, Deputy," he said over his shoulder. "Get behind that tree there, and get your rifle loaded and ready for argument."

"Listen, Prophet," McIlroy called. "I'm totin' a badge, remember. I have to give those men a chance to give themselves up."

Prophet turned, scowling. "You didn't feel the need back at the cabin!"

"That's because, after assessing the situation, I felt the girl was in imminent danger. But now, I'm—"

Prophet was angry—exasperated, in fact. "You call to those men before you start shootin', they'll have the upper hand . . . and you'll be the first son of a bitch I shoot next!"

The deputy sat his horse in the middle of the trail and shook his head, giving an exasperated pshaw. "Prophet, you're just plumb crazy, you know that?"

"That's why I've lived as long as I have, old son." Prophet dismounted behind Louisa, then helped her out of the saddle.

"Yeah," McIlroy admitted. "Yeah . . . I reckon it is."

Leading his horse, Prophet started guiding Louisa, shaky on her feet, back behind the hill. Over his shoulder he said to the deputy, "I figure it took 'em at least five minutes to get saddled. They should be along in a minute or two."

Behind the hill, Prophet tethered Mean and Ugly and the Morgan to some shrubs, then walked over to where Louisa had sat along the base of the hill. He was carrying his shotgun in one hand, his rifle in the other. Kneeling beside her, he set his shotgun against his knee and brushed her hair from her face with his right hand.

"The deputy thinks I'm crazy," he said. "What you did would get you locked up tight in a funny farm—jumpin' that train you knew was headed straight for the Red River Gang!"

She lifted her head and looked at him, but he couldn't see her eyes. "I reckon I didn't think it all the way through," she said, with a slight shrug of her shoulders.

Something about the shrug told Prophet she was all right. Relieved, he clutched her to his chest and kissed her head. He'd never known a girl such as her. Nope, never in his whole life. Few men had her kind of pluck. He was just glad that he and McIlroy had made it to the cabin in time to save her.

"Well," he said finally. "We ain't out of the woods yet. Anything funny happens here in the next minute or two, you get on that Morgan and ride like hell, you understand?"

"Give me a gun, and I'll help," she said, holding out her hand.

Prophet laughed and shook his head. "You rest right where you are, Miss Bonny-venture."

With that he picked up the shotgun, stood, and climbed the hill. When he was almost to the brow, he removed his hat, got down, and crawled to the crest, until he could see the trail snaking around below. On the other side of the hill was the cottonwood beside which McIlroy was waiting.

Prophet waved to the deputy, letting him know he was

in position. McIlroy lifted an arm, waving back. Then Prophet turned his gaze northward, the direction in which the gang would appear—if it appeared, that was. Prophet figured they would. Even if there were only one or two men left, Prophet figured they'd want revenge for the trick he and the deputy had pulled on them back in the cabin.

The thought hadn't left his mind before he heard the thunder of galloping hooves.

"They're comin'!" he yelled to McIlroy, just loud enough for the deputy to hear.

McIlroy waved and slipped behind the tree. Prophet hunkered down, bringing up his Richards's sawed-off. Hearing a rustling to his right, he turned sharply with a startled grunt.

"It's just me," Louisa said, crawling up beside him.

"What are you doin' here? I told you to stay where you were."

"Since when are you givin' the orders?"

"Where did you get that?" Prophet nodded, indicating the revolver in her right hand.

"Your saddlebags."

"That's my extra pistol."

"Thanks for letting me borrow it."

Hearing the horses more clearly now, and the squeak of saddle leather, he pushed her head down. "Be quiet! Here they come!"

Peering down the hill, Prophet saw six riders come into view around a bend in the trail, growing out of the darkness and moonlight, their spurs, bridle bits, and silver hat trimmings flashing. He brought the barn blaster to his shoulder and waited until the riders were within range.

Tripping both triggers on the ten-gauge, he watched the two lead men fly off the backs of their startled mounts. Beside him, Louisa opened up with the Smith & Wesson. Below him, McIlroy went to work with his freshly loaded

Winchester. Prophet tossed his shotgun aside, picked up his own rifle, and started firing down the hill at what was left of the Red River Gang being tossed this way and that by flying bullets and rearing, bucking horses.

Prophet, McIlroy, and Louisa had taken the group by such surprise that only two men had had time to squeeze off rounds before they were shot yelling and cursing from their saddles. In less than two minutes, all the riders were down and out of commission, their horses scattering and screaming off in the night.

Gunsmoke wafted and webbed in the quiet air, eerily illuminated by the still-climbing moon. Far off, wolves howled.

Prophet walked down the hill. Louisa followed, her strength returning to her legs though her swelling face was beginning to ache in earnest.

Prophet walked among the men twisted in all possible positions along the trail, making sure they were all dead. When he'd checked the last man, he turned to McIlroy.

"Well, it looks like we got 'em." To Louisa, he said happily, "The last of the Red River Gang, girl."

Louisa was walking among the bodies, her empty revolver held down at her side. She was studying each face in turn. "What about Handsome Dave?"

"We probably got him back at the cabin," McIlroy said.

"I hope so," Louisa responded, turning and heading around the hill toward her horse.

"Wait," Prophet yelled to her. "You shouldn't go back there alone, girl!"

As if she hadn't heard him, she disappeared around the hill. Prophet turned to McIlroy, frowning. "Let's get these bodies dragged off the trail."

They were dragging the cadavers into the brush when Louisa spurred the Morgan past them, heading back toward the cabin.

27

ONCE AGAIN CURSING the day he ever laid eyes on Louisa Bonaventure, Prophet rode hard toward the cabin. Mean was as durable a mount as you'd find in the West, but even the hammer-headed line-back was starting to blow and shake his head with exhaustion. McIlroy's horse was giving out, too, and had slowed to a floppy-footed canter a good hundred yards behind. It had been a long day for both horses.

Prophet was glad when the cabin appeared in the cove in the hills, its lanterns still lit and splashing their dim buttery light on the yard and over the back of the Morgan standing before the door.

A gun barked from within, stunning the quiet night.

Cursing, Prophet reined Mean to a sliding halt and slipped out of the saddle while drawing his six-shooter. Crouching, he dropped the reins and ran toward the cabin.

When a figure appeared in the door, he stopped and raised the Colt. But then he saw the long hair falling to the slender shoulders. Exhaling a sigh of relief, Prophet lowered the gun to his belly.

"Louisa, goddamnit! Why won't you ever listen to me?"

"He's not here," was all she said, standing on the stoop and looking around.

"What?"

"You heard me."

"What were you shootin' at?"

"One of 'em was still breathing."

Prophet stared at her, always surprised at the matter-of-factness with which such a harmless-looking young woman went about her killing. Shaking his head, he walked to the door and looked inside the cabin.

"You sure?" He raked his eyes around the blood-splattered room littered with bodies. "He's got to be here. I woulda hit him with my sawed-off when I first came through the door."

"See for yourself," Louisa said levelly.

Prophet walked around the room, stepping over bodies, broken chairs, cups, bottles, and the overturned table. Sure enough—the girl was right. Handsome Dave wasn't here.

Standing frozen in the middle of the room, glancing around disbelievingly, Prophet heard a muffled cry. He jerked around, saw the door to the other room, and re-membered the English women. Moving to the door, he opened it and saw the two disheveled women lying in heaps along the back wall.

"Sorry, ladies," he said, shucking his bowie knife. "Damn near forgot about you."

"Who are you?" one of them asked.

"Name's Lou Prophet, and what I'm doin' here's a long story. Suffice it to know you're safe. We'll take you back to your party in the morning."

The woman sobbed as Prophet cut the ropes binding her wrists and ankles. "Who were those men? Who were those . . . godawful . . . men!"

"That was the Red River Gang. And I mean 'was.'

They're all dead, except one, that is." He frowned, perplexed, at the idea that Dave Duvall had somehow slipped away.

Prophet heard boots thumping the floor behind him. Squatting beside the second woman, who was crying uncontrollably into the first woman's low-cut neckline, Prophet turned his head. The deputy was moving toward him while sweeping his gaze around the carnage-filled cabin.

"Is he here?"

"Nope," Prophet said crisply, sheathing his knife and moving out the door. "I must not have shot him because he was too close to Louisa; the ten-bore would've taken them both. He must've found him a good hiding spot after I nabbed the girl, and waited till we were gone to hightail it."

Prophet cursed loudly, wincing and shaking his head. "Take care of the women, will you? I'm gonna go out and see if I can track him."

The young deputy glanced at the women, frowning. "Now, wait a minute, Prophet. I'm a deputy U.S.—"

But Prophet was already outside, moving off the stoop and starting toward the corral off the lean-to, where the six remaining horses milled, pricking their ears, wide-eyed at all the commotion. Seeing a figure walking toward him from the south, Prophet stopped and turned that way. It was Louisa, walking fast if a little stiffly.

"I found a single set of horse prints branching off the main trail," she said, turning toward the Morgan. "He must've made like he was riding with the others after us, then branched off at the last minute. Probably figured we were laying for him."

Approaching the Morgan, she turned out a stirrup and began to mount.

"Where are you goin'?" Prophet asked her.

She reined the exhausted beast toward him, scowling.

"After Duvall!" she said, as though answering the dumbest question she'd ever heard.

"Not on that horse, you're not," Prophet said. "Look at him. He's ridden with me and McIlroy all the way from Fargo. He won't last another mile."

Louisa jerked her head around, looking for a fresh mount. Prophet shook his head. "All these horses have had it. They need grass, water, and a good night's rest."

"Well, the Morgan'll just have to do," Louisa said, giving the horse the spurs.

The black gave a halfhearted lunge off its back feet, but the gallop quickly wilted into a half-hearted canter. The Morgan blew and shook its head, flinging lather in the moonlight. At the edge of the yard, it stopped and turned broadside to Prophet.

"Goddamnit," Louisa said, her soft voice clear in the quiet yard, the moon nearly straight overhead. She looked around at the darkness around the cabin and corral, then turned to Prophet.

Her voice was small as she gave into her frustration and weariness. "He killed my family." She took her face in her hands and sobbed, slouched in her saddle.

Prophet walked to her, reached up, put his hands around her waist, and slipped her, crying, from her saddle.

"He won't get far, Louisa," Prophet assured her. "His horse is as tired as ours. Tomorrow, we'll track him . . . together."

"He killed my . . . he killed my whole family," she cried against Prophet's shoulder, releasing a flood of tears, her body racked with anguish.

Prophet held her tightly, surprised at how slight and slender she was, for all her vim and vinegar. He stood there, holding her, and let her cry.

Prophet awoke at dawn the next morning and lifted his head from his saddle. He looked around the camp he and

McIlroy had set up in the tall grass behind the cabin, away from the main trail.

The fire ring was a mound of gray ashes, the coffee pot cold. Directly across the dead fire lay the deputy, curled under his blanket. To McIlroy's left lay the two British women, nestled under the blankets Prophet had gleaned from the soogans he'd found in the lean-to. They'd both murmured in troubled dreams all night, but at the moment the women appeared to be resting contentedly.

So not to disturb them—he'd let them sleep another hour—Prophet turned quietly to his right, looking for Louisa where she'd spread her blankets the night before not far from his side.

All that was there, however, was a rectangular patch of matted grass. Louisa, her saddle, and her soogan were gone!

Resisting the urge to cuss aloud, Prophet tossed his blanket aside and climbed to his feet, looking around. There was no sign of her. Grabbing his gunbelt and hat, he headed around the cabin to the corral.

The horses snorted as he approached and looked over the top corral slat, sweeping the remuda with his gaze and setting his jaw when he saw the Morgan was gone.

Saddled up and gone, with Louisa on his back . . .

"The girl gone?"

Prophet turned to see McIlroy walking toward him, wrapping his gunbelt around his waist, his dusty, wrinkled frock coat flapping like huge bat wings.

"Yeah," Prophet groused, drawing the word out for emphasis.

"She's hell in a saddle, isn't she?"

"I could tell you stories." Prophet stared down at the fresh tracks leading from the corral and southward out of the yard. To McIlroy, he said, "See the Englishers back to Fargo, will you, kid? I'm going after Louisa."

Prophet started toward the lean-to for his saddle, but

stopped when McIlroy place a freckled hand on his shoulder. "Hey, wait a minute, Prophet. First off, I'm no kid. Second, it's my official duty to track Handsome Dave Duvall."

"Yeah?" Prophet said, a cunning twinkle in his eyes. "Who's gonna see the Englishers back to Fargo?"

McIlroy stared at him. Then he sighed. "I don't suppose you . . . ?"

Prophet shook his head, grinning. Placing his own paw on the crestfallen deputy's shoulder, he said, "Now you see why freelancing's the only way to go? I'm not responsible to anyone but myself." Seeing Mean and Ugly staring at him over the corral fence, Prophet added, "Oh, and my horse, of course."

He patted the deputy's shoulder and headed into the lean-to. Ten minutes later, he led the saddled horse out of the corral, McIlroy opening the rickety gate for him.

"Well, it was nice ridin' with you, Zeke," Prophet said, turning out a stirrup and poking his boot through. "Maybe see ya around sometime."

"You mean that?"

Prophet looked at the young man, McIlroy's face shaded by the brim of his snuff-colored Stetson. "Mean what?"

"That it was nice ridin' with me. I mean, not that I care what an old, down-at-heel bounty hunter has to say, but—you know—since you been down the river a few times . . ."

"Hey, I ain't as old as I look, kid," Prophet said with mock severity, leaning out from his saddle. "But after the sand you showed in the cabin last night, you can ride any river with me you want—though I'd just as soon you pocketed that shiny silver star when you did."

With that, Prophet reached out and tugged the deputy's hat brim over his eyes, then kneed Mean and Ugly into a canter.

He stopped when he heard a female voice call, "Say, there . . . can one of you direct us to the lavat'ry?"

The duchess stood beside the cabin, holding the hand of her glum friend. Both women were wrapped in their blankets, their tangled hair drooping past their shoulders, the hems of their expensive gowns soaked from the morning dew.

Prophet chuckled and glanced at McIlroy. "The deputy'll direct ye straightaway," he hollered to the women.

Craning around to grin at the deputy, he touched his hat brim in a mock salute, gave a laugh, and gigged his horse southward out of the yard. McIlroy watched him—a big, broad-shouldered man with a sawed-off shotgun hanging down his back, riding an ornery line-back dun.

"Be seeing you again soon, Prophet," the deputy said with a dry chuckle. "Lord help me. . . ."

ABOUT THE AUTHOR

Like Louis L'Amour, **Peter Brandvold** was born and raised in North Dakota. He's lived in Arizona, Montana, and Minnesota, and currently resides in the Rocky Mountains near Fort Collins, Colorado. Since his first book, *Once a Marshal*, was published in 1998, he's become popular with both readers and critics alike. His writing is known for its realistic characters, authentic historical details, and lightning-fast pace. Visit his website at www.peterbrandvold.com.